"I read that book."

Luz's father looked at her coldly. "You had no business to touch it."

"What does it mean, *penal colony*? A prison planet? Our ancestors were sent here as prisoners, is that right?"

Falco's face was getting whiter, but the danger exhilarated Luz; her mind raced, and she spoke her mind.

"The First Generation was sent here because they were all thieves and murderers. And most of them were men, that's why there were so few women to start with. That always seemed stupid to me, not to send enough women for a colony. And it explains why the ships were made only to come, not to go back. It's true, isn't it? We call ourselves Victoria Colony—but we're in jail!"

But Luz, as her father, his face heavy with anger, moved toward her, knew that for the first time in her life she was free.

MILLENNIAL WOMEN

Edited by
VIRGINIA KIDD

A DELL BOOK

Published by
DELL PUBLISHING CO., INC.
1 Dag Hammarskjold Plaza
New York, N.Y. 10017

Dell ® TM 681510, Dell Publishing Co., Inc.

ISBN: 0-440-16301-3

Reprinted by arrangement with Delacorte Press
Printed in the United States of America
First Dell printing—May 1979

You'll be
coming home alone on the AA
local from Canal St., 1 A.M.
Two black girls, sixteen, bushy
in plaid wool jackets, fiddle
with a huge transistor radio.
A stout bespectacled white woman reads
NOVY MIR
poking at a gray braid.
A thin blue blonde dozes on shopping-bags.
Tobacco-colored, hatchet-faced and square,
another mumbles in her leather collar.
Three sharp Latinas jive round the center-post,
    bouncing
a pigtailed baby, tiny sparkling
earrings, tiny work-overalls.
A scrubbed corduroy girl wearing a slide-rule
    eyes
a Broadway redhead wearing green fingernails.
A huge-breasted drunk, vines
splaying on cheeks, inventively
slangs the bored black
woman in a cop suit, strolling.
You'll get out at 81st St. (Planetarium)
and lope upstairs, traveling light-years.
The war is over!

Prayer for My Daughter,
by Marilyn Hacker

CONTENTS

MILLENNIAL
WOMEN

INTRODUCTION

A millennium is a simple time designation of one thousand years. The word "millennial," however, also has associations of the future and of hope. These probably stem from the belief (generally scoffed at) that the biblical prophecies in the Book of Revelations will be fulfilled with a thousand-year reign of universal peace and the triumph of righteousness.

The contributors to this anthology have created an array of possibilities for their millennial women. Not all of them are hopeful, however, and none pretends to be more than a lucky guess.

Will the year 2000 free women to reclaim the earth and explore space? Or will it bind them more tightly in unending oppression by the unrighteous? Science fiction writers don't have the answers—they're not in the crystal ball business. Like other writers, their primary interest is in people and ideas; but rather than delineate the familiar, they prefer to place their characters against hypothetical backdrops and explore questions of "what if?"

Cynthia Felice's futurescape might be no further away than the day after tomorrow. She describes the torment a young woman named Carol experiences when her successful meshing of household and career responsibilities is put to the test, and she's forced to choose between the two.

Diana Paxson makes use of an unvarying constant—the need for nurturing—under very special circumstances. Her story takes place in space among humans in extended family groups as they encounter five-sexed aliens who cherish their own young but have brutalized a human child. Paxson's heroine, Elana, strives for understanding in the tragedy that erupts.

Elizabeth Lynn takes us down a branching path. Her protagonist, Jubilee, gives us a fifteen-year-old's view of an America where militantly separate women lead a life of their own, offering shelter to others endangered by the collapse of a more traditional lifestyle.

Cherry Wilder considers the career of Mab Gallen, a medical officer adjusting to enforced retirement from the space service. Mab leaves it to others to sort out her experience, knowing that it's time to step aside for the next generation.

Joan Vinge creates a society that has descended to barbarism. Her heroine, Amanda, is a pariah among her own people. Having refused to marry the man her father chose for her, she finds a good life by defying him even further and befriending someone obviously cursed by God.

Lastly, Ursula Le Guin takes us off-planet again, to a world peopled by two communities of outcasts: One is nonviolent; the other is organized along very strict hierarchical lines. Her heroine, Luz, is confronted by a succession of choices and learns that there are ways to live other than the way in which she was brought up.

Six science fiction writers, all women. Since most of them are mothers and most have served as teachers, it is not surprising that the fate of young people should figure so prominently in the anthology. Love is another theme that echoes from story to story—love that needs to maintain its individuality, love that isn't ready to bloom yet, love that transcends ugly circumstance.

But what seems to me one of the most impressive aspects of the collection is that all of these science fiction writers avoid hard-core science fiction for sociology, soft-pedal radical feminism for humanism, and write about women simply as women. These, then, are their heroines: Carol, Elana, Jubilee, Mab, Amanda and Luz. Discover their lives and their ideas —tomorrow or well into the next millennium, in the confines of Earth as we know it or another world altogether.

In a recent *New York Times* review, the distinguished critic, Gerald Jonas, wrote about science fiction: "I don't know any other form of writing that, even in its lighter moments, demands so much from readers."

I agree. But at the same time, I don't know of any other form of writing that has so much to give.

—Virginia Kidd
Milford, Pennsylvania, 1977

NO ONE SAID FOREVER

Cynthia Felice

Carol stood on the balcony of the rented mountain home staring out over the dry meadow to the bus stop beyond. Squinting to see through harsh reflections, she watched people with yellow hard hats leaving the roadside. The aluminum bus flashed only a few seconds more, then was in mountain shadow as it sped toward the foothills. Carol could see that most of the passengers had walked to the juniper-lined parking lot provided by Consolidated Mines. One man separated from the others and struck out across the meadow on foot. Twenty steps into the meadow and he was lost in heat waves, a dancing apparition of a man floating over gold.

Carol turned and went into the house, drawing the drapes over the balcony window to cut out direct sunlight. The air coolers were blowing through the vents in the house, making it cool by comparison to the out-of-doors, but still too warm for comfort. Mike had forgotten to turn on the cooling system as he left that morning. It was chilly before sunrise when he got up and he forgot to ensure that it would be cool for her when she awakened in the sun-baked bedroom. But the house was the right temperature for him when he returned in the mid-afternoon. Carol always remembered to turn on the blowers before she left for Denver. Mike took for granted the conditions and circumstances that made his life comfortable, discarding burdens as easily as rubbish. He grasped impressions, absorbed ideas, sorted them with ease and never lost a moment of sleep over indecision. Carol had not slept for the past two nights. And today she'd forgotten the blowers until she returned home early and found it hot.

She greeted Mike at the kitchen door with open arms and a smile.

"Hey, Carol," he said, surprised but happy. "Off early today?" He tossed his hard hat to a cushioned chair and ran his hand through his sweaty hair. His sun-browned arms circled her enthusiastically as day-old whiskers scratched her cheek and pricked her lips.

Mike's smile faded at Carol's lack of response and he gathered her closer. "What's wrong, Carol?" he whispered.

Carol's answer was slow in coming. "I've been transferred, Mike."

"What!" He released her abruptly, brushed the hard hat from the chair and sank angrily onto the cushion.

He shook his head with disgust as he muttered a string of oaths. Then there was a choked sound of involuntary regret and fury. "Consolidated has let me transfer twice in two years to keep up with your transfers. I can't get another without losing seniority."

Carol opened the refrigerator and pulled out a can of Coors, set it on the table in front of Mike and sat down opposite him. The oaths, the loudness of his voice had nothing to do with her. When Mike vented anger, Mike did it here and now. No nerves, no ulcers for him. Still, Carol was extremely uncomfortable when he did. Mike sensed it now, took a few long gulps to cool himself and shook his head again.

"We're going to have to put up with this one, Carol," he said more moderately. "I don't see any other way . . . unless you can get out of it?" He looked up from the beer can, brows raised in query.

"No." Carol shifted uncomfortably in the chair. "I can't get out of it. That's the nature of the job, I knew it when I took it."

He shrugged and something useless fell away from him. (Herself?) "Well, then, we'll just have to make do with long weekends and vacations for a while. How long is the assignment?"

Carol hesitated. "Looks like two years minimum."

"Minimum!" Mike whistled. "It's going to be an expensive two years: two households . . . plane fares . . ."

"No, we won't have that to worry about," Carol said with a temporary external calm. She envied Mike's ability to decide so easily, to throw off pressure before he was even aware of its distorting effects. She didn't focus on the apparition she'd glimpsed from the corner of her eye. Then, unable to resist, Carol looked askance and saw herself, wide-eyed and trembling, staring at Mike. Carol frowned.

"What?" Mike finished the beer in two more swallows.

"I'm going to Antarctica . . . wintering over."

"Antarctica!" The can crushed easily; Mike's rage was rising again. "Damn Capitol Computer . . . they're inhuman! I can't go with you even if I want to and I sure as hell can't afford weekend visits!"

Carol knew his words were clipped by anger but she had heard each as if enunciated in the long, pausing voice of a stadium speaker. When, in utter frustration, he stamped out of the kitchen to the stairs in the hall, there was only the space of a heartbeat to measure the time. Yet in that measure she saw veins popping in his forehead, the glint in his narrow eyes, felt the breath of his passing envelop her, swirling along her skin and scalp. The floor seemed to vibrate with every maddeningly slow step.

"And they ask a hell of a lot from their employees, too!" he shouted over his shoulders. "If I were you I'd tell them to shove it!" Pause . . . eternity passed . . . Gently: "Carol?"

Carol's stomach flip-flopped as slowly as an iced fish. "I can't, Mike. There's no one else who isn't already on project they can send. Besides, it's a good assignment for me . . . one I ought to jump for. Hallerud's not going. It will be *my* project once Dr. Lincoln leaves Byrd Station." Carol followed Mike to the stairs; he was on the landing above—why had it taken so long for him to get there?—shirt off, pants unbuckled, ready for the shower. Time refused to accelerate when Carol wanted it to. This scene should be finished. It was eating out her heart.

"Promotion?" Mike said.

Rage was gone from him. She tried to ignore its lingering effects on her stomach. "Implied, but not firm. It'll come." That kind of confidence she had.

"Good for you, Carol," he said, almost sincerely. "So, you didn't even try to dodge it?"

"Not too hard," she admitted.

Mike stood quietly, grimacing with just a hint of comprehension. "Okay, babe, I understand. Look, I've some time coming. We'll take a vacation . . . fly to Acapulco, spend a week or two." He looked at her. "How long before you leave?"

"I'm sorry, Mike. They've given me the rest of the week off to get ready. I leave Sunday."

"S u n d a y ! T h i s i s . . ."

Another voice, her own, close by: "It's all right, Mike." Frantic notes, clearly her own: "I can't go through with it, I knew I couldn't." Shame, relief: "I'll call and tell them to find someone else." Carol knew the words were on her tongue, but. . . . She saw the one who had spoken, herself, stepping away from the stairs, hurrying to the kitchen phone. The listener at the top of the stairs sighed. He glanced toward the kitchen, nodded, satisfied. Carol blinked.

". . . i s T h u r s d a y a l r e a d y !" Mike ran the rest of the way up the stairs to the bathroom. Doors slammed and shower faucets were wrenched.

The other Mike was still nodding with satisfaction as he turned to the bedroom. Carol wondered why Mike had not bumped him off the stairs when he ran past. She glanced toward the kitchen; a sunshaft filled with blue dust motes where her phone was cradled. The other Carol would be standing on the patio composing a refusal. Carol went to hear her, knowing it would be poorly done, terribly lame. But the patio was empty. "I don't need to know what she . . . I . . . would say." She clutched her elbows. "I never said forever," Carol whispered. She was on the defensive without being aware of how she'd come there.

The sky was gold above the mountains. Suspended pink-orange clouds were shading the patio an hour before shade was due. Danny wolfed the steak dinner like the appreciative cub he was, hardly noticing his parents' lack of appetite. He managed the day's news between mouthfuls and was off to the meadow to play in the lingering daylight.

"We should have told him," Mike said, interrupting the peace of the evening.

Carol felt an unreasonable twinge of fear. "Tomorrow is soon enough. You and I need to . . . to talk things over."

"Like what? Absence makes the heart grow fonder? Or . . ."

"No. Like will you keep the house or move up to the mining camp? Shall I arrange for storage of my things or will you do that so we can spend the next few days together?" She was determined not to let him twist the knife that already had her guts in turmoil.

"I'll take care of all that," he said sourly.

"Then you're going to give up the house?" She felt vaguely disappointed.

"No sense in keeping a big place like this for Danny and me alone. I've plenty of seniority to get a nice place in camp."

"Schools are better down here," she pointed out.

"So, I'll lead a protest to improve the quality of education. It will give me something to do."

Carol's breath shortened in anticipation. "That sounds like you plan to wait for me." She suppressed cynical laughter and bit her cheek waiting for his answer.

Mike sighed as he looked out over the meadow. "I don't know . . . yes—you know damn well I will."

How do I know? Words are easy. No one is forever. Discard: irrational.

"Will you get leave?" He was musing aloud, considering chimerical hopes along with reality.

"No chance. I'm wintering over. I may get a week in New Zealand next summer . . . that'd be winter for you."

"Maybe we should have gotten married. Then they'd pay our fare or send you home to visit us." Mike's tone was bitter, his face dark with the stark brilliance of hindsight.

Carol laughed flippantly. "They know they're minimizing excess baggage by choosing a single person." Then suddenly it didn't seem so amusing. "My mother had to do that, you know." *Everything changed. Discard: irrelevant.*

Mike stared at her a moment. "You mean her leaving you?"

Carol shrugged. "I don't blame her. She had no choice and I adjusted. Children always do." *Do they? Don't they?*

The black elm by the balcony swayed with the first touch of evening breeze; each branch moved differently, each had the same origin, each branched from the same trunk but somehow each swayed individually. The tiny uppermost branches seemed fragile. Carol was unsure if they'd been wise to sprout from the sturdy trunk and seek the sun on their own. But the heavy limbs near the base of the tree hardly stirred, content, perhaps, over the years with their decision. Carol wanted to be strong, as were the oldest limbs, or better yet, as the trunk of the tree. But she felt as strained as the uppermost twig, brittle . . . *No!*

She shook her head. Mike was watching Danny pick himself out of the tall grass where a friend's none-too-gentle tag had dumped him. "Danny will be fine," Carol said softly.

Mike didn't look at Carol. "By the time you get back, he'll be as tired of batching as I will."

"It's such a long time," she said doubtfully.

Mike seemed surprised. "I just assumed . . ."

"You always do."

"You don't want to make a commitment, do you?"

"Two years is a long time . . ."

"Christ, Carol, you know I'm not asking for a vow of chastity, but we've got eight good years invested together that I'd like to double. Two years isn't forever." He slammed his coffee cup down.

Carol frowned. "I'd like to come back to you, but
..." *I never said forever, you never said forever. No
one says forever!*

"But," he prodded impatiently.

"Two years is a long time," she said helplessly.

"All right! No commitment . . . and if I'm busy
when you get back, I'm sure you'll understand."

No. I won't understand, but two years is a long time.

Mike lit a cigarette and walked to the edge of the
patio. Agitated, he puffed heavily. Mountain zephyrs
wafted the smoke away as quickly as he produced it,
but his own aura was enough to fog the whole patio.
He ground out the cigarette with his heel and crossed
his arms. "Is the pay good?" he finally asked.

"Astronomical. And no living expenses, either." She
wanted to sound proud but instead it came out as if
by way of explanation.

"Why do they need you at Byrd Station?"

He'd sounded genuinely interested. "You know I
can't discuss my work," Carol said unhappily. Mike
looked at her sharply and she turned away to avoid
his gaze, mopping up some spilled coffee with a
napkin.

"I thought there wasn't supposed to be any classified
work on Antarctica."

"There isn't." She put the wet napkin in the ash-
tray.

"But?"

Even with her back turned Carol felt the restraint
Mike was exercising. He didn't like pulling answers
from her. He expected—and deserved, she reminded
herself—openness and honesty. "Technically I won't

be breaking the treaty. I'll be observing the auroras
and working in the Space Disturbance Forecast net-
work."

"But you'll be making other observations too?
Applying research from your last project?"

"Mike!" she whined. She turned, made an exasperated gesture.

"I'm not being nosy about your damn top-secret
work! I'm concerned about your well-being," Mike
said angrily. "You'll be thousands of miles from aid.
People get killed in outposts! There are crevasses and
blizzards and maybe some Russians who won't like
what you're doing."

"People get killed detonating explosives too," Carol
said evenly.

"I don't have camps full of Russians around to screw
up my charges. There's a difference!" Carol's brow
had furrowed and her chin was set defiantly. "Okay,
okay, I'll knock it off." He realized that she'd related
as much as she could and that further baiting would
be futile. "I learned what I wanted to know anyway.
Lots of compensation to keep an employee happy on
a supposedly peaceful international project. It must
be important."

"It is."

"What the hell am I worrying about," he said.
"You can outfox any damn Russian anyhow." He
laughed nervously as he kicked a stone off the patio.
His gaze met Carol's. "I'm going to miss you," he said,
mistaking the fear in her eyes for tenderness and
longing. Or had he glimpsed the other Carol? The one
beside her who wanted to stay?

"You'll get over it, Mike . . ." She wasn't able to say more. Mike didn't seem to realize that it was an unfinished sentence.

"That's your experience, Carol, not mine. You've been separated from your loved ones so many times . . . two fathers, your mother, Frank . . ."

"I've learned to accept it," she said quietly. "At least this time it is I who will leave. It's not me being left behind." She felt a perverse comfort in that thought.

"Frank?"

"Even Frank. He didn't have to go on that last mission. His job was to train the men, not lead them."

"But you *have* to go?"

"Oh, Mike," Carol said unhappily. "Are we going to start that again?"

"No," he replied quickly. "Look, I'm going to call Consolidated and get the rest of the week off. Saturday we'll get you packed and we'll all fly to San Francisco together."

"There's little to pack." Carol fell silent. "Mike, this is so hard."

"Did you think being on the other side of the fence would make it easy?"

"Of course not. It's just that up to now we've managed our lives so well. Perhaps I never expected luck to desert me." The audacity of the lie struck her: She'd always expected to be discarded again.

Mike shrugged and she stifled a sob in response to his casual gesture. She barely heard him over the screams of pain filling her mind.

"Let's face it," he was saying. "We've been offered

promotions because the companies know we're willing to relocate and because it's cheaper to move a
single person than a household. Which of us would
have agreed to subjugate his job to the other's? Mine
would have been the logical one financially . . ."

"And mine would be, traditionally," she finished
for him. "Some people feel it's a wholesome approach.
My grandmother did it that way. My mother . . ."

"It works fine for cab drivers and interior decora-
tors. They can work anywhere. I can't and you can't.
It's as simple as that."

Carol hesitated, afraid to pursue memories of what
her mother had done . . . as simply as that. "It seemed
as if you were having regrets."

"Why? Because I was angry? I'm still angry. I don't
like it at all, but I don't see a choice open to us . . .
unless you want to turn it down."

Carols looked at him: one impatient, the other slow.

"My grandmother was right . . ." said slow Carol.

Impatient Carol stared, watched slow Carol receive
a rewarding smile from her Mike. She longed for a
smile for herself. She knew she could have the kisses
the other Mike was giving that Carol—that slow,
reprehensible Carol! Who was she? She certainly
looked and felt better than Carol did right now. Or
was it only Mike who looked so contented? Carol
eyed Carol and Mike as they walked hand in hand
into the meadow, fading there, too far removed from
her own reality. *That Carol is a fool . . . a happy fool.*

"I won't turn it down!" *I'm no fool.*

Mike nodded slowly. "I can accept that, Carol, but

I don't see why you don't want to come back." He was studying her from across the patio.

"There's always been some woman around you. You're good-looking, you have a sympathetic ear and charisma that won't stop. You've never lacked for company. I don't think it's practicable to make vows we might be forced to break."

Mike laughed. "I'm worried that you might die down there and you're concerned about me getting laid once in a while."

Carol flushed. "I'm not immune either."

"I don't care about your sex life. You know I'll never even ask. I just don't want this to be the end for us. I'm not ready to settle for that. I want to know you're coming back!"

"Mike, if you insist on pursuing this topic, we're going to have a lousy weekend," she said coldly.

"Then be prepared for the lousiest weekend of your life because I'm not going to let it all end here and now, clean and simple. Hell no! Forget it! You can't get off that easy!"

Mike was right. It was the worst measured period of time she'd ever spent in her life. A weekend she'd never forget. She never could, she never tried. Too many tender moments; speeding away from her like autumn leaves in a maelstrom. Too many dramatic confrontations, laggards in realtime, with the reprehensible Carol clinging to her Mike a thousand unrestrained times while Carol deliberately regarded her. The endless details: packing, papers, tickets.

Mike's relentless pressure (slow Carol yielding). Danny's stricken face when he came to realize that separation was imminent. Carol's own memories of exactly the same anguish so many times before. Acceptance that it was happening again.

And then they were sitting in the San Francisco terminal. The few personal items she deemed irreplaceable by company issue were already checked. The weekend was gone. A finality hung over her.

While Carol and Mike sipped coffee purchased from a dispenser, Danny roamed the terminal. The boy seemed to have a healthy excitement . . . he was looking forward to watching the jet take off. His disappointment had faded; he rallied quickly to the prospect of moving up to the mining camp with his father: new home, new school, new friends . . . he'd apparently decided it was fair compensation for losing a mother. Mike's influence, Carol decided; Mike's genes. She was sincerely glad for her small son . . . and envious. Sturdy as a tree trunk.

Mike reached across the small table where they were sitting and took her hand in his. "Carol, come back to me."

"I can't confine myself to a commitment like that," she said, trying to keep the snap out of her voice. (Slow Carol was melting again.) Carol closed her eyes in disgust.

"I don't want to confine you. But dammit, don't deny eight years of love."

Carol rubbed a tired eye with her free hand, looked at him curiously through the other. He was holding her hand with an urgency she'd never suspected he could possess at the finale. "I'm not denying it," she said tiredly.

The loudspeaker in the terminal began to make an announcement. Mike talked over it. "You are! You don't believe I wouldn't endanger what we've had while you're gone."

Carol shook her head. "We each have an independent existence, Mike." Slow Carol was staring at her. Carol was too tired even to snarl at the woman.

Mike was disgusted. "I never said we didn't."

"You made it clear that you wanted me to turn this project down."

"It was a legitimate alternative that needed to be explored."

"It wasn't to me." (Slow Carol listened carefully.)

"I understand that. But you needed to know how I felt."

"You were explicit, as I recall," she said with memories of the emotion-charged weekend running through her mind.

"We're digressing," Mike said impatiently. "It's got nothing to do with the project. It's you and me. I'm telling you I value what we've had enough to know I won't jeopardize it while you're gone. Two years *is* a long time, but it isn't forever."

(Slow Carol frowned.)

"It's hard to visualize you without a woman in your life," she said, without bitterness.

"I can't either, but I also know I'll be right here to meet you when you come back. Why is that so hard to accept?"

Carol felt dizzy, frightened and elated. *Why indeed?*

she asked herself. *Because it's never happened before?*
"It could destroy us," she said thoughtfully. "It could
change us," she protested.

"We're strong enough to risk it."

"I'm afraid . . ." Carol *who?* admitted that.

"I know, Carol." Mike squeezed her hand and let it
go, waiting for her to answer. His eyes searched the
terminal, found Danny standing at the drinking
fountain across the concourse. Carol followed his gaze.
"You won't drop out of his life. You endured that
yourself too many times to do it to him." Mike looked
back at Carol, who still watched her son. Her head
was nodding now. Mike bit his lip angrily. "I didn't
mean to say that. I only meant . . ."

"I know what you meant. You've been extremely
careful not to use Danny as a lever. I appreciate that,
but you're right. I can't abandon him. I've come to
expect it for myself, but I can't do it to him."

Mike frowned. He was uncertain of her meaning.
"But you can do it to me?" he finally ventured to ask.

"No, not to you either." Deep-rooted raptures of
expectation were building to almost painful intensity. "It is *me* doing this . . . not you, Frank or my
parents. It's me who's leaving. I *can* come back!" She
waited for the inner voice to denounce her words. It
was blissfully silent.

(Slow Carol smiled, then was gone.)

Carol smiled. *A risk is involved, perhaps.* . . . She
looked at Mike's self-satisfied grin. Perhaps not. Good-
bye wasn't going to mean forever; not to Carol and
not if she didn't want it that way.

THE SONG OF N'SARDI-EL

Diana L. Paxson

───────────

*I*t was quiet in the living area of our suite, but the screams of the child I had just seen in the ship's infirmary still echoed in my ears. I sighed and went over to dial a drink.

"What time is it?" came a sleepy voice from the other side of the living area. The clock flickered in the darkness, there was a muffled exclamation and the sound of someone getting up. "Where have you been?" said Jen, padding into the snackery. "I've been waiting."

"The vocorder and I were reciting poetry to each other—what do you think I was doing?" The machine beeped softly and I took my drink.

Jen looked at it and dialed one for himself. "What

you are usually doing doesn't usually take you till the middle of sleep-period, Elana."

I shook my head. "I was working on the Xicithali linguadisks . . ."

He closed his eyes momentarily, hiding the flicker of anxiety that mirrored my own. If we couldn't communicate with the natives on Cithal when we arrived, our last hope of getting enough credits to replace our ancient drive system was gone.

We had been almost desperate when we heard Center had opened up Cithal to trade. Cithal had barisidium, the only known source since the mines on Bari played out. They use it for something to do with faster-than-light communication, I think. The outfit that got the Xicithali to press a contract would never have to worry about credit again, but two other ships were racing us for the prize.

"You're supposed to be a hot-shot xenolinguist. What's the matter?" Jen said, finishing his drink a little too quickly.

"A language with five different genders, with every word in a sentence inflected according to its relationship to all the others, is hardly straightforward. They refuse to speak Tradetalk at all," I defended.

"Does that mean there are five sexes, too? No wonder you've seemed bored with us lately."

I stared at him, unable to tell if he were joking. "I stopped on my way back from the cubicle to chat with Korion Engener . . ." I said, leaning against the partition and swirling my drink around in my glass.

"That pill monkey! If you have to go outside the Family, you could at least show some taste."

"Taste? What sort of discrimination do you need to help a medic comfort a child terrified out of her mind from a nightmare? My dear mate, sometimes your automatic tendency to think the wrong thing makes me wonder why we ever opted you in."

"Sometimes I wonder why you stay in."

I smiled faintly. "I'm sorry, Jen, I guess we're both worried. I worked as long as I could and was on my way back here when I heard screaming and went into the infirmary to see if I could help. It was that girl they picked up off the *Alcantha*'s lifeboat, just before we heard about the opening of Cithal. She's had a rough time. I hope somebody opts her into a Family soon."

"I'm sure the Council will see she gets a good home," Jen replied without much interest. "You look exhausted. Let's go to bed." He smiled and held out a hand.

We tiptoed into the sleeping chamber, hoping that the others had left some room. We were lucky, there was space on the pad, but Stane woke up as we came in, so we didn't go right to sleep after all. Afterward I slept badly, seeing once more the heart-breaking curve of a child's tear-stained cheek, hearing her uncontrollable sobbing.

Another day passed. I had spent a bad half-hour with the captain, who wanted to know when the disks would be ready for the rest of the crew. Dinner was over, but I didn't feel like going back to the suite, and I couldn't face my work cubicle anymore. My mind was still running on that orphan girl, as a way of avoiding thinking about my own problems, perhaps. Korion had said visitors might do her good. . . .

They had given her drawing materials, and as I came in, she was sitting on her pad, covering the slate with tight concentric circles.

"Good—you decided to come!" Korion smiled, then turned to the child. "Jo—you have a visitor—this is Elana Driver."

The girl gave me a polite smile which did not reach her eyes. She looked about eleven—she had seemed younger, before. I held out my hand, and she greeted me in the dialect of our ship.

"You speak shipslang very well, Jo. I thought your own ship-language was System II—" I added, remembering words from her nightmare.

"System II . . . I don't know. I don't remember very well."

"She has always used our language with us," said Korion.

"Well, either she knew it already, or she's some kind of linguistic genius." I turned to the girl. "Is this the language you used to speak?" I asked in System II.

She looked at me as if I had hit her, and then the words tumbled out.

"What's she saying?" asked Korion.

"She wants to know if I know her Family—if I know what happened to them. Jo—do you remember what happened on the *Alcantha*?"

The girl stared at me for a moment, her face growing pale as the sheet.

"Yes. I couldn't remember before . . ." she whispered at last. "We took off at night. They didn't see us, and we were so happy because we had escaped. I was asleep . . . they must have blasted us then. I couldn't get to the control room. I saw their ship, a black ship, and it just went away—they didn't even look to see if anyone was still alive.

"I was trying to get the baby to the lifeboat, but my hands slipped, and he ran back into the fire . . . he was screaming, but I couldn't reach him, and then I got into the lifeboat and left them, and they are dead, all dead!" She had begun to cry uncontrollably, and I held her against me, patting her thin shoulders.

"There was nothing you could do, Jo," I murmured. "They were probably dead before you left your chamber. There was nothing you could have done." Then I foolishly voiced the question that was haunting my mind. "Jo, who did it? Where did you escape from? Who was in the black ship?"

She stiffened. "Monsters! The monsters—I hate them, I will kill them, I hate them, I . . ."

Finally Korion gave her a quieter, and the terrible shouting stilled. He glared at me. "What did you say?"

I told him.

"You should have known better than that, Elana. She didn't say who they were, huh? I should probably forbid you to see her again, but if you're careful you may be able to get her past the rest of her block. She won't be able to function normally until she accepts her loss. If we knew what had happened we could control the process, but as it is, you'll just have to be as careful as you can."

The next day I brought up the possibility of adopting Jo.

"Good heavens, don't you think four children are enough for any Family?" said Stane. "I'm nearly run ragged by the ones we've got!"

I smiled a little, thinking of them—Kendal, our oldest, beginning to fill out at last, and getting so independent we scarcely saw him anymore; Sonry, the budding engineer, who had "fixed" the snack dispenser on the average of every other week until we sent her down to learn the mysteries of Drive tech; Karane, whose ambition seemed to be to turn into an alien, preferably horned and scaly; and Wilis, who mainly got underfoot.

Darith added, "Why do you want a kid who's nearly grown? We don't know anything about her gene chart or her background."

"We know *something* about her, even if Elana doesn't want to admit it," said Jen. "We know the child's disturbed, if not incurably spaced. That's just what we need!"

"I admit it," I replied. "Maybe that's why I want her. Of course she'll probably need medical help for a while, but she also needs love. How would you feel if someone refused to take in one of our kids because he was sick with grief for *us*?" I waited a moment to let that sink in. "Besides, Kendal is almost ready to leave us. Haven't you noticed how often those two

Huller boys have been around? Before you know it they'll be opting out to form a Family of their own."

"I've seen this girl," Stane said slowly. "You know, she looks like you—maybe you share some genes. It could be, if her Family adopted its children from the crèche on Center, too. Is that why you want her?"

I thought about it for a moment. Was that the reason? Did I really want a smaller reflection of myself around the suite? That was an appalling thought, but I knew it wasn't a physical thing. I shook my head.

"I don't know. I think I could help her—she's good at languages—but the most important thing is that she needs us!"

"Well, let's not jump into anything," said Darith. "You of all people don't need anything else to worry about until we're through with Cithal . . ."

We all fell silent, thinking about the uncertainties of trading with an unknown race, and wondering what we would do for a ship if we failed.

The sticky prose of the xenological expedition's report made its way across the viewscreen in a series of spurts, as if the machine were having trouble getting it out.

The dominant life-form of the planet Korsky 28-C, also called Cithal, refer to themselves as the Xicithali . . . sentient . . . level-VIII culture, including in-system spaceflight . . . ruled by an emperor . . . five clans . . . wars. . . .

I pressed the "forward" stud, and the letters flowed by in a stream of light. After a few moments I stopped it again.

Physiology: pentapolar . . . five sexes . . . Interesting, but not what I needed. Slowly I turned the film back.

Sociology: all societal roles are dependent on gender. At the top of the hierarchy are the ovulators, who are also in charge of all religious affairs. The two types of inseminators handle arts, sciences, and mercantile affairs. The host sex, except when actually carrying eggs, do most of the domestic and servile tasks in the community. The stimulators appear to be born in larger numbers than the other four sexes, and are the warriors.

That was more like it. If the social structure of a species was sexually determined, the language was bound to reflect it. Basic, for instance, still retained traces of the sex-role differences that had been common in oldentimes, while our shipslang showed scarcely any evidence of it. If gender was really the key to Xicithalian, I could master it, but Terra, it was going to be a long haul! I looked despairingly at the two cases of viewframes and the four disks of native epics and speeches which the xeno team had also collected, and could not bring myself to pick them up. I turned off the viewer and headed down the corridor to see Jo.

They had brought two other kids to play with her. They had some game going on at a table in one corner, and Jo's eyes were bright with excitement. She was playing with an intensity I had never seen in a child her age.

"She's better, isn't she?" I said to the medic on duty.

"Yes. She's been a lot more responsive since you talked to her. You're ship linguist, aren't you?" she added.

I nodded, not noticing that Jo had finished her game.

"What does the language of that place sound like?" the medic asked.

I cast about for something suitably impressive and came up with what I thought was a formal greeting from one of the disks.

"*Idlen tinarri, pro Xicithaliarra,*" I pronounced.

There was a spurt of laughter behind me. I turned to see Jo staring at me with bright eyes.

"*Idla n'salich ala Xicithen!*" she said. "Your accent is terrible, and besides, you used the *saden* form."

For a moment I could not speak at all, and then, unthinking, cried, "Jo, were you on Cithal?"

The laughter went suddenly from her face. "Cithal ... Cithal ..." she said slowly. "Yes, that is what they called it."

"How did you get there, Jo?" I asked, my head whirling. There was so little traffic in this quadrant, was it really so strange that they had been coming from Cithal? And yet . . . Perhaps our luck had turned at last.

"We went to the mountains of Cithal to prospect. Sari was afraid, because it's illegal to go there, but Maris said it would be all right—the Xicithali would never know we were there—but they did, and they took us to prison in their big town, Tasain."

No wonder there had been no record of the

Alcantha's course. If they were planning an illegal try at the barisidium mines, they would hardly advertise their flight plan.

"Were you there a long time, Jo? Did they treat you well?"

"I don't know how long it was. They took us and our ship to a Nahaina clanhold and the pentiarch's personal retainers guarded us, but they let us kids run free—that's how I learned to speak their language."

I did not dare ask how they had managed to get away, and who had blasted their ship, but there was something else I wanted to know, right now—

"Jo, will you help me? I would like to learn Xicithalian, too," I said.

She nodded. I glanced at the medic, who smiled approval.

"Would you like to come with me and see where I work?"

Jo nodded again and followed me out of the infirmary to my work cubicle.

It was easy after that. I simply told Jo what phrases we needed and recorded her translations, feeding the information into the computer so that the training disks for the negotiators could be run.

I soon discovered that Jo's idea of recreation was to listen to the Xicithali epics the Center xenologists had recorded, and each of our work sessions usually ended with an hour or so of heroic literature. With Jo's help, I was soon able to understand them pretty well.

They were heady stuff. The Xicithali bards went in

for long, ringing lines with half-sung refrains.
"K'Salna-el and the Chorizan" was one of her favorites,
the *chorizan* being a wormlike monster which added
to the excitements of travel in the highlands of Cithal.
"The Song of N'Sardi-el" and "K'Pot-el's Death-Ride"
were also on the disks, and we played them many
times.

Sometimes we just sat and talked. Young as she was,
Jo seemed to have an instinctive grasp of linguistic
principles. She became as cheerful as any other kid,
and most of the time we both forgot the blank places
in her past.

"It was not bad in Nahain," Jo told me one day. "I
got to be good friends with N'Tal-el, one of our regular
guards. 'Tal used to sing this stuff all the time, you
see, which is how I got to know it, and even to learn
some—

> *N'Sardi-el Nahaina li/ sinta chanasta Xithen sa,*
> *Qua idlachti sintana wonoten/ Norenik litane ala*
>   *falarr.*
> *Ori qua xicith sinta, sinta-el,*
> *Nahaina norae norae.*

" 'N'Sardi-el, of the Nahaina clan, of the warrior-
sex, strongest in the land he was. When he grasped
his five weapons, none could beat him, so quick he
was. Alas for the warrior, the warrior who served his
clan. The Nahaina weep, they weep.' That is not a
very good translation, of course," she added.

"The story is about a *sintael*, a warrior, who was the
teacher, or special friend, of the child of the pentiarch.
But he was careless, and it was stolen by a rival clan.

N'Sardi-el went into the enemy clanhold alone to rescue it—he had to, or he would have been *shilel*." She paused, unsuccessfully seeking a translation, then went on. "He got the child out, but he died of his wounds on the way home."

"Why didn't the other parents go, too?" I asked, since among the ships, any mate who didn't fight alongside the others would have been opted out. I have heard that some of the dirtsiders have different ways.

"Oh, they couldn't! They were not warriors. . . . The *tarna* could not be risked, the *leneri* found out where the child was, the *saden* waited outside and helped them get home, and the *leneff* made the song about it.

"N'Sardi-el was from N'Tal-el's clan, you see, so 'Tal was very fond of the song. 'Tal was even teaching me to use the *xitasi*—it's a sort of bladed thing they throw—when. . . ." She stopped. We had come to the part she would not remember yet.

We were about two days away from Cithal, and our work was nearly done. The crew had the learning disks and were doing well. The negotiating team had been chosen. It occurred to me that we might produce a dictionary, something we could publish later on. I started by taking Jo on a tour of the ship, recording her words for everything the Xicithali had a word for. Then we went back to the cubicle to go through the videos of Cithal.

The first set of frames was straightforward enough— buildings, tools, a marketplace with goods. The second held portraits of natives of various ranks and sexes.

"That's a *tarna*, but not of a very high class," said Jo, brushing her heavy hair back from her face and leaning forward to see better. "See, she's wearing no jewelry. The *tarna* gets gifts from her mates at breeding time, but if they are poor they have to sell them again afterward."

I looked at the picture curiously, being an egg-producer myself, though not in the Xicithali fashion. The *tarna* had a slender, upright body much like our own and was draped in a loose garment which covered three of "her" five arms and fell nearly to the ground. The head had a single mouth and breathing hole, and three eyes, topped by a stiff brush of fur.

The next frame showed two natives together. These, Jo informed me, were a *leneri* and a *leneff*. They were taller than the *tarna*, but otherwise much the same in form, the *leneri* being a little heavier in build than "his" companion. They wore cloths twisted around their midsections which left all five legs free. This was followed by a picture of a native as short as the *tarna*, but very muscular and broad, with no clothing at all. I was not surprised to learn that this was a *saden*, a host. I pressed the stud for the next frame.

This must be a *sintael*, like the one who had befriended Jo. I examined it, trying to match it up with the heroic figures of the epics. It was formidable enough—tall, well muscled, with a spear in the top hand and a molded corselet covering the torso. There was an emblem on it, a double pentangle of yellow with a red sphere in the center.

I turned to ask Jo what it was, and realized that she

was staring at the screen, as rigid as if someone had slipped her a hypnosting. Feeling suddenly cold, I touched her arm.

"What's wrong, Jo—it that a *sintael?*"

"The emblem! The Nahaina emblem! It was on the black ship. . . . Monsters, murderers, you blasted my Family! Oh N'Tal, how could you do it . . . I hate you, I will kill you for this, child of N'Sardi-el . . . oh 'Tal . . . 'Tal . . ." Her voice trailed off into a wordless sobbing. I tried to comfort her, but she did not seem to hear. After a little I carried her back to the infirmary, where the medic gave her a quieter that brought a semblance of peace. Then I went to report to Captain Teck.

"There's no reason for you to blame yourself, Elana," said the captain, her blue eyes softening a little. "You could not have known she would react this way."

"Well, it was pretty obvious that it must have been the Xicithali who attacked them, but I thought that was just something she would have to face. I should have realized it would be the warriors who manned those ships, and knowing how close she had been to that guard, considered the possibility of its having been his clan. I should have known!"

"Surely, given proper rest and care, Jo will recover. Both of you were working too hard." She brightened. "But everyone has almost completed the linguadisks now. We will be ready by the time we arrive."

"Will we? I've been listening to the disks the xenologists brought back. To the Xicithali, war is a way of life. Their only soft spot is for their young, possibly because they don't develop identifying sexual characteristics until quite late, and so any child is a potential *tarna*. They even have a special set of inflections for children to use. I was lucky to catch that, or we would have had the whole crew speaking like cubs!"

The captain put her hand on my shoulder. "What gender-speech are *we* going to use?" she asked gravely.

"Oh, the *tarnaeti*, the speech of the rulers, of course," I replied. "But seriously, we have got to be careful with these people. It's true that the *Alcantha* had no right to be near Cithal in the first place, and she did try to escape, but did they have to blast her right out of the sky?"

"All right, Elana, I understand. I'll suggest to the Council that we issue weapons to anyone going planetside, and we'll insist on having the first meeting with them here."

Cithal glowed amber below us like a safety beacon. Beyond us our two rivals held orbit, hoping that although we had won the race to the planet, we might fail in negotiating the contract.

Our people were confident, but I found it hard to rejoice. Jo remained in the infirmary, under constant care. I had seen her on the remote screen, but they would not let me go in for fear of upsetting her. Korion told me about the psychiatric facility on Center, holding out hope for a cure if we could take her there. He had smiled sympathetically and blamed himself for not having kept her under closer observa-

tion, and I winced, hearing the words of blame for me
that he was too professional to say.

Five stars of light blossomed on the viewscreen, expanded, and turned into five black ships, each with
the emblem of one of the Xicithali clans emblazoned
on its hull. The Xicithali were about to arrive. I followed the others from the viewroom to the Council
Hall.

In person they were more impressive than I had
expected. Their brightly dyed and embroidered robes
of state flowed around them as they glided forward. I
recognized the pentiarchs of the five clans, with their
retainers, both assistants and guards. I stared at them,
remembering the heroic figures of the legends Jo had
told me, and wondered if one of those warriors was
N'Tal-el.

We had prepared a display of our goods at one end
of the hall, but the aliens declined even to turn their
heads in that direction as they moved toward the
negotiating table. The long, formal phrases of the
opening speeches rang out, and I listened with some
pleasure to the negotiating team's fluent replies. I
had done all I could—it was up to their skill now. One
of my mates, Darith, was among them, and Jen and
Stane sat beside me on the balcony watching proudly.
It was my success, too, but the taste of it was bitter-
sweet.

Eventually the good faith of both parties was accepted, and the visitors got up to view the trade goods.
The captain signaled for a recess, and I saw Korion
raising his hand in greeting a few rows away. I made
my way over to him.

"How is Jo?"

"She seemed a little better this morning." He smiled. "She was talking to us quite calmly, and asking for you. For a moment there we were afraid she would try and find you herself."

"Kori, you must let me see her!"

"I think you may be right. I gave her a quieter, which should last until after the meeting, but why don't you come down later on?"

We were still smiling at each other when there was a murmur from the main floor and heads around us began to turn. We turned, too, and I felt cold sweat form on my back and forehead. Jo, still in her hospital coverall, stood motionless in the doorway, eyes haunted and face set. I wondered why no one had grabbed her, until she moved and I saw what was in her hand.

"My oath!" whispered Korion. "Did Lin leave her alone? I'll have her rating for this!"

I did not answer. I was trying to reach the door. There was no telling how Jo had gotten the thing. Miners used Sally charges, but I had not known we had any on the ship. Had she seen it when we toured the ship that day? The green arming light was on. The Xicithali were still examining the goods, their impassivity cracking a little as they fingered this item or that.

As I reached the portal and started down the slide, I glimpsed Jo beginning to walk across the floor. She is only a child, I told myself, they love children, surely they will not harm her even if she . . . please, please let me be in time . . .

I had just reached the bottom when I heard her

clear young voice call out, *"Idlel ara kilus, ara wonoti, sintael, ara shilel!,"* the enemy's taunting of the warrior from "The Song of N'Sardi-el," and then the pattering of her bare feet. I ran out onto the floor of the hall and saw the warrior she was heading for turn as the Sally left Jo's hand.

The warriors of Cithal are trained to be fast. I could even admire the fluidity with which the *sintael* blasted the Sally to dust with something held in one of his hands while with another he let out a stream of blue fire that bathed Jo in an eerie radiance. It took a long moment for her to fall.

I got to her quickly then. The hall was in an uproar around me, but I scarcely heard. I held Jo against me, and bent to hear her whisper, *"Shilel, shilel . . ."* before she went still. I got up, Jo's limp body in my arms, and found myself staring at the Nahaina emblem blazoned on the breastplate of the alien who stood before me.

"Shilel!" I echoed her.

It was very strange. The *sintael*'s eyes were fixed on Jo. The others had drawn away from him as from one struck by plague. I was vaguely aware of Captain Teck striding by me to face them, but I didn't care. I turned and carried Jo's body out of the hall.

N'Tal-el wanted to see me.

"I know how you feel," the captain had said, "but the barisidium is already being loaded. They are giving it to us free, as reparations, I think. We should be generous, too. They will send a ship to take you to the prisoner in Nahaina."

The Xicithali guard led me through the fortress to the cell. The *sintael* lifted his head as I came in, and seeing his dull skin and drooping brush, I felt a flicker of pity disturb the fog which had surrounded me since Jo died.

"You are the one who cared for her . . ." he stated. I winced, hearing in his accent the echo of Jo's, and searched for the Xicithali words I had been rehearsing all the way down.

"Why did you do it? Jo said you love children— but your people fired on her ship . . . you killed her . . . yourself!"

He grew a little more gray. "The ship—that was bad, but such things happen in war. They should have stopped when we ordered them to. They should not have tried to escape. I was not on that warship," he added, looking away. "But I am a trained warrior. You must understand . . . my hand moved of itself." He paused. "The grief is mine, too . . ." he whispered. "I was her guardian, and now I am . . ."

He did not finish, but I knew the word he could not say. *Shilel* is a hard name to bear on Cithal. Our languages have no equivalent. Since the *sinta* do not contribute genes to the making of children, they must relate to them in a special way, and the name for those who betray such a bond is the worst epithet in the warrior's vocabulary. N'Tal would have found death less hard to bear.

But I could not bring myself to say it for him. In a way, I too was *shilel*.

JUBILEE'S STORY

Elizabeth A. Lynn

---

*J*ubilee, Apprentice Historian, to Dorian, Historian of the White River Pack: Greetings.

I wanted to make this History very orderly, very formal, as you taught me. But it's hard to do that, sitting here in a strange room, trying to write, trying to remember. Memories aren't orderly. Hannako, the Historian here at Ephesus, says that confusion always happens when one is newly come to the page. She says I should write the story any way I want to. So I will just set it down as I would tell it, pretending that I am home, talking to my little sister. Today is Tuesday, June eleventh. We entered the territory of Upper Misery Friday evening.

Elspeth was going to Ephesus to live with Josepha

for a while. Josepha was going to have her fourth baby. I was going with Elspeth because I wanted to see Josepha, too, and because I love going to new places. Ruth came with me so that we could be together. And Corinna traveled with us to take care of us, because not all of the territory between White River and Ephesus is safe. Corinna is an amazon.

The territorial markers for Upper Misery were very odd. They were only pieces of old wood, with scribbled chalk words across them, as if a child or someone very feeble had put them up. I asked Elspeth, when we first saw them, "Why would anyone choose to name a place Upper Misery?"

She shrugged. "Overweening pessimism."

It was very quiet. Birds screamed sunset challenges at us from all the trees. Corinna went on ahead of us. She came back to tell us, "There's no town." There was just a jumble of ramshackle buildings surrounded by scored farmland. I think the road had once been paved, but now it was all chopped up with holes, and covered with dust and brush. It looked rarely used. No one had tried to repair it.

We went past the buildings. There was one well-kept house. "I wonder where the people are," Ruth muttered. "It's weird."

"In that house," Corinna said. I thought I saw a face look through a window at us. But no one came out.

We found an abandoned barn to sleep in. "Maybe they think we're devils," Corinna said. "Gah, this place stinks of horse dung!"

"They can't be that ignorant," Elspeth said.

"Though we are surely dangerous to them, if they follow the old customs. Free women!"

We all smiled. Ruth stretched, showing off her muscles. Ruth is very strong, and very beautiful. "Even living in this pigsty, they must believe they're free," she commented. "What is the opposite of us?"

Elspeth was suddenly somber. "Slaves."

The visitor came while we were eating breakfast. "Well?" Elspeth said.

He flushed under his red beard. They are not used to women talking to them like that. Then he said: "My wife—Kathy—she's going to have a baby. Maybe today. She's thin, very small, maybe too small to bear a child—" He stopped in mid-spate. "We are all alone here," he said.

Just looking at her face, I knew what Elspeth would do. "How old is Kathy?" she asked him.

"Seventeen," he said. Elspeth looked at me. That is only two years older than I am.

"I will come," she said.

Ruth said, "You will go into his house?"

Elspeth said, "What do you think, Corinna?" We all turned to her. She is tiny, like a fist, or an arrowhead. She seems lazy, until you see her move, and then she's fast as a thrown knife. I would not like to get in Corinna's way.

"What about Josepha?" she said.

"Josepha is not alone," Elspeth said.

"I think it will be all right," Corinna said.

"Thank you," the boy stammered. I could see that

behind the beard he was probably not much older than seventeen himself.

We went with him into the travesty of a town, to that one unbroken house. As we entered the hallway, a man with a big gray-and-red beard came out of a door. "Jonathan—I told you I didn't want them," he said angrily.

Jonathan said, "Kathleen is *my* wife."

The older man scowled and then seemed to change his mind. He said, "Since you've done it, it's done." And went back into the room he'd come out of. On its door was a piece of board with a word chalked on it, like the markers. It said: *Library.*

"He is my father," Jonathan said. "He is sick, and tired. Mostly he sleeps and reads. But he likes to think that he is still master of the house, and we let him think so."

Corinna asked, "Who else lives here?"

"Me," said Jonathan, "and Kathy. And my brother Simon."

We heard, then, from back inside the house, a wailing call, a woman's voice. Jonathan tensed. "That's Kathy," he said.

"Take us there," said Elspeth.

They had her trussed up in the old way, lying flat on the bed, with sheet strips hanging limp and ready for her to pull upon. She was breathing in raggedy chops. When we came in, she scrabbled for a sheet to cover herself, as if there were something to be ashamed of in being ready to give birth! It made me angry, but I pushed the anger out. It is not a useful tool to deal with fear. She was looking at us with wild eyes, as if her fear and Jonathan's fear for her had driven her a little mad.

I sat down on the chair by the bed. "Hello," I said. I took her hand. It was cold, despite the heat of the room. She gripped my fingers as if she would tear them off.

"Can you help me?"

"We came to help you," I said. "Jonathan brought us. My name is Jubilee. That is Elspeth. The tall woman is Ruth, and the short one is Corinna."

"She is small, too," said Kathy.

"Yes," said Elspeth, over my shoulder, "and so am I small, but I have three children." I tried to get up to give Elspeth my seat, but Kathleen kept hold of my fingers so tightly— "You sit, Jubilee," Elspeth said. "You are doing fine." I was pleased. I have seen births before, of course, even difficult ones. But this was different. Elspeth was really saying to me: *I trust you not to make a mistake.* That is a real compliment from one's mother.

Just then Kathleen gripped my hand so painfully that I wanted to yell, too. Her fingers were thin as twigs—but strong! "It hurts!" she cried.

"Let me see," Elspeth said. I moved my chair. She drew the covering away, and put her head between Kathy's drawn-up legs. Then she straightened up and laid a hand gently on the woman's belly. Kathleen moaned—from fear, I think, not because it hurt. Why should it? "Your pains just started, right?"

"Yes," said Kathleen.

"Are they close together?"

"N-no."

"Good," said Elspeth. "Very good. I don't think this is going to be as hard as you think."

Jonathan came up to the bed. "You hear that, Kathy?" he said.

I let Jonathan have my seat (and Kathy's hand). Her contractions were coming about every ten minutes, but I knew they could go on for hours like that. She didn't know how to breathe; she was breathing with her neck and shoulders rigid and her belly tense. And she kept looking at Jonathan with this loving-guilty glance, as if she was ashamed of what was happening to her.

There was a sudden noise outside the door of the room, and it opened, hard, banging back against the wall. Kathleen shrank into the bed. A man walked in. Like Jonathan, he had red hair; it was the thing I noticed about him first of all. He looked at Kathy, and then at us, and then at Jonathan, who stood up.

"Hello, Simon," he said.

"Who let *them* in here?"

"Papa said they could come," said Jonathan.

The other man made a brushing motion with one hand. "Papa can barely see to piss," he said. "You brought them."

"Yes."

Simon clenched a fist and stepped forward. Jonathan didn't even put up his hands. The blow caught him on the side of the face and sent him back against the wall.

I saw Corinna move close to Elspeth.

"You ask *me*," said Simon. He turned toward the

bed. I could smell his sweat. "Kathleen," he said. "You want them here?"

"Yes, Simon. Please." He stared at her. Her hands were twisting the sheet. Her breasts were bare. She didn't cover them up.

"They can stay," he said. "For the baby—they can stay."

"Thank you," she said.

Jonathan waited until Simon left before he moved. Then he came and sat in the chair by the bed and reached for Kathleen's hand. "We shall have to go away," he said. "When the baby is born, Kathy, we'll go away."

Kathleen tensed, and then cried out softly, as a contraction came and went. "Not now," she said. "Not now."

Jonathan was little help, but we couldn't tell him to get out. Elspeth let me sit with Kathleen, talk to her, rub her back, and show her a little about breathing. Her water broke, and it made her feel better. The contractions began to come faster, and that made her feel better, too. "I just don't want it to last too long," she said. She tried to breathe like I told her, what we call sea breathing, long and steady, rising with the contraction. "Hours and hours, they say. I can stand anything as long as it doesn't last too long." Every once in a while Elspeth came to look at her and reassure her. "Please," Kathy said to her, "keep him out."

"Who?" Elspeth asked.

"Simon. Keep him out."

Jonathan looked hard at her. Then he looked away, at the floor.

She was in labor for about twenty-four hours. We stayed, of course. She gripped my hand, and talked to me. "We're all alone. The old man's crazy, writing his words all over the walls. No one comes here any-more. . . . Jonathan visited Ephesus. I've never been there. We farm. There's no one here to talk to. Who will the baby play with here? All alone . . ." Jonathan sat in the room and grew paler and paler. Every so often Elspeth sent him out to get himself or one of us water or food.

Around four in the morning, I went out for a breath of air. Simon was there. He saw me and came over to me. "She's all right." It was not a question but a demand. "And the baby?"

"Still coming. Everything seems fine." I tried to sound sure, as Elspeth always sounds sure, even when she is saying "I don't know."

"It's too long."

"Not for a first labor."

"Is my brother in there now?"

"I don't know," I said.

He turned and made for the house. I followed him.

He went right into Kathy's room. She was wet with sweat and some tears, but she had learned that it made it worse to fight the pain and was trying to ride it out. Jonathan was not there. Simon bent over her. She put up a hand to thrust him off. "Get out of here!" she said with lovely fierceness. "I don't need you now."

"Bitch," he said to her, "the baby's mine. You can say it now. He's mine."

She slowly shook her head from side to side. "No," she said. "It's Jonathan's."

"Jonathan was away in September," he said. "All month."

"It's early," she said. "Eight months. Happens all the time."

"You can't know that," he said angrily. "You're just saying it."

"I'll say it," she said. "And say it and say it and say it." A contraction came. She breathed it down. They were coming every three minutes now. "Get out."

I thought he would hit her. But then he whirled and left the room, nearly knocking Elspeth down. Jonathan was just outside the doorway and moved aside to give him room.

At last the baby began to move fast. I always imagine it as a little worm, pushing and shoving down the birth canal, even though I know that's not what happens at all. As the head crowned, Kathy screamed, a wide open-throated yell of triumph. The baby slid into Elspeth's hands. I was ready with the bath. In the warm water Elspeth stroked him, and he smiled, and we brought him to Kathy so she could see that luminous ecstatic smile of the newborn. Jonathan, who had been almost fainting, pulled himself together and came to look. "A boy," he said. "I must tell Papa."

Kathy said, "I want to wash." We brought her a towel and a clean sheet. She wiped the sweat from

her face and neck and breasts, and held out her arms
for her son—and Simon came in.

"Let me see him."

Jonathan stood in his way. "Simon," he said, "go
away. Leave us with our son."

Simon laughed at him. "*Your* son," he said, with
contempt. "Mine, Jonny. Who do you think kept
Kathy sheltered from the cold, September, while you
were away buying supplies in Ephesus? Papa?"

Jonathan's face worked like a child's. "It doesn't
matter," he said finally. "Kathy's *my* wife."

Simon stepped up to him and pushed him. "*You*
go," he said. "Go keep Papa company, him and his
books. He'll be all that's left, when winter comes.
Kathy and I'll be gone."

Jonathan flailed at him like a windmill, all arms.

Kathy grabbed for the baby as Simon fell across the
bed. Simon sprang up again and lunged for Jonathan.
The baby started to howl. The two men struggled,
panting, Simon cursing. Jonathan had his hands
around Simon's throat. Simon seized the oil lamp from
the table and struck at Jonathan, once, twice—and the
third time Corinna caught his arm and twisted the
weapon away, very calmly, just as if it were practice.

Jonathan's cheek was bleeding. Oil slithered across
his throat and his shirt. He lurched and fell down
suddenly, and just lay there. I could see a crease
across his skull, where the metal base of the lamp had
hit him.

Simon looked down at him. He looked young, and
afraid, and dreadfully like Jonathan.

The door opened. The old man stood there.
"Jonathan," he said. He looked at Simon. His voice
was very hard. "Go away," he said.

Simon said hoarsely, "I'm going nowhere."

The old man took a step. "You will go. This is my
house. I built it, with my two hands. Now it is stained
—" His voice fumbled with that word, then picked up
cadence again. "You *will* go." He pulled the door
open with one hand. "Leave now."

Simon might have fought or defied another man.
But with all of us looking on, and the force suddenly
back in his father's voice, as it had not been for a long
time, maybe, and his brother dead by his hand, he
couldn't. He walked through the door, and we heard
him go down the hall.

The father knelt. He tried to turn the body. Blood
and oil smeared his hands. He looked up at us, and
then spoke directly to Ruth. "Excuse me, sir," he said,
"would you help me bury my son?"

They dug a grave for him, back of the house. We
waited. Later Ruth told me about it, crying a little
in the circle of my arms. "He talked to me about the
farm, and how much work needed to be done on it
before the winter, and how hard it would be, now that
he was alone. He didn't mention Simon's or Jonathan's
name, once."

After they finished the burial, the old man disappeared for a while. I heard hammering. I went toward
it. It was him—he was hammering a piece of wood
onto the door of Kathy's room, an old piece of wood
chalked with a word.

The word was *Whore*.

* * *

Kathy would not open her door to us. Ruth raged at Elspeth for leaving. "How can you leave her there? With a newborn baby, and that hideous mad old man?"

Elspeth would only say, "She has to make her own choices."

We passed the old barn. For a moment I thought I saw someone standing in its doorway. We passed the last of the markers and went round a bend in the road—and Kathy was standing there, with the baby in her arms.

"Here!" she said. "Take him!"

Automatically Elspeth's arms went out. I grabbed the corked jug just as Kathy let that go. It dropped into my hands.

"Ephesus will be better for him than Upper Misery," she said. She pointed to the jug. "That's milk."

"Come with us," urged Ruth. "You don't have to stay."

"Simon's in the barn," Kathy said. "Skulking there. The old man will forget his strength soon. Simon will come back. I used to be Jonathan's wife—I'm still Simon's whore."

We took him with us, of course. We named him Nathan: it means "gift." He is going to live with Josepha—she says she always has enough milk for two. Did I say that he had red hair?

But Ruth and I keep thinking about Kathy, alone in that house, with Simon and that old man. We have talked about it. Ruth has decided: She wants to be an amazon. So we will be able to travel anywhere, just the two of us by ourselves.

One day, after winter is over, we will take that road again, to come home.

Kathy had said to me: "I can stand anything, as long as it doesn't last too long."

She will come. I am sure of it. She will come.

MAB GALLEN
RECALLED

Cherry Wilder

———————

When I returned from my final tour of duty, I
found that fashions in dress had changed
completely. People on the concourse, in the shuttles,
seemed to be heading for a masquerade. There were
colors that I had never seen before. One might have
emerged from the Bastille after its fall . . . like de
Sade . . . or between the Terror and the Directory . . .
like Josephine. My daughter Valentina, happy to take
charge of her mother's wardrobe, put me into a pleated
cloak; it looked strange on top of the old gray coverall. I saw other middle-aged faces rising oddly from
shining pleats.

I cannot recall what was worn, what I wore, five
years ago, ten . . . About the time we were passed
out there might have been a holiday outfit: purple

bandit breeches and a silver bandolier. My great-grandparents lived out their lives in blue denim. On Arkady the poor colonists wear wooden shoes and drawstring pants of cycadic fiber. I have seen a linen robe from the system of 70 Ophiuchi, embroidered with thick spiderweb and slit to the waist so that air can come to the young in the mother's pouch. These people, the Moruia, find placental birth difficult to comprehend. Moruian females have no breasts; they give birth painlessly to a six-inch embryo. A class of female laborers exists among the Moruia; they become porters or miners; they carry no children.

I am old and doubly old "before my time." My metabolism alters queerly, my blood-sugar plays tricks; I must gulp OSV, orange concentrate with supavite, even when I am on Earth. My years of active service have been spent in the long sleeps, the twilight, the blur of inactivity that is deep space. I have read the history of the world fifteen times by artificial light. I can draw breath more gently than a buried fakir; I can slow my own heart, lower my blood pressure, suppress my secretions by taking thought. At Port Garrett I learned to keep pace with the barrel-chested Arkadians on their morning walks. I crawled on Ida, went lightly upon Philomel; for a part of my working life I was weightless. Here on Earth I have weight but little substance; I am transparent . . . an old woman, a ghost reflected upon the night sky, outside a window pane.

Memories are solid. I see Barnes, Blake . . . I see Garrett himself, hacking away at the stubborn ground of some asteroid of the Alpha system. I see a young ensign's body floating; he had hooked the toe of his boot into a cabinet to steady himself. The blood from the throat wound hung in a flat, irregular mass over the face; droplets were spreading through the cabin like the molecules of a gas.

I see Ivanov . . . I have never recorded this before . . . I see my Ivanov walking away from the ladder of our ship and deliberately taking a path through the flowers to the riverbank. The Russian ship stood waiting a hundred meters away; it was at Riverfield outside Port Garrett, a blue evening in the month called Chet. Alexei had intercepted the recall message in our own comcen; he walked away toward the river, into the wastes of his own planet, Arkady. They say he is still there, on one continent, on both; Arkady is the place for gossip. Is this the reason I have never told this story?

I have a vision of three persons in a winter landscape: tall conifers with their trunks bare for several meters. Snow on the ground, three dark figures in long, skirted coats standing beside a low building. A shed. A railway carriage. What is this, memory or dream? An old still from World War II? Is it a Russian scene because I have been thinking of Alexei Ivanov?

The girl, the wunderkind, Valentina Ivanova Gallen, is twenty-five years old, going on forty. When the tests showed that I was carrying a girl child I had thought of her as an artist, a marine biologist; I didn't consider anything so absorbing and dangerous as my own trade of space medicine. She goes about, old head on young shoulders, changing her silk capes, working out in the gym. Brings back a stack of tapes and printouts after a twelve-hour day. What does she do? Coordinates, bargains. Her secretary is her bodyguard, may even be her stud. I took a call once, saw him on the tube. Not bad. Valentina is a union organizer. She feeds me tidbits of information:· infarction, which soared among female construction workers during the past century, has been controlled by voluntary arterial implantation. The operation is performed on men and on sterile women between the ages of twenty-five and thirty. (I think of the *omor*, the empty ones among the Moruia.) Valentina says to me one night, "Where are you thinking of going?" I dare not tell her; clouds obscure the night sky; the sea serpent is invisible.

I travel a thousand miles on two successive days to address young graduates in search of a specialty. I give them facts—drug schedules, casualty breakdowns—but they prefer travelers' tales. My field is like a bad definition: too broad and too narrow. The capsule and beyond it "the expanded stars." There are two rows of medical missionaries in the audience; boys and girls wearing neat cream or navy zippersuits and gold crosses. They look like floor nurses in a cult clinic. I believe I have a story for them, but when I come close to these young people in the reception area, they are too well nourished, too immunized. Not one has the scrawny, vulnerable neck, the chapped fingers of the priest in my story.

This priest was a commissariat officer, a cook-sergeant on the failed Titan station. There was a full complement on this station, dying by numbers, and they were being ferried aboard the rescue ship *Delta Oregon* in an old Class E transporter, larger than a shuttle. There was a minor docking error during the last transshipment: twenty refugees were squeezed to safety through a whistling valve, then the pilot uncoupled, returned to Titan orbit for a second try.

I was medical officer on the *Delta*, assisting with the rescue. I was aboard the Class E with a stretcher case: Swain, the station's provost marshal, had fractured both ankles. This was dangerous as well as painful ... "space shock" or "supershock" is a clinical entity. I was setting a casein emergency pack and watching the man carefully when I saw we had company. Skinny, set-faced creature, commissariat flash on an unused silversuit.

"Docking shouldn't take long," I said.

The Class E heeled right over, made a 180-degree roll and came partway back; the lights went out. They extinguished in banks, seconds at a time, and we watched them. I was bracing the stretcher and the suction cups held. Two lights stayed on in the last bank.

"Holy hell, Doc ..." said the provo feebly, "what they playing at?"

The cook-sergeant swooped down like a scrawny bird. I said to her, "Keep this stretcher braced if we roll."

I went up the wall to the intercom; it crackled and spoke as I raised a finger to tap on the box.

"Doc?"

The pilot was Barnes, our own senior, picked for

one tricky maneuver—the rescue operation—and left
with another.

"Charlie? I'm in B-Lock with two rescued."

"Damage?"

"Lights out, some tilt."

"Hang in there. We have . . ."

The line went dead. I never did hear what we had.
I checked pressure and atmosphere, both dials still
functioning, readings normal, then I went back to the
stretcher.

"Under control," I said confidently. "Lieutenant
Barnes will dock as soon as he can."

Swain was greenish, quiet; I fed him oxygen from
the puffer pack attached to the stretcher. The cook-
sergeant swung, half in shadow, one leg hooked
around a stanchion. There was a passivity in her
attitude that I didn't like, a resignation that made me
think of shock again. I held out a hand.

"Gallen, M.O."

"Fahey. How is Mr. Swain doing?"

"Fine. Too bad you didn't get off with the others."

"I stayed . . . in case of emergency."

While I was working this out, the cook-sergeant
pressed a metal object into my hand. I felt it, in
shadow, for some minutes before I recognized the
shape. My attention was divided between the crucifix
and the living face. Thin, pale wedge of a face . . .
"homely," as they used to say.

"I am a priest."

I shook my head; there was not much I could say. I
was younger then, more wary, more ambitious. Reli-
gion has always interested me as one of the great

anomalies of the service. It is a local option: one ship, one station might have a Vedantist prayer group, a Bible-banging skipper, while another suppresses all traces of "cultism." Even the Russians have this experience; the *V. V. Tereshkova* made its "emergency landing" on Arkady because there were Baptists in the crew. Ivanov, that godless man, attracted visionaries.

I stared at this priest with clinical interest but little comprehension.

"That must be difficult," I said.

She was graceless, unable to deprecate. "Yes, pretty rough."

She glanced at the provost marshal and added, "I was in solitary."

"How long?"

"Ten days."

"For . . . preaching?"

"Offering sacraments."

Before handing back the crucifix I held it up in the feeble light. The injured man stirred and instinctively I lowered my hand. Even without the implications, I didn't consider a human figure nailed to a cross a therapeutic sight. Fahey thought I was protecting her.

"It's okay. He let me keep it."

She went on awkwardly. "We have difficult jobs . . . I guess. You and me both."

I could not take this very seriously but I began to see what she was driving at.

"What are you called?" I asked.

"Prester. Old word for priest."

I thought of the fabled empire of Prester John and,

by contrast, the uncomfortable legend of Pope Joan.

This *was* Fahey's point. The ordination of women had been accepted in principle by her church fifty years before, but the last-ditch stand of the fathers and brothers was a determined one. Fahey had been subjected to sex discrimination of a medieval harshness. Female priests, particularly those of the Seton Society, her order, often went underground, worked in defense, in the peace corps, in factories.

"Christ's heroes . . ." Fahey was quoting her old preceptor. The cavernous tilted hold had strange acoustics that muffled our voices. "Little soldiers of the Lord . . . we are the last of the urban guerrillas."

There was no irony in the halting voice; no fanaticism, not much spirit or sweetness. I tended the injured man when he grew restless. We were perched on the surface of B-Lock like flies; outside was the long night of space. Fahey droned on, yawning.

"Millions . . . still not free . . ."

Our situation was eerie, unnatural; I felt the power of the vacuum ready to crush us like the hand of God. But it had nothing to do with being a woman.

"We have simply taken the extreme case . . ." I said and yawned.

I fell into a dream of Arkady: on the savannah of Oparin a thundering cloud, a herd of ungulates. Alexei shouted my name: Mab . . . Mab Gallen . . . you are recalled . . .

I dug my nails into my palms, exhaled from my boots and twisted into the helmet. Prester Fahey hung nodding from the stanchion . . . I slapped her, had her helmet on before she could turn the other cheek. A helmet and an empty backpack; I set in my spare tank. We breathed rich and deep; I was already checking the provost marshal.

The mask of the puffer pack had slipped down. He had lost his pallor, looked healthier, which was bad. I thumbed the button for the oxygen tent on the stretcher, watching his vital signs. Swain was wide awake and hearty in seconds; he had his intercom working first and nearly blasted my eardrums.

"Some foul air . . . huh, Doc?"

"Getting a little soupy," I grinned.

"Who else is here?" He swiveled his eyes under the tent and answered his own question. "I might have known. Fahey never quits, Doc."

I reckoned this was about all the encouragement the Prester received on Titan station; she made the conversation three-cornered with a voice small as static.

"Feeling okay, Mr. Swain?"

I was conscious of Fahey at my elbow as I checked and rechecked the damned stretcher dials. I was afraid of something more deadly than "foul air"; the sudden onset suggested CO. Which meant we were absolutely dependent on our bottled air. The puffer pack had depleted the supply to the stretcher tent; the injured man had exactly ten minutes left on half-flow. Automatically I filled my helmet, shut the valve and gave the tent a blast from my tank.

"Doc . . ." said Prester Fahey.

I closed off the provost's intercom; I had a powerful instinct to shield him from alarm.

"Let me give him some air," she said.

"No need, yet," I said. "Fahey . . . don't alarm him. For heaven's sake take it easy."

For answer Fahey began fumbling with the clamps of her helmet.

"Stop that! Leave it, Fahey!"

"I can breathe shallow. This air ain't bad . . . why, back there on the station . . ."

"You can't breathe carbon monoxide."

Swain was quiet again; his respiration was up and I guessed that he had sensed the crisis. I was numb; my reflexes had slowed. I knew what my next move must be and it seemed like a forlorn hope. I did not, dared not calculate the amount of air left for each one of us—thirty minutes maybe. I felt the seconds tick past as we sat encapsulated. Fahey reached out for the valve of the oxygen tent and I caught her wrist.

"My duty . . ." she said in a strong, flat voice. "My duty to give him air."

"Be damned to you!" I snapped. "*My* duty to keep us all alive as long as possible."

She resisted; the two of us were surreptitiously Indian wrestling for a few seconds; her wrist was wiry and strong. I wondered about giving her a sedative; a bubble of laughter caught in my chest. Fat chance.

I had to leave her alone with the patient and she was bent on self-sacrifice. I had a horrific vision of Fahey snatching off her helmet, floating in the hold, her face turned cherry-red. One thousandth of one percent CO would do it, a smoldering electrical connection leaking combustion products into the hold.

"You're under my orders, Prester Fahey," I said wearily. "Don't interfere with Swain's air supply or your own."

I left them and vaulted away to a place where four fan ribs met on the interior port wall. A- and B-Holds lay parallel, but there was this one spot where B-Hold, for less than a meter, gave directly onto control. I pounded on the square of gray paneling with my fist, then tapped with the end of a penlight. Went on tapping, forgetting letters, overlapping, still foggy, it was like Poe, tapping, musically rapping. A long rigmarole that began SOS in my rusty international code. I repeated the message several times and tried to call Barnes on my suit intercom. My ESP is only average but I shouted to him inside my head. There was not much hope of a reply; I leaned down with my helmet pressed to the gray panel, and at some point I felt satisfied that Barnes had heard and understood.

I went back to the stretcher with the fear of death like a cold compress on the back of my neck. The provost marshal had plenty of air, too much; I evened the pressure in the tent, fed in the last of his thinners. If I was right—and my judgment was all to pieces— the man was sliding into shock and I could do nothing. Prester Fahey was hanging from her stanchion like a bat in a cave. Relaxed, resigned, holding her crucifix. She had given Swain more than half of her air supply. My own tank had been down to begin with.

We drew breath gently; I tried to return to Arkady. I took the child back and we walked, mother and daughter, together into the river fields. After a long time there was a grating of metal, then strong light, a burst of sweet air. The docking was just as bad this time; the valve whistled as we were squeezed aboard the *Delta Oregon*. By the time Barnes brought in the Class E, there was a lethal buildup of CO in both holds, but the priest survived and so did Swain.

The stubborn image of Prester Fahey persists as I move among the crowd of young missionaries. Perhaps my ESP has sharpened up, for here comes a big coincidence; time trips me by the heels.

"Hey, Doc! Doc Gallen!"

A tall black man with cropped white hair; he wears the uniform of a security officer.

"Charlie! Charlie Barnes!"

We walk through the reception area, talking up a storm. It is not in the least like old times; we are Earth-bound, old. Charlie Barnes is five long Earth years older than myself; he commutes from the old town, where he has a wife, grown sons, grandchildren. He makes me proud.

"Doc, I voted for your girl. V. I. Gallen, that's her, right? She got me a pay hike."

We walk out into a sunlit court with fountains playing.

"Charlie . . . whatever happened to Fahey, that cook-sergeant from the Titan station?"

"Still out there," says Charlie Barnes, "last I heard."

He squints at the sunlight and asks politely: "Ever hear any more of that explorer . . . the Russian captain who defected?"

"Still out there, so they say." Why should I mention

that one of those he left behind was V. I. Gallen, our
wunderkind?

"What will you do, Doc?"

"Travel about . . . take a look at their clinics."

"Veterans take a while to settle."

"I know it."

The sunlight is filtered through a glass dome; the
students swarm around us in their pleated cloaks. I
know it now; the people of Earth are and always have
been my proper study. I will never again see the
Moruia; I will not go back to Arkady. Some historian, writing for other sleepless travelers, will make
a correlation between gender and culture, fitting
Prester Fahey and Doc Gallen into some grand design
. . . end products, forerunners . . . but I cannot do it.
My orientation is over; I will get back to work.

PHOENIX IN THE ASHES

Joan D. Vinge

---

*T*he sun's blind, burning face pushed upward past
the scarred rim of the river canyon; brands of
light seared Hoffmann's closed eyelids. He stirred, and
sighed. The temperature rose with the sun; flies and
red ants took the day shift from the mosquitoes.

Hoffmann kicked free of the blankets and sat up.
He brushed flies from his face, sand from his watch
crystal: "Six A.M. . . ." Something stung his foot. "God
damn!" He crushed an ant, felt the familiar throbbing
begin to spread up his foot; he was allergic to ants.
There was no antidote—it meant half a day's nag-
ging pain and nausea. He put on his pants, hobbled
down to the river to splash his head and shoulders
with the still-cool waters of dawn. The river moved
sluggishly past him, only two hundred kilometers

from the Gulf; the water was silted to the color of coffee with too much cream. But Colorado meant "the color red." He wondered whether it had been different, in the past, or whether, somewhere upstream, the river still ran red. . . . "Someday we'll get to find out, Hoffmann." He stood up, dripping, noticed a piece of scrap metal half-buried in the sand. He squatted down again, dug with his fingers. "Steel . . . talk about the middle of nowhere! Yeah. Looks good. . . ." He went back up the bank.

He gathered brush for a fire, cooked rehydrated eggs and bacon. A final bat surrendered to the day, chirping shrilly overhead on its erratic return to the shadowed caves on the far canyon wall. Sparrows rustled in the dusty trees behind him. He tossed out stale bread, watched the birds drop down to peck and wrestle; the sun's heat burned away the wetness on his back, faded the ends of his dark, shaggy hair. He studied the roll of USGS map reproductions again, laboriously translating from the English. "Huh! Los Angeles basin! San Pedro; nice bay . . . wonder what it looks like now? Probably like a crater, Cristovão: navy yards, at Long Beach." He pronounced it "Lona Becha." "Well, we'll know by nightfall, anyhow . . ." He laughed suddenly, mocking. "They say talking to yourself means you're crazy, Hoffmann. Hell, no—only if you answer yourself."

He forced his swollen foot into a hiking boot, pulled on his wrinkled shirt and drooping leather hat, and threw his bedroll into the cockpit behind the 'copter's single seat. The bulge of oversized fuel tanks made the 'copter look pregnant: he called it the

Careless Love. He brushed the blazing metal of the
door. "Don't short on me again, machine—they didn't
build you to give me trouble. Get me to the basin,
one more day, then I'll check the wiring; promise. . . ."
His eyes found the starry heavens in the Brasilian flag
on the door. He looked past the ship at the smoothly
rising gravel of the slope, toward the barren, tortured
peaks, basalt black or the yellow-gray of weathered
bone. He remembered pictures of the moon; pictured
himself there, the first man to walk another world
since before the Holocaust; the first man in two hundred and fifty years. . . . He smiled.

As he climbed into the cockpit, he struck his aching
foot on the door frame. "Mother of God!" He dropped
into the pilot's seat, grimacing. "This day can only
get better." He started the engine. The 'copter rose
into the sky in a swirling storm of sand.

Amanda sipped tea, watched sun sparks move on
the water of the bay through the unshuttered window
of her sister's house. She set down her beaker, returned to brushing the dark, silken hair of Alicia, her
niece. Red highlights flickered between her dye-stained
fingers like light on the water, a mahogany echo of the
auburn strands that escaped around the edges of her
own head-covering. Alicia twisted on her lap; sudden
impatience showed on the small snub-nosed face. "Ow!
Aunt Amanda, tell us another story, please?" She
tugged at the laces of Amanda's leather bodice, untying
them.

Amanda shook her head. "No, Alicita, I can't think
of any more stories; I've already told you three. Take

Dog outside, you and Mano can make him chase sticks." She slid the little girl down, steadied small, bare feet on the floor, and retied the laces of her vest. Dog whined under the table as the children pulled at the scruff of his neck. He raised a bristled yellow face, his jaws snapped shut over a yawn with a *clack* of meeting teeth. He scratched, and sighed, and obeyed. She heard his toenails clicking on the floor tiles, and then happy laughter in the courtyard: sounds she seldom heard.

Her sister returned from the fire, moving slowly because of the clubfoot invisible beneath her long dress. She propped her crutch against the table and sat down again in the high-backed chair. "Are you sure it's all right for them to play with Dog, Amanda? After all, he was . . . well—"

Amanda smiled. He was a snarling, starving mongrel when she had hurled rocks at him for stealing eggs and broken his leg. And then, in remorse, she had thrown out food to him, and given him shelter. When he stood on his hind legs he was as tall as she was; his mustard-brown hide was netted with battle scars, his flopping ears were torn. He would attack any man who gave her trouble, and that was why she kept him. . . . But he slept peacefully at her feet through the long, empty hours, and rested his ugly head against her knee as she sat at her loom; and whomever she loved, he loved . . . and that was also why she kept him. "It's all right, Teresa. I'm sure."

Her sister nodded, turning her cup on the plate. Rainbows revolved in the beaker's opalescent glaze. Teresa put her hands to her bulging stomach suddenly. "Ah! I'm kicked night and day. The little devil . . . I have bruises, would you believe it?" She sighed.

Amanda laughed sympathetically, covered her envy, because Teresa tried to cover her pride.

"How do you ever think of those stories you tell the children?" Teresa pressed on, too brightly; Amanda felt her own smile pinch. "All those wondrous cities and strange sights, balloons big enough to carry men in a basket . . . honestly, Amanda! Sometimes I think José enjoys them more than the children. . . . You're so good with children. . . ." Amanda watched the brightness break apart. "Oh, Amanda, why didn't you obey Father! You'd have children too, and a husband—"

"Let's not bring that up, little sister. Let's not spoil the afternoon—" Amanda studied the dark wood of the tabletop; the fine lace of the cloth Teresa had made by hand caught on her calloused fingers. *To have the money, to have the time.* . . . "I made my choice; I've learned to live with it." *Even if it was wrong.* She looked away abruptly, out the window at the sea.

"I know. But you're wasting away . . . it breaks my heart to see you." Teresa's brown eyes rested on Amanda's hands and were suddenly too bright again with brimming tears. "You were always so thin."

But once there was a man who had called her beautiful; and when he touched her—Amanda felt her cheeks redden with shame. "By the Word, Teresa; it's been eight years! I'm not wasting away." Teresa jerked slightly at her oath. Embarrassed, she picked up her beaker.

"I'm sorry. I'm very . . . moody, these days."

"No . . . Teresa . . . I don't know what I would ever have done without you and José. You've been so kind, so generous to me. I never would have managed." No resentment moved in her.

"It was only justice." Old indignation flickered on Teresa's face. "After all, Father gave me your dowry as well as mine; it wasn't fair. I wish you'd let us do more—"

"I've taken enough already. Truly. It was more than I deserved that Father lets me have the cottage. And that José lets you give away his possessions like you do. He's a kind man."

Teresa patted her stomach, smiled again. "He treats me very well. I don't know why I deserve it."

"I do." Amanda smiled with her, without pain. The wind carried the sound of bells from the temple tower in Sanpedro town.

"The evening bells; José should be coming home . . . now." Teresa reached for her crutch, pushed herself up from the chair. Amanda rose, pulling up her veil as she heard a commotion in the courtyard, shrill delighted voices and a barking dog. José came in through the hall, dark and smiling, a child trailing on each arm. Amanda dropped her eyes, as Teresa did, peeked upward to see José gently raise his wife's chin with a fingertip. Longing pierced her; she pressed her own rough hands against the lavender weave of her shapeless dress.

"My husband . . ."

"My wife. And Amanda: it's good to see you, wife's sister."

She raised her eyes, looked down again, made awkward as she always was by the warm concern in his eyes. "José. Thank you."

Two more figures entered, crowding the small room. Amanda's breath caught on anger as she recognized her other sister, Estella, with her husband Houardo.

"José, why didn't you tell me we were having more guests!" Teresa pulled at her veil, flustered.

"I thought since Amanda would be here, Wife, there'd be plenty to eat for two more." José beamed at his unsubtle inspiration.

"Yes, there will be, José," Amanda said, meeting his gaze directly, made reckless by resentment. "I can't stay. I have too much . . . work . . . to do." She glanced away, at Estella. She could only see the eyes, scornful, beautiful and coal-black, above the fine cloth of Estella's veil. Memory filled in the face, pale, moonlike, flawless; the body, soft, sensually cushioned, with none of the sharp, bony angles of her own. Estella was two years older, but looked two years younger now. Houardo's hand was on Estella's shoulder, possessively, as always; a touch that stirred no longing in her. Teresa had said that Houardo beat his wife, without cause, in fits of jealousy.

But if there was no longing, there was also no sympathy in her now, as she endured their stares. Estella had loved not well, but wisely, marrying the son of the town's wealthiest merchant; a thing which she never let her disinherited sister forget. Amanda noticed that the rich cloth of Estella's dress was the muddy rose color of imitation, not the pure, fragile lavender-blue that only her own dye could produce. She smiled, safe behind her veil. "I have to finish a piece of cloth, if I'm to get it to market."

"Amanda . . ." Teresa started forward, leaning on José's shoulder.

"Good-bye, Alicita, Manolito . . ." She slipped out through the hallway, into the fading heat of the desert afternoon. Dog joined her as she left the shaded courtyard, licked at her hands and her bare, dusty feet. She stroked his bony back. Dog would not share a room with Houardo.

Amanda followed the palm-lined road that led to her father's fields, her toes bunching in the warm dirt; trying to outdistance her own futile resentment. She slowed at last, breathing hard, a cramp burning her side from the long rise of the road. She looked back over the bay, saw ships, like toys, moving under the wind. *And they go away, forever. . . .* "He will come back!"

Dog barked, his tail waving.

She looked down, her shoulders drooped as she reached to pat his head. "And what would he find, if he did . . . ?" Her calloused hands knotted, loosened. *They go away forever.* But the futility, the bitterness, the sorrow and the dreams never left her, never gave her rest. Still looking down, she saw a wrinkled, thumb-sized lump in the dirt; she crouched to pick it up, seeing more scattered across the road in the reaching shadows. Dates hung in bulging clusters below the green frond-crests, in the trees above her head. The crop was turning, the earliest to ripen were already falling along the road. She picked them from the dirt eagerly, filling the pockets she had sewn into the seams of her dress.

As the track wound through the last of the fields before the pasture, she saw her father standing in the road. She stopped; he was not alone, but with three other men. Other merchants, she supposed, come to dicker about the shipment of his grain. . . . She saw that one wore the inlaid ornamental chain of the mayor: he had come to designate the tribute to be sent to the fortress in the hills of Palos Verdes. Her heart lurched; the men of the mayor sometimes took women, as well, for tribute. But they had seen her; she could not turn back now. She moved toward them again, walking on hot coals.

The agent of the mayor turned back to the fields, disinterested, as she drew closer. She felt the other men's eyes on her, vaguely curious, and on her father's broad, unyielding back. He had not looked at her; would not look at her, or speak, ever again. She kept her eyes carefully downcast, seeing only the edge of his long vest, the rich earth-red of his longer robe beneath it, his sandaled feet. *I have only two daughters*, he had said. She did not exist, he would not speak to her, and so she could never speak to him again. Her feet made no sound in the road; the men began to talk of wheat as she passed them.

Suddenly they fell silent again. Amanda raised her head, looking out across the fields toward the river. A high throbbing sound in the air; she frowned, searched her memory, but no recognition came. One of the men muttered something. She saw him point, saw a dark spot on the sky, a bird's form, growing larger and larger, until it was no longer a bird form, or the form of anything she knew. The noise grew with it, until she imagined that the air itself broke against her eardrums like the sea. She covered them with her hands, frozen inside her terror, as the monster swept over the green leaf-wall of the olive orchards. The workers in the field began to break and run, their shining scythes falling in the wheat, their shouts lost in monstrous thunder . . . that ceased, abruptly, leaving a shattered silence.

The monster plummeted toward the half-mown wheat, keening a death song. At the last moment a tearing cough came from it, it jerked upward, its wings a blur . . . and smashed down again into the field, with the grinding crunch of a ship gutted on the rocks. Fingers of sudden flame probed the crumpled corpse, pale smoke spiraled. In the eternity of a heart-beat, she realized that the broken thing was not alive, that it was a ship that flew, like the balloon-ships in the south. And then she saw a new movement, saw the flames give birth to a human form. The man fell, fire eating his arm, crawled, ran desperately. Behind him the flames spread over the ship, the stink of burning reached her, and a cracking noise. The machine exploded, split by God's lightning, impaling on her eyes the image of the running man struck down by a mighty, formless hand. Blinded and deafened, she toppled in the road, while the sky rained blazing debris. "Mercy . . . have mercy on us, sweet Ángel . . . !" Dog began to howl.

One of the merchants came to take her arms, helped her to her feet. She blinked at his stunned face, lost to her behind splotches of dark brilliance as he let her go.

"Are—are you all right, maid?"

She could barely hear him. She nodded, hearing other voices fogged by her deafness.

"Angel, Son of God—" Her father turned away as she looked toward him. "Did you . . . it, Julio? An accursed thing . . . down by God in my own field! My wheat field; why did this—miracle happen in my field?" He shook his head, to clear his eyes, or his regret. The others shook their heads with him, murmuring things she couldn't hear. The mayor's man stood at the edge of the irrigation ditch, his face gray with shock.

Amanda looked out across the field again at the smoking ruins of the machine spread over the flattened wheat. There were no field-workers at all that she could see now, only the sprawled form of the man struck down by God. Her hands wadded the cloth at her stomach as a sound pierced the fog of her ears, and the man in the field lifted his head. She saw only redness—her blindness, or blood: ". . . help . . ." She shut her eyes.

"Look! Listen—" The mayor's man pointed. "He's still alive, in the field. We'll have to kill him."

"No!" her father said. "You'll make my field barren if you shed blood." He shriveled slightly as the other turned back coldly toward him. "He'll die anyway. Let God punish him as He sees fit. Let him die slowly; he's a sorcerer, he deserves to suffer for it."

Amanda's fingers twisted on her dress, sweat tickled

her ribs. The stranger's head fell forward, his hands moved, clutching at the golden, broken grass.

"... help me ... for Christ's sake ... help me ..."

"Listen! He's calling on devils," one of the merchants said. "If you go into the field, he might lay a curse on you."

"God will punish him."

"The metal thing—"

"... *ayuda* ..."

"Don't go near it! God only knows what demons are still left inside it ..."

"... please ..."

Amanda heard a sob, choked back her own sob of anguish. *Father, he sees us! Please, help him—* She turned imploringly, but no one looked at her.

"... that such a thing happened here. We must consult the Prophet's Book ..." Their voices droned on, the cries from the field grew weaker, broken by hopeless silences.

"... *pelo amor de Deus*, please ..."

Amanda started toward the ditch. She heard an oath, looked back at the startled faces of the men, froze as she saw her father's face. *Will you humiliate me again, Amanda, before the mayor and God?* She stopped, stepped back into the road, her head down.

The merchant who had helped her up came toward her, said kindly, "This is no place for you, maid; there is evil here, these things are too strong for a woman's mind. Go home."

She faltered; she glanced again at her father, signaled to Dog and turned away down the road.

Amanda entered the cool, shuttered darkness of her

cottage. She slammed the bottom half of the door,
leaned against the lime-washed adobe of the wall,
feeling the bricks erode under her fingers, tiny flecks
of clay. In the yard Dog harried chickens, barking.
"Dog, stop it!" He stopped, silence fell around the
fading clutter of the chickens. She heard a gull's cry,
as it wheeled above the river, heard in it the cry of
the man in her father's field. *It isn't right—*

But it wasn't right for her to feel this way: It was a
sin to meddle with magic, to harness the power of
demons. It was unnatural. The Book of the Prophet
Angel taught that these things must be denied, they
had been damned by God. And surely she had seen the
stranger struck down, before her eyes, by God's wrath.
Surely—

She moved away from the door, pulled down her
veil, unfastened the ties of her stiff, constricting
bodice. The damp folds of her worn dress beneath it
fell free. She sighed in relief, stretching. The weaving
must be finished tonight, or she would never have the
cloth dyed by market day. . . .

He woke in darkness, retched with the blinding
pain in his head. The matted wheat was sodden with
blood under his cheek. Weakness settled his stomach;
he lay without moving, shivering in the warm air,
staring at his own groping hand. There was one
memory, like a beacon on a black sea of pain: They
would not help him. . . . His eyes closed, the wheat
between his fingers became the stuff of dreams, became
the endless, rippling grass of the Pampas:

He was fifteen, living on his uncle's ranch in the

Argentine province. His cousins had gotten him drunk on the nameless liquor that the ranch hands sucked out of hollow gourds. He had bragged, and they had saddled the half-wild mare who was the color of blood. . . . And she had reared and thrown herself over on top of him, spraining his back.

He lay in the crumpled grass, every breath searing in his chest; stared at his uncle's black, gleaming boots, like bars against the endless freedom of the sky. "Help me, Uncle Josef—"

Get up, Cristovão.

"I can't; it hurts too much, please help me."

Help yourself, Cristovão. You must learn to be strong, like my sons. You must be independent. Get up.

"I can't. I can't."

Get up. The boot lifted his shoulder; he cried out.

"I can't!"

Get up, Cristovão. You can do anything you have to do.

"Please help me."

Get up.

"Please . . ."

Get up. Get up—!

Amanda rose from her stool, began to work the finished piece of cloth free from the loom at last. The candles flickered, her shadow danced with her on the wall. The weaving soothed her in the quiet hours of the evening, patterned her thoughts with its peaceful rhythm. Often she sang, with no one but Dog to hear, and the crickets in the yard for a chorus.

She folded the cloth carefully, kept the edge from

sweeping the floor . . . and noticed that the crickets were silent. She stood still, listening, heard an unidentifiable noise in the yard. Dog stirred where he lay sleeping, growled softly. He climbed to his feet, went to the door and snuffled at the crack. Another small sound, closer to the cottage. Dog's hackles rose, her skin prickled. A coyote or wildcat out of the desert, hunting . . . a drunken herder or field hand, who knew she lived alone—

Something struck the door, struck it again. Dog began to bark, drowning her cry of surprise. "Dog, be quiet! Who's there? What do you want?" No answer came. "Go away then! Leave me alone or I'll set my dog on you!"

She heard a fumbling, a scratching, slide along the wood, and a sound that might have been human. She moved toward the door stiffly, caught in a sudden, terrifying prescience. Her hand shook as she unlatched the top of the door, pulled it open— "No!" Her hands covered her unveiled face, denying the nightmare that was the face before her.

The man from her father's field clung to the lower door with blistered, blackened hands. A gash opened the side of his head, slashed his cheek, oozing sluggish red; his eyes showed white in a death mask of crusted blood and filth.

"Sweet Ángel!" Amanda whispered, stumbled back, hands still covering her face. "I can't help you! Go away, go away—" Dog crouched, his muscles coiled.

"Please . . ." Tears spilled down the stranger's face, runneling the crusted mask. She wondered if he even saw her. "Please."

She dropped a hand to Dog's neck, rubbed it, felt his crouching tension ease. She unlatched the bottom door and pulled it open.

The stranger stumbled forward into the room. Amanda caught the bruising burden of his weight, led him to her pallet and let him slip down her arms onto the blanket that covered the straw. He lay weeping mindlessly, like a child, "*Obrigado, obrigado . . .*" Dog nosed his tangled legs.

She poured water into a bowl from the *olla* by the door, crossed the room again and took up the newly woven cloth from the loom's stool. *He'll die anyway—* She hesitated, looking back; then biting her lip, she began to tear the cloth into strips.

He sank through twisting corridors of smoke, lost in the endless halls of dream, where every convolution turned him back into the past and there was no future. He opened the doors of his life, and passed through. . . .

He opened the door to the crowded outer office, pushed his way through the confusion of milling recruits around the counter. He felt his blood pressure rise with every jarring contact, at every sight of an army uniform. He broke through, almost ran down the hall to Mario Coelho's office.

"Where the hell is Hoffmann?"

He slowed, hearing his name, and the voice of Esteban Vaca from the Corps of Engineers.

"Relax," Coelho said. "If he's half an hour late, he's early; you know that. I think he makes a point of it."

"Mother of God; I just don't understand why you put up with it!"

"You know why I put up with it. He's the best damned prospector I've ever seen; he knows more about metals than half the chemists in Brasil. He's uncanny at ferreting out deposits . . ." Coelho's chair squeaked.

"How much of an instinct does he need to find the Los Angeles basin? I suppose only some crazy fool who talks to himself in a crowd would even want to go look for it."

Laughter.

"You'd talk to yourself, too," Coelho said, "if you spent most of your life in the middle of nowhere. . . ."

"And besides, I know I'll never talk behind my back." Hoffmann grinned as he entered the room, saw Coelho's thick neck redden with embarrassment. "So, you want me to scout the Los Angeles basin." He straddled a chair, resting his arms on the hard back. "That's news. I thought we didn't have the fossil-fuel resources to mine clear up in the Northwest Territory. Or did we take over Venezuela while I was asleep?" *The Los Angeles basin.* . . . He felt a sudden eagerness, the sense of freedom and fulfillment that only prospecting brought into his life.

"We didn't; but they estimate it won't take us much longer. If that's so, the Corps of Engineers is thinking of reopening the Panama Canal: If it's feasible we've solved the transportation problem. And the coast's inhabited—which gives us a local pool of gook labor, to do the dirty work in the ruins." Vaca smiled.

"You stink, Vaca," Hoffmann mumbled. Vaca looked up sharply.

"Come on, Hoffmann." Coelho tapped his fountain pen wearily on the blotter. "Nobody makes you work for us. All we need from you is a report on whether the Los Angeles basin is worth our while."

Hoffmann shrugged unapologetically, felt them assessing his rumpled civilian clothes, the battered hat jammed down over his shaggy hair, his muddy desert boots. Even Coelho, who ought to be used to it, and to him, by now. Hoffmann said absently, "I use you, you use me. . . ."

They looked at him.

"All right, I do want the job. I'm ready whenever you are. What background stuff can you . . ." He watched as Coelho's face dissolved into the milky white globe of a street lamp; got up, staring, as Vaca's face became the face of his uncle. The desk was a spreading, formless darkness, a gaping mouth to swallow him. Ragged teeth tore into his flesh as he fell through the doorway of another dream. . . .

Amanda started out of a nodding dream at the stranger's cry. The candle before her on the bare wooden table was half burned away, like the night beyond the door. She got up from her stool, stumbling over Dog at her feet, and went to kneel again beside the pallet. She had stripped off the bloody rags of the stranger's clothing and bathed him, picked metal from his torn flesh, bound his wounds and burns with the healing pith of aloe vera leaves broken from the serrated bush in the yard. And she had prayed, as she worked, that he would die, and God would take away the torment of his suffering from them both. . . .

But he did not die, and he lay now huddled between

her blankets, shivering and sweating, his face on fire under her hand. She wiped it again with cool water, saw fresh blood on the white linen that swathed his head. He mumbled words that she almost understood, altered strangely. She whispered reassurance, tried to still his restless motion. His blistered hand closed spasmodically on her dress, jerking her down. "*Mãe*, I'm cold . . . s-so cold, *mãe* . . ." She struggled as his other hand trapped her wrist, and she heard the threadbare cloth begin to tear. ". . . cold . . ."

She went limp on the straw beside him to save her dress, shuddered as he pressed against her. "No—" She felt the fever heat even through her clothing; but there were no more blankets to keep him warm. "Angel, Son of God, forgive me. . . ." She put her arms around him and let him find the comfort of her own warmth. He sighed, and quieted, touching her in his delirium as a child seeks its mother, as a husband seeks his wife. Amanda heard the steeple bells sound midnight in the town below, remembered them on too many nights, when she lay alone with sleepless sorrow. Slowly her rigidness softened; her hair slipped free of its cloth as she moved her head, and spread across her shoulders. Memory caressed her with a stranger's unknowing hands, and Amanda began to weep. . . .

Diego Montoya was a merchant, dealing with the captains of the ships that sailed the long coast to the southern lands. He had no sons but only the burden of three daughters who must be dowried for marriage. But he was a wealthy man, by the standards of Sanpedro, and he had determined that his daughters would marry well . . . and so recover his losses in giving them away. His eldest daughter, Estella, was a beauty, and he had managed to match her to the wealthiest heir in town. And then he had begun to negotiate a match for his second daughter, awkward, reed-thin Amanda.

He had protected his daughters, like the valuable property they were, particularly keeping them from the sailors with whom he dealt and whom he knew too well. Again and again he impressed on his daughters the need for chasteness and obedience, the Prophet's warnings about the sins against natural law that damned the souls of the footloose sailors and their women.

But Amanda had drawn water from the well in the courtyard, and the handsome, black-haired boy drank as he waited while his captain spoke with her father inside. He was different from the sailors she had seen, somehow in her heart she felt he was not like any man she had ever seen—and he looked at her over the cup's edge in a way no man ever had, hesitantly, with pleasure. She stole glances at him, at his bare brown arms, his rough gray tunic, the laces of his sandals hugging his calves. He wore golden plugs stretching his earlobes.

"Thank you, maid." He set down the cup, caught at her with his eyes as she began to turn away. "Are you"— he seemed to be trying to think of something to say— "are you the daughter of this house?" He looked embarrassed, as if he'd hoped it would be something more profound.

"The second daughter." Knowing that she should not, she stayed and answered him.

"What's your name? I'm Miguel," he acknowledged his effrontery with a bob of his head. "I—I think you are very fair."

She blushed, looking down again, twisting the soft laces of her bodice. "You shouldn't say that."

"I know . . ."

"My—name is Amanda."

Her father saw them together by the well as he came to the doorway and ordered her sharply into the house.

But the next afternoon she slipped away, to meet Miguel on the path that wound along the river, and every afternoon, through the week that his ship was in port. Miguel answered questions her heart had never known how to ask, that had nothing to do with the limits of the world she knew. He was eighteen, hardly older than she was, but he had left his home in the far south years before, longing to see what lay beyond the headlands of the harbor. He told her tales of the peoples of the south and their strange cities, strange customs, strange beasts. He told her of men who flew, suspended beneath great bags of air; who crossed mountains higher than the shimmering peaks she could see at the desert's limits, to visit the southern lands. He said that they came from a land where there were wonders even he could not imagine, boasted that someday he would find a way to steal aboard one of the airships and explore all the new wonders that hid behind the mountain wall.

Amanda found herself dreaming with him; dreaming that she would be with him forever, share in his adventure, have his love, and his children. . . . For she had always been afraid of the things that passed between a man and wife, things a maiden hardly dared to whisper about. But lying on the warm river-bank, he had unfastened her veil to kiss her lips, freed her hair from its covering, sighing in wonder and calling it flame. And his fingers had touched her breast through the cloth of her gown, and started another flame, inside her. That night she had gone to the temple, heavy with guilt, and prayed to God for guidance. But the next afternoon, she let him touch her again . . . and only the impossibly knotted cord that pinioned her cotton drawers kept her a maiden, at last.

And then, suddenly, the week they had shared was gone, and they clung together in the shadowed heat of the olive grove. "How can I leave without you, Amanda? Come with me—" His fingers lifted tendrils of her hair.

"Stay here, with me, Miguel! Let me speak to Father, he'll let us marry—"

"I can't. I can't stay in one place, there are too many places I still haven't seen. Come away with me, let me share them with you. . . . You want to see them, too; I see them in your eyes! I'll buy you strings of opals, to match the fire in your hair . . . sky-blue butterfly wings that shine with their own light. . . . We'll cross the mountain wall in a balloon. Come away with me, Amanda!" He caught her hands, kissed her hungrily, drawing her toward the road.

The temple bells began to sound for evening prayer

in the village. She pulled free, tears welling in her eyes. "I can't—the Prophet forbids it!" Afraid of God's wrath, and her father's, afraid of the shame it would bring on her family, and to her . . . afraid that none of those things mattered enough to keep her from his arms, she ran, sobbing, back through the trees.

"Amanda . . . I love you! I'll come back; wait for me! Please wait for me—"

Amanda woke up, aching with stiffness and remembered grief, to the sound of the morning bells. She gasped as she focused on the stranger's naked side lying against her own; stilled her urge to leap away, as memory stilled her terror. His head rested on her shoulder, pillowed on her spreading hair; the stains on the bandage were dark now, but his face still burned with fever. He lay quietly, his ribs barely rising, falling. With infinite care she drew her numbed arm from beneath him, covered him again and stood up. Dog scratched at the door; she let him out into the dawn, let in the pungent, sage-scented air to cleanse the smell of sickness. She noticed a line of dark stains across the hard dirt floor, tracing the stranger's path from door to bed. *Oh God, why must you send me this new trial?*

The stranger lived, on the edge of death, through the long day; and that night again she held him in her arms, startled from her sleep by the ghosts of his haunted fever dreams. Names of people, cities and objects, words in a meaningless tongue, filled her own unquiet rest with strange, unnatural dreams. And yet, time and again he spoke the names of places she knew: Losangeles, Palos Verdes, her own Sanpedro.

The dreams clung to him like death's shroud while two days passed, and three, and four. Amanda carried water from the river, heated it, washed bandages and dressed his wounds. She bathed his parched body, forced liquids down his throat. He was damned, but in his willfulness and sinful pride he struggled for his own destiny, defying the powers of nature and God. She shared in his defiance of fate, afraid to stop and question why.

At last a night came when he slept in her arms breathing quietly and deeply, unharrowed by dreams; and, touching his face in the morning, she knew that he had won. She cried again, as she had cried on the first night.

Late in the afternoon the stranger woke: Amanda looked up from her loom to find him staring silently at her face. She pulled up her veil self-consciously, wondered how long she had been sitting revealed to him, and went to kneel down at his side. He tried to speak, a raw noise caught in his throat; she gave him water and he drank, gratefully.

"Where . . . where am I?" The words were thick, like his swollen tongue.

"You are in my house." Habitually she answered what a man asked, and no more.

His hand moved under the blanket, discovering his nakedness. He looked back at her, confused. "Have I been . . . were we—? I mean, are you a—" She flushed, stiffening upright. "I'm sorry . . . I can't seem to remember, my head—" He lifted his hand with an effort; his fingers grew rigid as they brushed the thick, swathing bandages. He stared at his hand, also bandaged. *"Meu Deus . . .* an accident? Was I in an accident?" He looked away, taking in the small, windowless room, the streaming dusty light that struck her loom from the open door. "Where is this place?"

"This is the village of Sanpedro." She hesitated. "You fell from the sky, into my father's field. God . . . God struck you down. You nearly died."

"I did?" He sighed suddenly, closing the eye not covered by bandage. "I can believe it." He was quiet for a long time; she thought he had fallen asleep. She started to get up; his eye opened. "Wait! Wait . . . don't go—"

She kneeled down again, feeling the tension in his voice.

"Who are you?"

"Amanda. Amanda Montoya."

"Who am I?"

She blinked, shook her head. "I don't know."

"I don't know either . . ." His hand pressed his head again, the words faded. "Christ . . . I don't remember anything. Not anything—" He broke off. "Except . . . except . . . the field; people, standing in a road, looking at me . . . but they wouldn't help me. They saw me, they knew, but they wouldn't help me." He trembled. "God . . . they wouldn't help me. . . ." And he slept.

"I know the name San Pedro . . ." he said stubbornly between sips of broth as she fed him. She had killed a chicken while he slept, and made soup to give him strength. "I saw it, somewhere . . . the Los Angeles basin? Does that mean anything?" He looked up at her, hopeful, swallowed another mouthful of soup. His eye was as gray as sorrow in the candlelight, and fear lurked in it.

"Yes. It's the desert, all around us, to the north, to the mountains— We only go out into it for metals."

"Metals!" He pushed up onto his elbows, spilling soup, sank back with a groan. "Metals—" His hand reached for something, found it gone. She wiped soup from his half-grown beard and his chest. "Damn it," he whispered, "it will come back. It will. When I'm stronger I'll go to the—the place where it happened, and I'll remember."

"Yes," Amanda said softly, thinking he expected an answer. "Yes, I'm sure you will."

The gray eye glanced at her, surprised; she realized that he had not been speaking to her. She offered him more soup; he shook his head carefully. "Why do you cover your face—Amanda? You didn't before . . . or your hair; I remember, your hair is red."

"You weren't supposed to see it!" She wondered, mortified, what else he remembered. "The Prophet Ángel teaches us that it isn't modest for a woman to show herself to a man who is not her husband."

He smiled stiffly with one side of his mouth. "I'm sleeping in your bed, but you won't let me look at your face. . . . Who is this 'Ángel'?"

She felt irritation prick her at the tone of his voice. "No wonder you practice sorcery, if you've never received his Word. Ángel is the son of God, who led our people here from the south. He revealed that the only true and righteous life is one within the pattern of nature, the life all creatures were meant to live. To do sorcery, to try to put yourself in the place of God, from false pride, is to bring down ruin—as you were shown. That's why my father and the other men wouldn't help you. It was God's punishment."

His expression doubted her, changed. "You were there—"

"Yes." She looked down.

He took a deep breath, held it. "But—when I came to your door, you helped me. Why? Weren't you afraid of God's punishment, too?"

She sighed. "There's little more that God could do to me, or I to God. . . ." She got up and moved away, gave the last of the soup to Dog where he lay under the table, her own hunger forgotten.

"Amanda?"

She straightened up, looked back at the stranger.

"When I'm well—"

"Then you must leave." She rubbed her arms inside the loose sleeves of her dress. "Or people will call me a harlot." *And they call me too many things already.*

"But what if I can't—" He didn't finish it.

She went back to her loom. When she looked up again, he was sleeping.

Days passed; the swollen redness slowly went out of his wounds, the sight of his blistered arm no longer turned her stomach. But still he sometimes dropped off to sleep in the middle of a sentence, to wake minutes or hours later, out of a mumbling, delirious dream; a dream that he could never remember.

He pressed her angrily, almost desperately, for the details of his dreams, old ones and new, swearing at her once because she couldn't write them down.

"Women are not taught to write," she had snapped. "Women are taught to serve their husbands, and—and their fathers. Only men have a need to write."

"What kind of garbage is that?" He struggled to sit up, propping his back against the cool wall. "*You* need to write, so you can tell me what I say! This place is the damnedest, most backward piece of real estate in the entire Northwest Territory!" He frowned, analyzing. "In what's left of it—"

She glared at him. "Then it's a pity you'll have to stay here. Perhaps that's God's final punishment to you." She dared many things, in her speech with this stranger, that she would never have dared with a man of her own village or one strong enough to strike her.

He looked up sullenly. "What makes you think I'll stay in San Pedro?"

"Because your flying ship is broken. You'll never get back to wherever you came from, across the desert and the mountains, without it."

He was silent; she saw tension drawing the muscles of his hollowed cheek. "I see," he said finally. "What . . . what happens to 'sorcerers' in San Pedro?"

"Anything." She hardened her voice, and her heart. "They're outcasts. They can pray for forgiveness, and do penance at the temple, if someone will sponsor them. But you're an outsider. You have no family, and no money; no one will protect you. If you offend people, they will stone you. If not, they'll ignore you;

you'll have to beg to live. Some walk out into the desert, and never come back—" *The silent, burning mirror of light; the scented, fevered wind; the shimmering, unattainable peaks of Sangabriel. . . .* It had drawn her away, as she gathered brush, more than once; but never far enough.

The stranger sat, stricken, his uncovered eye expressionless with the confusion of his emotions. Almost defiantly he said, "What if I won't leave here?"

"Then Dog will tear your throat out."

He slid down the wall onto the straw, pulling the blanket up over his shoulders, and turned his back on her. That night she lay sleepless on her own new pallet of straw, hearing the hard, bitter voices of the midnight bells.

The next morning she knelt at her *metate,* watching the sun rise over the distant peaks as she ground the grain she had gleaned from her father's fields. Dog lay stretched on the cool dirt, tongue lolling, looking half-dead in his eye-rolling ecstasy. She smiled, glanced up as he raised his head and barked once, inquiringly.

The stranger stood in the doorway of the cottage, wearing his torn, close-fitting pants and nothing else. The pants hung precariously around his hips; his ribs showed. He sat down abruptly against the house, sighed in satisfaction, smiled at her. "It's a beautiful morning."

She looked down, watching the motion of the smooth granite *mano* beneath her palms, made ashamed at the sight of him and by the memory of her cruelty.

But if he was angry, or afraid, he showed no sign,

only stretched his scarred limbs gingerly in the soothing heat of the early sun. He watched her form the flat, gritty loaves of unleavened bread. "Can I help?"

"No," she said, startled. "No, enjoy the sun. You—you need to go slowly, to recover your strength. Besides, this is women's work." She chided, mildly.

"It doesn't look too complicated. I expect I could learn."

"Why should you want to?" She wondered if the blow on the head had driven him mad, as well. "It's unnatural for a man to want to do women's work. Don't you remember anything?"

"I don't remember that. But then," he shrugged, "I don't think I was ever an Ángelino, either. I only thought—maybe I could help out with some of the work around here. You never seem to rest. . . . You'd have more time for your hobby." His voice was oddly cajoling.

"Hobby?" She struck her flint against the bar of steel, saw sparks catch in the tinder-dry brush beneath the oven. "What hobby?"

"Your weaving." He scratched his bandaged head, smiling cheerfully. "Mother of God, this itches." He scratched too hard, winced.

She turned to stare at him, at the linen that bound his head, in stunned disbelief. "It's not my hobby! It's how I stay alive: by weaving cloth. It took me two months to finish the piece I tore into rags, to bind your wounds!"

His hand froze against his head. "I'm sorry. I didn't know that—people wove cloth by hand. . . ." He looked down at his pants. "Let me make it up to you, Amanda. Let me work while you weave; it doesn't matter if it's women's work. I'm just grateful to have my life."

Smoke blew into Amanda's eyes, brought stinging tears. She wiped them away and didn't answer.

But she let him help her with the endless, wearying tasks that wove the pattern of her life so that she could weave cloth, instead. At first he was too weak to do more than toss the sparse handful of grain to the sparse handful of scrawny chickens, hunt for their occasional eggs, sit on a stool in the sun tending her cooking pot. He ate ravenously, never quite seeming to realize how little there was, and she was glad that it was the autumn harvest, when the little was more than usual. And she was glad that he would soon be gone. . . .

But as his strength returned he began to do more, though he still collapsed into dreaming trances sometimes while he worked. He mumbled to himself, too, as though he really were a little mad, as he fetched water up the long slope from the river, walked out across the brown pastures to the desert's edge, bringing back brush and deadwood to chop up for her fire. She was afraid to send him to town, or even into her father's fields to glean—for his own sake, or hers, she didn't know. But, of his own accord, he began to fish from the riverbank: He gutted and scaled his glassy-eyed catches, spitted them over the fire for her dinner; and as the days passed she began to feel a trace of softness cushioning the sharp edges of her bones. She watched the stranger's own emaciated body fill out;

saw, unwillingly, that he had a strong and graceful build. She cut a slit in one of her blankets to make him a poncho; to protect him from the hot sun, to protect herself from the shameful embers the sight of him began to stir within her.

At last, as though he had postponed it as long as he dared, the stranger asked her to take him to the place where he had fallen to earth. She led him back through the rustling shadows along the palm-lined track, to the field where his machine lay in pieces in the amber sea of grain. He stopped in the road, stared, his face burning with hope . . . but he only shook his head and crossed the irrigation ditch, dry now, into the field. He began to search through the grasses, forgetting her, hunting for his past as Dog hunted for squirrels.

She followed him, strangely excited, afraid to interfere, and heard his sudden exclamation. "What is it?" She came hesitantly to his side, tugging at her snagged skirts.

"I don't know. . . ." He kneeled down by a flat piece of metal, warped at one end. She saw a rectangle of green paint, a yellow diamond inside it, a blue circle filled with stars. A band of white, with lettering, arced across the sky. "But that," he pointed at the rectangle, "is the Brasilian flag!"

"What's Brasil?"

"A place. A country."

"Where? Beyond the mountains? Is it like the mayor's domain?"

"I don't know." He frowned. "That's all I can remember. But the words *Ordem e Progresso*: that means 'order and progress' . . . I think it does. Brasilian must be the other language I speak—for whatever good that does me." He got up.

Dog came bounding to them, something large and brown flopping in his jaws. Amanda grimaced, "Dog! Don't bring your carcasses to me—!"

"No, wait, it's not an animal. Come here, Dog! Bring it here, good boy . . ." The stranger held out his hand; Dog came to him obediently, tail beating. Amanda wondered if Dog knew a fellow outcast by instinct, or why he gave this one other person his trust. "It looks like a hat—" The stranger pried it loose from Dog's massive jaws, pounded his back in appreciation. Dog smiled, panting. "Could it be from around here?"

He turned it in his hands: "It must be mine," and he looked inside. His breath caught. " 'Cristovão Hoffmann,' " he said quietly. "Cristovão Hoffmann . . . I'm Cristovão Hoffmann!"

"Do you remember—?"

"No." His mouth pulled down. "No, I don't remember! Hell, for all I know Cristovão Hoffmann's the man who made the hat!" He looked back at her, defeated, set the hat on top of his bandages; it fell off. "But it doesn't matter. I'll be Cristovão Hoffmann; it doesn't feel so bad. I have to be somebody. Christ, maybe *I* made the hat." He started away across the field to the main wreckage, the mutilated skeleton of the flying ship. She picked up his hat, began to strip wheat from the stalks to fill it up.

When she reached the charred hulk of the flying ship, she found him lying senseless in the grass.

* * *

The clouds closed around him like soft wings as he reached the wreck, stealing him away from the dream world of his waking reality, back into the reality of his dreams. He chose a door: The clouds parted, and he was flying. . . .

Hoffmann followed the frayed brown-green ribbon of the river out of the mountains, looking down on the sun's anvil pocked with skeletal shrubs: the desert that stretched to the sea. "If anybody's crazy enough to live here now, they've got to be sane enough to stay by the water. . . ." On every side, for as far as he could see, a faint rectangular gridwork patterned the desolation. He caught occasional flickers of blinding whiteness, the sun mirrored on metal and glass. This was the Los Angeles basin: hundreds of square miles of accessible aluminum, steel and iron . . . copper, tungsten, rare earth elements . . . all the riches of a benevolent nature, waiting for discovery and recognition. Waiting for him. Waiting for him. . . . His skin itched with desire; tomorrow he would begin to explore.

But with the desperate scarcity of one thing—fossil fuels—no one would ever make use of his discovered bounty, unless there was an available pool of local labor to do what machines could not. He knew small primitive villages and colonies stretched northward up the coast from the South American continent, cut off from all but the most fragmentary dirigible contact with the Brasilian Hegemony: Today he would search for those. If there was an available subsistence agriculture the specialists could upgrade, then the local

population, and even imported laborers, could be put
to work mining the treacherous, possibly radioactive
ruins. The people would have more food, better
medical care—and lose their freedom of choice, and
their lives, in grueling servitude to the government.
It had been the way of governments since the first
city-state, and though it troubled Hoffmann somewhat
that he had a part in it now, he seldom thought about
why. Prospecting was the one thing that gave any real
meaning to his life, that evoked any real emotion in
him: He endured his fellow men to the extent that
they made it possible for him to live the way he did;
beyond that, he chose to live without them.

He began to see the form of San Pedro Bay, promis-
ing for shipping. From the air, the land was visibly
patterned by ruins beneath the amorphous sand-piled
pavement of desert. The bay was more deeply incut
than he remembered on the maps, with a scalloped
rim. " 'Like a crater, Cristovão. . . .' " he repeated.
"Jesus, what a beautiful harbor!" He could see signs
of habitation now, a small mud-brick town, bright sails
in the harbor, fields and pasturage along the river. He
used his binoculars, thought he detected other signs of
habitation farther along the northwestward curve of
the coast; pleased, he dropped lower, buzzing the
fields. "Some irrigation, primitive . . . bet they don't
rotate their crops. . . ." Tiny figures huddled, staring
up at him, or fled beneath the 'copter's shadow in
terror. They were as nonessential to him as the rest of
humanity, less real than the shining, lifeless wilderness
of the desert. . . .

And then, abruptly, the umbilical of vibrating roar

that gave him life within his glass-and-metal womb was cut. Faint cries of fear and disbelief reached him through the windshield glass, echoed in his mind, as he began to fall. . . .

The stranger jerked awake, sitting up from Amanda's lap in the shade of the broken ship. His breath came hard; he rubbed his sweating face. *"Mãe do Deus. . . ."* He looked back at her, at the shadowing hull above them. "It happened again?"

She nodded.

"I was falling . . . *that* was falling, the—the *Careless Love.* The electrical system was . . . was. . . . Damn it! Damn it! It's in there, my whole life! But every time I reach for it, it slips between my fingers . . . like mercury. . . ."

"Maybe if you didn't try, it would come. Maybe you try too hard." She wondered what good it would do him to know, but knew that even she would need to know.

"How am I supposed to stop trying?" He covered the frustration in his voice. "Did I—say anything?"

"You said, 'Cristoval.'" The name wasn't quite the same, when he pronounced it. "You said, 'Craters.' And that we didn't . . . turn our crops around." She made circling motions with her hand.

"Rotate your crops," he said absently. "Alternate them, from field to field, season to season, to let the fields rest. It's good for the soil. . . ." He stopped. "Maybe I was some kind of advisor. Maybe I could teach your father better farming methods—"

A small, sharp laugh escaped her. "I don't think

he'd listen to you. Not after he watched you struck down by God."

He grimaced, got up, staring at the burned-out wreck. He leaned down to pick up a handful of charred papers. "Maps. They're in English . . . but I can't read it anymore." He bunched them in his hand, didn't drop them, looking south across the bay. "It's a good harbor. And that's important. . . ."

"Yes, it is." She answered, knowing now that he didn't need an answer.

"Where do the ships go from here?"

"Mostly south, for a long way. In the southern lands there are airships that fly with balloons, not sorcery, and cross the mountains to a strange land." Her heart constricted.

"There are?" he said, suddenly excited. "If I could find a ship in port, to take me—"

"Not unless you could pay for it."

"How much?"

"More than nothing, which is all you have. And all I have."

"How am I supposed to get the money? I can't *do* anything!" His hand struck the blackened frame. "*Tamates!* I can't do anything . . . it's never going to come back. Let's go." He started abruptly back toward the road.

When they returned to the cottage, he took the leather hat and stood before the broken mirror on the wall. He began to unwrap the bandages that covered his head. As he pulled the final clinging strips away from his skin, she saw his hands drop, nerveless, to his sides; the streamer of bandage fluttered down. She saw his face in the mirror: the half-healed scar that gaped along his cheek and scalp, the stunned revulsion in his eyes.

"Cristoval," she whispered, "it was worse, before. It will be much better, in time. Much better. . . ." She met his eyes in the mirror, eyes as gray as sorrow.

He looked away; went to the door, and out, word-lessly.

She sat weaving, waiting, through the hot autumn afternoon, but he did not return. She watched the cloth grow as she passed the shuttle back, and back again, through the taut threads; thinking how much it had grown, in so short a time, because the stranger had come into her life. She went down to the river, but he was not there; she bathed, and washed her hair. Suppertime came, and passed. Dog sat in the door-way, whining into the twilight. Hungry for broiled fish, she drank water and ate dry bread. . . . He would fell the dead orange tree, he had said, before it fell on her house . . . he would build her a palm-leaf canopy in the yard to shade her while she cooked. A fence of adobe bricks . . . a henhouse . . . a shower . . . a real bed. A life for a life. . . .

She blew out the candle, lay down on her pallet of straw and in the darkness remembered the feel of his body against her, the touch of his hands. He had gone out into the desert; he would walk toward the un-reachable mountains, trying to go home. And he would lie down at last and die, alone, and the buz-zards would pick his bones. She heard the tolling of the midnight bells: Pitiless and unforgiving, they mocked her, and named her, *Amanda, Amanda.* . . .

* * *

"Amanda?" The door rattled; Dog leaped to his feet, barking joyfully. "Amanda? Will you let me in?"

She ran to the door, wrapped in her blanket, her hair streaming. She unbolted it, threw it open; the light of the full moon struck her face. Cristoval's shadowed eyes looked long on her, in silence. At last he stepped forward, into the house. She lit a candle as he bolted the door, brought him bread and a pitcher of water. He drank deeply, sighed. She sat across from him at the table, covering her face with a corner of her blanket, but feeling no embarrassment. She didn't ask where he had been, he didn't tell her; he kept his face slightly averted, hiding his scar.

"Amanda—" He finished the bread, drank again. "Tell me why you're not married."

She started. "What, now?"

"Yes, now. Please."

"I have no dowry," she said simply, hoping he would understand that much and let it go. "No man would take me."

An unreadable expression crossed his face. "But your father must be a wealthy man, he owns all these fields—why does he treat you like this; why do you live in this hovel?"

She reddened. "He's very generous to let me live here! I defied him, and he disowned me. He didn't have to give me anything; I would have been like you. But he lets me stay in this cottage, and glean in his fields. I suppose he would have been ashamed to watch his daughter become a beggar or a whore."

"Why did you disobey him? What did you do?"

"I wouldn't marry the man chosen for me. He was a good man; but I thought—I thought I was in love. . . ." She tasted bitterness, remembering the red-haired girl she had once been: who sat with her embroidery for hours at the window, gazing out over the bay, who wept with unconsolable loss, for her heart had been stolen, and she had not had the strength to follow it; who found that the staid ritual of life in Sanpedro was suffocating her, and her dreams were dying. *He said he would come back* . . . and she had believed him, and vowed that she would wait for him.

But her father had known none of that, thinking only that his spindly, homely daughter longed to marry any man; that it was high time to get her a husband, to make order out of her foolish maiden's fancies. And when he had told her of the match, she had run sobbing from the room and sworn that she would never marry. Her father raged, her mother scolded, her sisters wept and pleaded. But she sat as still and unreachable as her aged grandmother, who rocked endlessly by the fire, blind with cataracts, and deaf: who had had hair of flame, like her own, once, in youth. . . .

And at last her father had given her an ultimatum, and in her childish vanity she had spurned the marriage, and he had disowned her. He had given her dowry to Teresa, ungainly of body but fair of heart, and for Teresa he had chosen well—a man who desired her for her soul, and not for her riches.

"And so I came to live here, and learned what it

is to be poor. My vanity starved to death, long ago. But by then it was too late." She glanced down at the rough hand holding the blanket edge. "There is no end to my sin, no end to my punishment, now." Her hand slid down, taking the blanket with it; Cristoval looked at her strangely. She pulled it back up, defensive. "I am still a virgin; my marriage sheets would not dishonor my husband. But I don't have a maiden's soul . . ." She felt her words fading. "In my mind, lying alone at night, I have sinned, and sinned. . . ." She reddened again, remembering her thoughts this night. "Sweet Ángel; I'm so tired!" Her voice shook. "I would gladly have married, a hundred times over, by now! But what man would have me now?"

She heard Cristoval draw a long breath. "I would have you. Amanda . . . will you marry me?"

Her blush deepened with anger. "You! Do you think I don't know why you're asking me? I may be just a woman, but I'm not such a fool that I can't see what you've been trying to do to me. You've smiled, and wheedled, and tried to make me depend on you, so that when you were well I wouldn't make you leave. And so you'd even marry me, to save yourself?"

"Well, what the hell's wrong with that?" His scarred hand knotted on the table. "You just told me you'd marry anybody, to save yourself from the hardship, and the loneliness. Why is it wrong for me to want the same thing? I don't want to die a friendless beggar in this self-righteous hell, either! I'm not asking you to love me—I don't love you. I want to marry you to save myself, because there's no other way I can; that's all. If you accept, take me out of your own need. I'll be a good husband to you. I'll carry my share of the weight. Together, maybe we could even make a decent life for ourselves." He glanced down, turned his face squarely to her in the light. "God knows I'm not much to look at, now, Amanda. But . . . but in the dark—"

She studied his face, her eyes catching only once on the scar, used to it from dressing his wound. Apart from it his face was pleasant, almost handsome now with familiarity, under the short, sun-faded hair. He was no more than thirty, perhaps no older than herself: He was strong and, behind the strangeness of his peculiar habits, somehow gentle. She did not think he would beat her. And— "And I'm not . . . much to look at, either, now; I know." She sighed. "Love is not a right to demand in marriage. Love is a reward. Yes, then, Cristoval; I will be your wife. Tomorrow we will go to see my father." Her shoulders sagged; pulling the blanket close around her, she rose and went to her bed.

Cristoval followed her with his eyes before he blew out the candle. She heard him lie down on his own pallet, heard his voice in the darkness: "Thank you."

They walked slowly along the road to town, silently. Amanda listened to the creaking gulls and the twittering waking sparrows. *This is my wedding day,* she thought, surprised. *Will I be different tomorrow, if we're wed? Will he?* She glanced at Cristoval, his face turned away toward the sea. He didn't touch her but walked as though he were entirely alone, brooding. *Everything will be different. I've lived alone for so long. . . .*

"Amanda," he said suddenly, startling her. "Do we have to go to your father?" Her breath caught; she saw that they were passing the field where his ruined ship lay. "I mean, isn't there—a priest, or somebody, who could just marry us quietly, instead?"

She saw the unhealed wound that still lay behind his eyes, felt her own fear drain out of her. "Each man is his own priest, with the Prophet's Book to guide him. My father must give us his blessing, or we will be living in sin, and no better off than we were alone. We'll go to my sister first, she can speak to Father for me; and, I hope, make him listen—"

He sighed, nodded. " '*Casamento e mortalha, no céu se talha. . . .*' "

"What?" She looked up at him.

He shrugged. " 'Marriages and shrouds are made in heaven.' "

José came to the door of his house; surprise showed on his face, and then incredulity. "Amanda!"

"José. This is . . . this is my betrothed, Cristoval . . . Hoffmann." She struggled with the word.

"By the Book. . . . Teresa! Amanda's here? And"— he laughed —"by the Prophet Ángel, she's brought a man with her!"

Teresa, José, and the laughing children went ahead of her as they reached her father's courtyard at last; Cristoval walked grimly beside her. Her heart fluttered like bird wings under the wedding vest, beaded with pearls, that Teresa had given her to cover her faded dress: Cristoval wore one of José's robes, a vest and head-covering, in place of his poncho and his flopping hat. He could pass for a townsman; but she knew that it would not fool her father. The sun's heat made her suddenly giddy.

The heavy door of the house swung open, and Diego Montoya came out into the yard. His broad, jowled face widened with a smile at the sight of his grandchildren; they danced around him, chanting, "Aunt Amanda's getting married!"

Her father's obsidian eyes flickered up, seeing her in her wedding vest, seeing the scarred stranger beside her. "Teresa, what's the meaning of this?" Behind him her mother came to the door, and her sister Estella.

Teresa hung on her husband's shoulder, his arm around her waist, steadying her. "Father, Amanda has asked me to speak to you for her. This man would take her for his wife, even though she hasn't any dowry. Please, Father, she begs your forgiveness for the past; she asks you to give her in marriage, so that she may live as a dutiful wife, and—and make amends for the grief that her willfulness has caused you."

Her father stared at Cristoval, the words lost in the rising fury of his realization. "Amanda!" He spoke directly to her for the first time in eight years; she dropped her eyes, despairing. "What new mockery is this?" He came toward them; his hand closed on the cloth of Cristoval's head-covering. He jerked it off, revealing the ragged wound and the short, sun-faded hair. Her father threw the cloth to the ground, disgusted, moved away again. "Why do you shame me this way?" He turned back, his voice agonized. "How have I offended God, that such a creature was born a child of mine? How can you come here, and tell me you would marry this—" He gestured, his hand constricted into a fist.

"Father!" Teresa said, appalled, not understanding. The children hung on her skirts, eyes wide.

"By the Son of God, I won't stand for it! No more; no more humiliation, Amanda!" He reached down, caught up a stone. He lifted his hand.

Amanda cried out, cringing. Cristoval pressed against her, his body as rigid as metal.

José moved forward, caught his father-in-law's arm. "Father, no!" He pulled the hand down, his arm straining; Montoya glared at him. "Forgive me, Father. But I won't let you do such a thing before the children." He shook his head. "What's this man done to make you hate him?"

Amanda's father looked at the stone. "He's the sorcerer whose machine fell into my field. He is despised by God; it was God's will that he should die; no man would raise a hand to help him. But my —daughter," the word cut her, she flinched, "would defy natural law, defy God, again, to help him. And now she asks to marry him. Marry him! God should strike them both dead!"

"Perhaps He's punished them enough," José said quietly. "Even a sorcerer can repent and be forgiven."

Cristoval put his arm around Amanda. "Sir—" She heard a tremor in his voice, very faint. "God—God has stripped the evil thoughts from my mind; I can't remember anything of what I was." He touched his head. "I only want to marry your daughter, and live quietly; nothing more."

"Nothing?" Montoya said sourly.

"I don't demand a dowry. In fact, I'll give you a . . . a bride payment for her, instead."

Amanda's eyes widened; she saw every face turn to stare at her, at Cristoval.

"What kind of a payment?" The merchant pressed forward into her father's eyes.

"You use metals, don't you? Aluminum? Steel? I'll give you my ship in the field, what's left of it."

"It's accursed; it's full of demons."

"You have rituals to purify metals. If the ship was your own to make into . . . natural objects, the curse could be lifted. . . ."

The merchant weighed and considered.

"There must be at least half a ton of usable scrap metals left there. Maybe more."

"Oh, please, Father!" Teresa burst out. "Think of the honor it does you. No one has ever made such an offer, for anyone's daughter!" Amanda saw tears wetting her mother's veil, felt the look of astonished envy in Estella's dark and perfect eyes. She suddenly saw that one of the eyes was not perfect, swollen by a black-and-purple bruise. Amanda looked away.

"Half a ton . . . ?" her father was saying. He drew himself up. "The mayor's men came here looking for you, you know. In case you were still alive."

"No," Cristoval said. "I didn't know." His hand tightened on Amanda's shoulder. "Why? What does that mean?"

"Nothing." Her father shrugged. "Your body was gone from the field. I told them God had taken it away to hell—what else could I say? I thought you were dead. So did they; they seemed relieved." A smile struggled in the folds of his face. "The mayor has halved my field tribute this harvest, because of the miracle." He dropped the stone, sighed. "Half a ton. It must surely be God's will in the matter. . . . All right, Amanda, I will see you wed. But that is all. We'll go to the temple now. And then I will call a gathering, to bless the machine."

Amanda knelt by Cristoval before the altar in the silent temple while her father pronounced the words above them, and her family looked on. There would be no ritual, no feasting, no celebration. It was nothing like her dreams. . . . *But the dreams go away forever*. She remembered how long it had been since she had prayed in the temple; it had been too far to walk into town, to be met by stares and whispered scorn. She gazed without emotion at the rainbow of light that broke across the dusty tiles, below the altar window fused from colored shards of glass.

And then she followed her husband home, walking two paces behind him, eyes downcast.

He caught fish for their wedding supper while she finished the new piece of cloth on her loom, trying to recall the habits of a dutiful wife. Silent, patient, obedient . . . she had not been any of those, to her stranger-husband, until now. She must please him, now, and learn to make the best of it.

But as the evening passed she felt his irritation at

her awkward deference, and, not understanding, she tried harder; felt her tension grow, and her resentment.

"Damn it, Amanda, what's the matter with you!"

She looked up at him meekly. "Forgive me, my husband. Have I displeased you?"

"Yes." He frowned from his seat at the table. "What the hell is this silent treatment? And why wouldn't you walk beside me today?" His hand covered his cheek, unconsciously. "Are you that ashamed to be married to me?"

"No!" Tears of exasperation blurred her eyes. "No. You've honored me greatly, in the eyes of my family. But it's proper for a woman to defer to a man, in speech, in actions . . . in all things."

"Even if he's wrong?"

"Yes." Her hands clenched on the cloth of her dress. "But, of course, a man is never wrong."

"Mother of God, Amanda—you don't believe that?" He looked at her. "I'm a man. Up until now I've made plenty of mistakes, and you haven't been afraid to let me know about them."

"I—I'm sorry. It's just that I've lived alone for so long . . . but I'll change. I want to be a good wife to you." A tear burned her cheek, caught on her veil.

"You can be; just stay the way you were. Do what you want, talk when you feel like it. Don't hang on me! I haven't got the patience for it. I—I think I've lived alone for a long time, too, Amanda, and I don't want to have to change my habits; I don't expect you to change yours. We're sharing space in time, that's all. Let's do it as painlessly as possible."

"If that is what you wish, my husband . . ."

"Amanda!" His anger slapped her. "None of this 'my husband,' 'my wife.' It's just Cristovão, and Amanda. And in the future, walk with me, not behind me; I felt like I owned a servant, a slave. . . ." He rubbed his head, staring into space.

"But it's the custom; every wife follows her husband." She felt a terrible relief begin to loosen her knotted muscles.

"Not your sister Teresa."

"She's crippled. José has to help her walk."

"She does fine on a crutch. I don't think that's why he does it at all. I think it's because he wants her there."

Amanda wiped her eyes, startled, amazed. "But—but, you and I, people would . . . laugh at us."

"So what? After a while they won't even notice us anymore." He stood up, came toward her; her heart beat faster. "And the veil—"

She jerked away from him, appalled. "Would you humiliate me so, before every man in town—?"

"No." He caught her arm. "No, Amanda. But in our home you can let me see your face, can't you? You *are* my wife, now." He drew her veil down gently, pulled the cloth from her hair. Her hair came undone, spilled loose over her shoulders; he filled his hands with it. "Like spun copper . . . spun gold . . . like flame. . . ." She stood very still. His hands found the laces of her leather vest, untied them; his voice was husky. "I . . . just want you to know that, in town today, you were the most beautiful woman I saw."

Like flame. . . . She heard nothing more. On her

wedding night she lay at last with her husband, and dreamed that the man who made love to her was someone else.

The days passed, and the weeks, and the months; Sanpedro entered the gentle season of winter. Amanda did as her husband wished by doing as she always did, self-consciously at first, but easily and gratefully again, in time, as she came to realize how much her independence had grown to be a part of her, a source of pride and integrity, a defense against the indignities of life.

As he had promised, Cristoval worked hard, sharing the endless tasks of her daily existence and freeing her to make the cloth that was their only item of trade for the village market. He walked with her, too, for miles along the sea's shining edge, on the days when she gathered the tiny fluted shells she used to make lavender dye. He questioned her about her discovery; she told him how she had boiled them in salty water, desperate with hunger; how the tiny sea snails had been inedible, but how, because they turned the water purple, she had never been as hungry again. Cristoval had looked out across the bay, where Dog plunged beside them, shattering the foam. "You'll never be hungry again, Amanda; we'll never be hungry, if I can help it."

Farther along the beach they had come on a dead fish mired in a clot of greasy black scum. Cristoval squatted down beside it, took some up on his fingers and sniffed it, fascinated.

"It's the sea filth, that fouls the water's surface and

can kill fish and birds." She waved Dog back. "It happens farther up the coast, too; at Santabarbara."

Cristoval wiped his fingers on the sand. "Does it?" His voice was wondering. "But that's good! It's oil, Amanda; don't you know what that means? It means they can establish a major outpost here, they can put in wells . . . they can mine metals with—with gook labor. . . ."

"Who can?" she asked, frightened.

He stopped, staring at her strangely. He touched her arm for a moment, as though to reassure her, or reassure himself of her reality. "I don't know," he muttered. "Nobody, I hope."

Late in the winter he had gone to her father and asked permission to till a part of the grassy pasture-land adjoining the wheat fields in return for half the crop. Amanda had protested unhappily, saying they could glean enough to get by on and that it was too much extra work. But he had said it would be an investment in the future and worth it a hundredfold: "You were right in what you told me once, Amanda. With a man like your father, you don't tell him things. You show him. . . ."

And when the wheat grew up past her knees, past her waist, almost up to her breasts, she had begun to understand the method in the madness of tilling fresh ground. And the method had not escaped the merchant's eye of her father, either, for he began to ask Cristoval questions, rewarding them with a cow and, in time, even asking them into his home.

Amanda had blossomed with the spring, the ache of hunger forgotten, and the aching weariness that had aged her before her time. She would never be plump and comely like her sisters, but she took a secret pleasure in the new soft curves that she discovered in the broken mirror on the wall. Cristoval fished and worked their field; she wove and tended the green sprouts in the garden patch; the work was still unending, but now it filled her with hope and pride instead of hopeless despair. At night she no longer lay sleepless hearing the midnight bells, but fell into dreams quickly and easily. And if in her dreams she sometimes found a face that she reached for with longing and could never forget, she knew that her regret was nothing to her husband's in his longing for the things he might never remember. He was a thoughtful and satisfying lover; he brought peace and fulfillment to her body, if not her soul.

The sudden fits of haunted sleep that took him through the locked doors of his mind to walk in his forgotten past grew more and more infrequent; though his hair grew in pure white along the seam of the scar. As the dreams faded, his interest in them seemed almost to fade as well; he no longer grew angry because she couldn't describe their details to him, and the projects and problems of his new life left him little strength or time for seeking after the old one.

But as he stopped pressing to remember, more and more the bits and fragments of his life began to rise unbidden to the surface of his mind. A rare animation would take him, and carry her with him, when he remembered a place he had traveled to see and described to her the brief, bright flashes of its terrifying wonder: A forest of tree and shrub that grew

so densely that he had hacked his way through it
with a hatchet, to find a gleaming mound of shattered
glass, stitched with vine, embroidered by fragile
blossoms in the colors of dawn. . . . A ruined city
filled with bones, on a treeless plain beneath a sullen,
metallic sky; a wind so bitterly cold that the rain froze
into stinging pellets. . . . The shadow of a man long
dead, imprisoned by some ancient sorcery forever in
the surface of a building wall. . . .

He rarely mentioned people or memories of his own
land, only the memories of searching the strange and
alien ruins of the "Northern Hemisphere." He never
seemed to wonder whether someone was searching for
him, or waiting for him, or mourning for him. She
wondered whether he chose not to tell her of a wife or
lover or friends, or whether there was truly no one he
wanted to remember. For, at first, he had seldom
spoken to her at all about things that didn't directly
concern her; instead he would mumble to himself,
answering himself, oblivious. She discovered gradually
that it was not because he believed that, being a
woman, she would have nothing to say; but rather because he lived, somehow, completely within himself—
as though two men lived together in one, behind his
eyes: Perhaps, she thought, there were two men; the
old one, and the new.

But his solitary conversations aggravated her, as her
own traditional behavior had aggravated him; she
had learned not to be silent, and so she began to
answer him, stubbornly, chipping at the shell of his
isolation. And after a time, as though, like herself, he

had had to learn that he could, he began to talk to her instead; became a companion for her lonely days, and not just a silent presence in her house.

Spring passed into summer, blistering summer moved again into fall. Amanda let herself be carried by the flow of unnumbered days, thoughtlessly, unquestioningly. At last one day she left the marketplace in the heat of noon, climbing slowly past the shuttered houses along the curving street. The sea breeze was strong, tangy with salt and the tartness of seaweed, sweeping her skirts ahead of her. She was poorer by one piece of cloth, richer by a basket of fruits and cheese, a razor and a new pair of leather sandals for Cristoval, a bangle of copper and colored stones: She looked down at her wrist, bare for so many years; touched the bracelet, feeling as light-footed as a girl with joy. Brightness danced along it like sunlight across the sea; she kept her eyes on it and forgot the hot, weary journey home to the cottage.

She looked up only once, stopping in the shadow of the date palms to gaze out at the field where Cristoval's airship had lain. There was no sign now that it had ever existed; the freshly turned earth lay waiting for the winter crop. She smiled briefly and went on her way.

She opened the gate in the new-made fence, her eyes searching the yard for Cristoval . . . heard voices from behind the cottage, strangers' voices. She walked quietly through the shadow beside the house, looked out again into brightness, shielding her eyes. She saw

Cristoval sitting on the milking stool beside the spotted cow, listening to two men she had never seen before. Dog lay warily beside him.

". . . report to the Brasilian government on the feasibility of mining the Los Angeles basin. But you never came back, and so we came looking . . ."

Amanda dropped her basket. Her hand rose to her mouth; she bit her knuckles to keep from crying out.

". . . the fossil-fuel situation is too critical, we can't afford to clean out the canal now. The Venezuelan war's reached a stalemate; we'll have to stop all further plans for expansion of our mining operations, unless someone like you can discover an independent source of oil or coal—" The speaker looked at Cristoval hopefully.

Cristoval shrugged, his face polite and expressionless, his hand covering his scar. "How did you—find me, here?"

"The 'miracle' of your crash filtered down the coast. We didn't know if we'd find you alive or dead, or not at all. But we had to come and see; you're that important, Hoffmann."

He laughed uncomfortably. "I don't know why . . ."

"Because you're the best damned prospector in Brasil—"

"It doesn't matter, for Christ's sake," the second man said. "You know you don't belong here, Hoffmann. Let us get you out of this dirty, godforsaken hole. There are doctors in Brasil who can treat your problem; you'll remember everything, in time. At least you'll be back in civilization again, living like a human being, and not like a dog." He glanced down, his disgust showing.

Cristoval stood up slowly.

Amanda shut her eyes; Cristoval's face patterned on her eyelids. And in her mind she saw him clearly for the first time: her husband; the strange and gentle stranger who had come to her door, accursed, hopeless, and changed her own accursed, hopeless life forever. She pressed back against the warm wall, not breathing.

"No. I'm sorry." Cristoval shook his head. "I'm not going with you."

"*Diabo!*" the first man said. "Why not? Coelho didn't risk coming six thousand kilometers on a sailing ship, dressed like a peon, for you to turn him down!"

"He didn't come for me at all. He came for the . . . government."

"We need you, Hoffmann. We can force you to go with us—"

Dog growled where he lay, the hair on his back ridging.

"I don't think so." Cristoval smiled faintly. "I don't know what you want of me; I don't think I ever will. I don't even know what oil looks like anymore. I might as well be dead, for all the good I'd be to you. I'm content here; let's just leave it at that."

"Hoffmann." The second man looked at him with pity and dismay. "Can't you *feel* what you're giving up? If you could only know what your old life meant to you: Can't you remember, don't you know the discoveries you've made; the things you must have seen;

the knowledge that's still locked inside your mind . . . how important you were to your people?"

Cristoval kept his smile. "I only know how important I am, to someone, now—and someone is to me."

The second man looked puzzled. He produced something from inside his sleeveless coat. "You're right; you might as well be dead. Take this, then; in case you ever . . . remember, and want a way out. It's a distress beacon; they'll pick it up in El Paso; we'll try to send someone to you."

"All right." Cristoval took the dark, hand-sized box. *"Seja feliz, Hoffmann. Adeus."*

"Good-bye."

The two men turned, started back across the yard toward her. Amanda picked up her basket, stood stiffly, with dignity, as they noticed her and, staring, passed on by.

"Hoffmann's?" the first man said, incredulous.

"Será possível—!" the second man murmured, looking at her, shaking his head. *"Deus dá o frio conforme a roupa. . . ."*

When they were gone from the yard, she ran to Cristoval, clung to him, wordless. The strange box jabbed her back as he put his arms around her.

"Amanda! What's the matter?"

"Oh, my husband." She sighed, against his robe. "Who—who were those men?" She glanced up, watching his face.

"Nobody . . . nobody important." He smiled; but the old sorrow showed in his eyes, like a colorless flame. He pried himself loose from her gently, looked down at the hard, almost featureless box still clutched in his hand. He threw it away over the fence. "Nobody who'll ever hurt you now. My prospecting days are over. . . ." He sighed, put his arm around her again, drew her close; he reached down to scratch Dog's leathery ears. "But you know, Amanda, in time, if we ever have any money, we could take a ship along the coast, see the south. Maybe we'd even find those balloon airships of yours." He laughed. "But we won't take a ride in one! Would you like that?"

She nodded, resting her head on his shoulder. "Yes, my husband; I'd like that very much."

"Amanda . . ." he said, surprised, wonderingly. "My wife. My wife."

THE EYE OF

THE HERON

Ursula K. Le Guin

1

In the sunlight in the center of a ring of trees Lev sat cross-legged, his head bent above his hands.

A small creature crouched in the warm, shallow cup of his palms. He was not holding it; it had decided or consented to be there. It looked like a little toad with wings. The wings, folded into a peak above its back, were dun-colored with shadowy streaks, and its body was shadow-colored. Three gold eyes like large pinheads adorned its head, one on each side and one in the center of the skull. This upward-looking central eye kept watch on Lev. Lev blinked. The creature changed. Dusty pinkish fronds sprouted out from under its folded wings. For a moment it appeared to be a feathery ball, hard to see clearly, for the fronds or feathers trembled continually, blurring its outlines. Gradually the blur died away. The toad with wings sat there as before, but now it was light blue. It scratched its left eye with the hindmost of its three left feet. Lev smiled. Toad, wings, eyes, legs vanished. A flat mothlike shape crouched on Lev's palm, almost invisible because it was, except for some shadowy patches, exactly the same color and texture as his skin. He sat motionless. Slowly the blue toad with wings reappeared, one golden eye keeping watch on him. It walked across his palm and up the curve of his fingers. The six tiny, warm feet gripped and released, delicate and precise. It paused on the tip of his fingers and cocked its head to look at him with its right eye while its left and central eyes scanned the sky. It gathered itself into an arrow shape, shot out two translucent underwings twice the length of its body, and flew off in a long effortless glide toward a sunlit slope beyond the ring of trees.

"Lev?"

"Entertaining a wotsit." He got up, and joined Andre outside the tree-ring.

"Martin thinks we might get home tonight."

"Hope he's right," Lev said. He picked up his backpack and joined the end of the line of seven men. They set off in single file, not talking except when one down the line called to indicate to the leader a possible easier way to take, or when the second in line, carrying the compass, told the leader to bear right or left. Their direction was southwestward. The going was not hard, but there was no path and there were no landmarks. The trees of the forest grew in circles, twenty to sixty trees forming a ring around a clear central space. In the valleys of the rolling land the tree-rings grew so close, often interlocking, that the travelers' way was a constant alternation of forcing through undergrowth between dark shaggy trunks, clear going across spongy grass in the sunlit circle, then again shade, foliage, crowded stems and trunks. On the hillsides the rings grew farther apart, and sometimes there was a long view over winding valleys endlessly dappled with the soft rough red circles of the trees.

As the afternoon wore on a haze paled the sun. Clouds thickened from the west. A fine, small rain began to fall. It was mild, windless. The travelers' bare chests and shoulders shone as if oiled. Water-drops clung in their hair. They went on, bearing steadily south by west. The light grew grayer. In the valleys, in the circles of the trees, the air was misty and dark.

The lead man, Martin, topping a long stony rise of land, turned and called out. One by one they climbed up and stood beside him on the crest of the ridge. Below a broad river lay shining and colorless between dark beaches.

The eldest of them, Holdfast, got to the top last and stood looking down at the river with an expression of deep satisfaction. "Hullo there," he murmured, as to a friend.

"Which way to the boats?" asked the lad with the compass.

"Upstream," Martin said, tentative.

"Down," Lev proposed. "Isn't that the high point of the ridge, west there?"

They discussed it for a minute and decided to try downstream. For a little longer before they went on they stood in silence on the ridge top, from which they had a greater view of the world than they had had for many days. Across the river the forest rolled on southward in endless interlocking ring patterns under hanging clouds. Eastward, upriver, the land rose steeply; to the west the river wound in gray levels between lower hills. Where it disappeared from sight a faint brightness lay upon it, a hint of sunlight on the open sea. Northward, behind the travelers' backs, the forested hills, the days and miles of their journey, lay darkening into rain and night.

In all that immense, quiet landscape of hills, forest, river, no thread of smoke; no house; no road.

They turned west, following the spine of the ridge. After a kilometer or so the boy Welcome, in the lead now, hailed and pointed down to two black chips on the curve of a shingle beach, the boats they had pulled up there many weeks before.

They descended to the beach by sliding and scrambling down the steep ridge. Down by the river it seemed darker, and colder, though the rain had ceased.

"Dark soon. Should we camp?" Holdfast asked, in a reluctant tone.

They looked at the gray mass of the river sliding by, the gray sky above it.

"It'll be lighter out on the water," Andre said, pulling out the paddles from under one of the beached, overturned canoes.

A family of pouchbats had nested among the paddles. The half-grown youngsters hopped and scuttered off across the beach, squawking morosely, while the exasperated parents swooped after them. The men laughed, and swung the light canoes up to their shoulders.

They launched and set off, four to a boat. The paddles lifting caught the silver light of the west. Out in midstream the sky seemed lighter, and higher, the banks low and black on either hand.

> O when we come,
> O when we come to Lisboa,
> The white ships will be waiting,
> O when we come. . . .

One man in the first canoe began the song, two or three voices in the second picked it up. Around the brief, soft singing lay the silence of the wilderness, under and over it, before and after it.

The riverbanks grew lower, farther away, more shadowy. They were now on a silent flood of gray half a mile wide. The sky darkened between glance and glance. Then far to the south one point of light shone out, remote and clear, breaking the old dark.

Nobody was awake in the villages. They came up through the paddy fields, guided by their swinging lanterns. They smelled the heavy fragrance of peat-smoke in the air. They came quiet as the rain up the street between the little sleeping houses, until Welcome let out a yell: "Hey, we're home!" and flung open the door of his family's house. "Wake up, Mother! It's me!"

Within five minutes half the town was in the street. Lights were lit, doors stood open, children danced about, a hundred voices talked, shouted, questioned, welcomed, praised.

Lev went to meet Southwind as she came hurrying down the street, sleepy-eyed, smiling, a shawl drawn over her tangled hair. He put out his hands and took hers, stopping her. She looked up into his face and laughed. "You're back, you're back!"

Then her look changed; she glanced around very swiftly at the cheerful commotion of the street, and back at Lev.

"Oh," she said, "I knew it. I knew."

"On the way north. About ten days out. We were climbing down into a stream gorge. The rocks slipped under his hands. There was a nest of rock scorpions. He was all right at first. But there were dozens of stings. His hands began to swell. . . ."

His hands tightened on the girl's; she still looked into his eyes.

"He died in the night."

"In much pain?"

"No," Lev said, lying.

Tears filled his eyes.

"So he's there," he said. "We made a cairn of white boulders. Near a waterfall. So he—so he's there."

Behind them in the commotion and chatter a woman's voice sounded clearly: "But where's Timmo?"

Southwind's hands went loose in Lev's; she seemed to grow smaller, to shrink down, shrink away. "Come with me," he said, and they went in silence, his arm about her shoulders, to her mother's house.

Lev left her there with Timmo's mother and her own mother. He came out of the house and stood hesitant, then returned slowly toward the crowd. His father came forward to meet him; Lev saw the curly gray hair, the eyes seeking through torchlight. Sasha was a slight, short man; as they embraced Lev felt the bones beneath the skin, hard and frail.

"You were with Southwind?"

"Yes. I can't—"

He clung for a minute to his father, and the hard, thin hand stroked his arm. The torchlight blurred and stung in his eyes. When he let go, Sasha drew back to look at him, saying nothing, intent dark eyes, the mouth hidden by a bristly gray mustache.

"You've been all right, Father?"

Sasha nodded. "You're tired. Come on home." As they started down the street he said, "Did you find the promised land?"

"Yes. A valley. A river-valley. Five kilos from the sea. Everything we need. And beautiful—the mountains above it— Range behind range, higher and higher, higher than the clouds, whiter— You can't believe how high you have to look to see the highest peaks." He had stopped walking.

"Mountains in between? Rivers?"

Lev looked down from the white visionary heights, into his father's eyes.

"Enough to keep the Bosses from following us there?"

After a moment Lev smiled. "Maybe," he said.

* * *

It was the middle of the bog-rice harvest, so that many of the farming people could not come, but all the villages sent a man or woman to Shantih to hear what the explorers reported and what the people said. It was afternoon, still raining; the big open place in front of the Meeting House was crowded with umbrellas made of the broad, red, papery leaves of the thatch-tree. Under the umbrellas people stood or squatted on leaf-mats in the mud, and cracked nuts, and talked, until at last the little bronze bell of the Meeting House went *tonka-tonka-tonk*; then they all looked at the porch of the Meeting House, where Vera stood ready to speak.

She was a slender woman with iron-gray hair, a narrow nose, dark oval eyes. Her voice was strong and clear, and while she spoke there was no other sound but the quiet patter of the rain, and now and then the chirp of a little child in the crowd, quickly hushed.

She welcomed the explorers back. She spoke of Timmo's death, and, very quietly and briefly, of Timmo himself, as she had seen him on the day the exploring party left. She spoke of their hundred-day trek through the wilderness. They had mapped a great area east and north of Songe Bay, she said, and they had found what they went to find—a site for a new settlement, and a passable way to it. "A good many of us here," she said, "don't like the idea of a new settlement so far from Shantih. And among us now are also some of our neighbors from the City, who may wish to join in our plans and discussions. The whole matter must be fully considered and freely discussed.

So first let Andre and Lev speak for the explorers, and tell us what they saw and found."

Andre, a stocky, shy man of thirty, described their journey to the north. His voice was soft and he did not speak easily, but the crowd listened intently to his sketch of the world beyond their long-familiar fields. Some, towards the back, craned until they saw the men from the City, of whose presence Vera had politely warned them. There they were near the porch, six men in jerkins and high boots: Bosses' bodyguards, each with a long sheathed knife on the thigh and a whip, the thong neatly curled, tucked into the belt.

Andre mumbled to a close and gave place to Lev, a young man, slight and rawboned, with thick, black, bright hair. Lev also began hesitantly, groping for words to describe the valley they had found and why they thought it most suitable for settlement. As he spoke his voice warmed and he began to forget himself, as if he saw before him what he described: the wide valley and the river which they had named Serene, the lake above it, the bog-lands where rice grew wild, the forests of good timber, the sunny slopes where orchards and root crops could be planted and houses could stand free of the mud and damp. He told of the river mouth, a bay full of shellfish and edible kelp; and he spoke of the mountains that stood above the valley to the north and east, protecting it from the winds that made the winter a weariness of mud and cold at Songe. "The peaks of them go up and up into the silence and sunlight above the clouds," he said. "They shelter the valley, like a mother with a child in her arms. We called them the Mountains of the Mahatma. It was to see if the mountains kept off the storms that we stayed so long there, fifteen days. Early autumn there is like midsummer here, only the nights are colder; the days were sunny, and no rain. Holdfast thought there might be three rice harvests a year there. There's a good deal of fruit in the forests, and the fishing in the river and the bay shores would help feed the first year's settlers till the first harvest. The mornings are so bright there! It wasn't just to see how the weather was that we stayed. It was hard to leave the place, even to come home."

They listened with enchantment, and were silent when he stopped.

Somebody called, "How far is it, in days of travel?"

"Martin's guess is about twenty days, with families and big pack loads."

"Are there rivers to cross, dangerous places?"

"The best arrangement would be an advance party, a couple of days ahead, to mark out the easiest route. Coming back we avoided all the rough country we went through going north. The only difficult river crossing is right here, the Songe, that'll have to be done with boats. The others can be forded, till you get to the Serene."

More questions were shouted out; the crowd lost its enraptured quiet and was breaking into a hundred voluble discussions under the red-leaf umbrellas, when Vera came forward again and asked for silence. "One of our neighbors is here and wishes to talk with us," she said, and stood aside to let a man behind her come forward. He wore black, with a broad silver-embossed belt. The six men who had stood near the porch had come up on it with him and moved forward in a semicircle, separating him from the other people on the porch.

"Greetings to you all," the man in black said. His voice was dry, not loud.

"Falco," people murmured to one another. "The Boss Falco."

"I am pleased to present the congratulations of the Government of Victoria to these brave explorers. Their maps and reports will be a most valued addition to the Archives of the State in Victoria City. Plans for a limited migration of farmers and manual workers are being studied by the Council. Planning and control are necessary to ensure the safety and welfare of the community as a whole. As this expedition makes clear, we dwell in one corner, one safe haven, of a great and unknown world. We who have lived here longest, who keep the records of the early years of the Settlement, know that rash schemes of dispersal may threaten our survival, and that wisdom lies in order and strict cooperation. I am pleased to tell you that the Council will receive these brave explorers with the welcome of the City, and present them a suitable reward for their endeavors."

There was a different kind of silence.

Vera spoke; she looked fragile beside the group of bulky men, and her voice sounded light and clear. "We thank the representative of the Council for his courteous invitation."

Falco said, "The Council will expect to receive the explorers, and examine their maps and reports, in three days' time."

Again the pent silence.

"We thank Councillor Falco," Lev said, "and decline his invitation."

An older man tugged at Lev's arm, whispering hard; there was much quick, low talk among the people on the porch, but the crowd before the Meeting House kept silent and motionless.

"We must arrive at decisions on several matters," Vera said to Falco, but loud enough that all could hear, "before we're ready to reply to the invitation of the Council."

"The decisions have been made, Senhora Adelson. They have been made by the Council. Only your obedience is expected." Falco bowed, to her, raised his hand in salutation to the crowd, and left the porch, surrounded by his guards. The people moved wide apart to let them pass.

On the porch, two groups formed: the explorers and other men and women, mostly young, around Vera, and a larger group around a fair, blue-eyed man named Elia. Down among the crowd this pattern was repeated, until it began to look like a ringtree forest: small circles, mostly young, and larger circles, mostly older. All of them argued passionately, yet without anger. When one tall old woman began shaking her red-leaf umbrella at a vehement girl and shouting, "Runaway! You want to run away and leave us to face the Bosses! What you need is a spanking!"—with a whack of the umbrella in demonstration—then very rapidly the people around her seemed to melt away, taking with them the girl who had annoyed her. The old woman was left standing alone, as red as her umbrella, brandishing it sullenly at nothing. Presently, frowning and working her lips, she joined the outskirts of another circle.

The two groups up on the porch had now joined. Elia spoke with quiet intensity: "Direct defiance is violence, Lev, as much as any blow of fist or knife."

"As I refuse violence, I refuse to serve the violent," the young man said.

"If you defy the Council's request, you will cause violence."

"Jailings, beatings maybe; all right. Is it liberty we want, Elia, or mere safety?"

"By defying Falco, in the name of liberty or anything else, you provoke repression. You play into his hands."

"We're in his hands already, aren't we?" Vera said. "What we want is to get out."

"We all agree that it's time, high time, that we talk with the Council—talk firmly, reasonably. But if we begin with defiance, with moral violence, nothing will be achieved, and they'll fall back on force."

"We don't intend defiance," Vera said, "we shall simply hold fast to the truth. But if *they* begin with force, you know, Elia, even our attempt at reason becomes a resistance."

"Resistance is hopeless, we must *talk* together! If violence enters in, in act or word, the truth is lost— our life in Shantih, our liberty will be destroyed. Force will rule, as it did on Earth!"

"It didn't rule everybody on Earth, Elia. Only those who consented to serve it."

"Earth cast our fathers out," Lev said. There was a

brightness in his face; his voice caught at a harsh, yearning note, like the deep strings of a harp plucked hard. "We're outcasts, the children of outcasts. Didn't the Founder say that the outcast is the free soul, the child of God? Our life here in Shantih is not a free life. In the north, in the new settlement, we will be free."

"What is freedom?" said a beautiful, dark woman, Jewel, who stood beside Elia. "I don't think you come to it by the path of defiance, resistance, refusal. Freedom comes with you if you walk the path of love. To accept all is to be given all."

"We've been given a whole world," Andre said in his subdued voice. "Have we accepted it?"

"Defiance is a trap, violence is a trap, they must be refused—and that's what we're doing," Lev said. "We are going free. The Bosses will try to stop us. They'll use moral force, they may use physical force; force is the weapon of the weak. But if we trust ourselves, our purpose, our strength, if we hold fast, all their power over us will melt away like shadows when the sun comes up!"

"Lev," the dark woman said softly, "Lev, this is the world of shadows."

2

Rainclouds moved in long dim lines above Songe Bay. Rain pattered and pattered on the tile roof of the House of Falco. At the end of the house, in the kitchens, there was a far-off sound of life astir, of servants' voices. No other sound, no other voice, only the rain.

Luz Marina Falco Cooper sat in the deep window seat, her knees drawn up to her chin. Sometimes she gazed out through the thick, greenish glass of the window at the sea and the rain and the clouds. Sometimes she looked down at the book that lay open beside her, and read a few lines. Then she sighed and looked out the window again. The book was not interesting.

It was too bad. She had had high hopes of it. She had never read a book before.

She had learned to read and write, of course, being the daughter of a Boss. Besides memorizing lessons aloud, she had copied out moral precepts, and could write a letter offering or declining an invitation, with a fancy scrollwork frame, and the salutation and signature written particularly large and stiff. But at school they used slates and the copybooks which the schoolmistresses wrote out by hand. She had never touched a book. Books were too precious to be used in school; there were only a few dozen of them in the world. They were kept in the Archives. But, coming into the hall this afternoon, she had seen lying on the low table a little brown box; she had lifted the lid to see what was in it, and it was full of words. Neat, tiny words, all the letters alike, what patience to make them all the same size like that! A book—a real book, from Earth. Her father must have left it there. She seized it, carried it to the window seat, opened the

lid again carefully, and very slowly read all the
different kinds of words on the first leaf of paper.

FIRST AID

A MANUAL OF EMERGENCY CARE
FOR INJURIES AND ILLNESS

M. E. Roy, M.D.

The Geneva Press
Geneva, Switzerland
2027

License No. 83A38014
Gen.

It did not seem to make much sense. "First aid"
was all right, but the next line was a puzzle. It began
with somebody's name, A. Manuel, and then went on
about injuries. Then came a lot of capital letters with
dots after them. And what was a geneva, or a press,
or a switzerland?

Equally puzzling were the red letters which slanted
up the page as if they had been written over the
others: DONATED BY THE WORLD RED CROSS FOR THE USE
OF THE PENAL COLONY ON VICTORIA.

She turned the leaf of paper, admiring it. It was
smoother to the touch than the finest cloth, crisp yet
pliable like fresh thatch-leaf, and pure white.

She worked her way word by word to the bottom of
the first page, and then began to turn several pages
at once, since more than half the words meant nothing

anyway. Gruesome pictures appeared: her interest revived with a shock. People supporting other people's heads, breathing into their mouths; pictures of the bones inside a leg, of the veins inside an arm; colored pictures, on marvelous shiny paper like glass, of people with little red spots on their shoulders, with big red blotches on their cheeks, with horrible boils all over them, and mysterious words beneath the pictures: *Allergic Rash. Measles. Chicken Box. Small Box.* No, it was *pox*, not *box*. She studied all the pictures, sometimes making a foray into the words on the facing pages. She understood that it was a book of medicine, and that the doctor, not her father, must have left it on the table the night before. The doctor was a good man, but touchy; would he be angry if he knew she had looked at his book? It had his secrets in it. He never answered questions. He liked to keep his secrets to himself.

Luz sighed again and looked out at the ragged, rain-dropping clouds. She had looked at all the pictures, and the words were not interesting.

She got up, and was just setting the book down on the table exactly where it had lain, when her father entered the room.

His step was energetic, his back straight, his eyes clear and stern. He smiled when he saw Luz. A little startled, guilty, she swept him a fancy curtsy, her skirts hiding the table and the book. "Senhor! A thousand greetings!"

"There's my little beauty. Michael! Hot water and a towel! —I feel dirty all over." He sat down in one of the carved wooden armchairs and stretched out his legs, though his back stayed as straight as ever.

"Where have you been getting dirty, Papa?"

"Among the vermin."

"Shanty Town?"

"Three kinds of creature came from Earth to Victoria: Men, lice, and Shanty-Towners. If I could get rid of only one kind, it would be the last." He smiled again, pleased by his joke, then looked up at his daughter and said, "One of them presumed to answer me. I think you knew him."

"I knew him?"

"At school. Vermin shouldn't be allowed into the school. I forget his name. Their names are all nonsense, Sticktight, Holdfast, Howd'youdo, what have you. . . . A little black-haired stick of a boy."

"Lev?"

"That's the one. A troublemaker."

"What did he say to you?"

"He said no to me."

Falco's man came hurrying in with a pottery basin and a jug of steaming water; a maid followed with towels. Falco scrubbed his face and hands, puffing and blowing and talking through the water and the towels. "He and some others just came back from an expedition up north, into the wilderness. He claims they found a fine town site. They want the whole lot to move there."

"To leave Shanty Town? All of them?"

Falco snorted in assent, and stuck out his feet for Michael to take off his boots. "As if they'd last one winter without the City to look after them! Earth sent them here fifty years ago as unteachable imbeciles, which is what they are. It's time they relearned their lesson."

"But they can't just go off into the wilderness," said Luz, who had been listening to her thoughts as well as to her father's words. "Who'd farm our fields?"

Her father ignored her question by repeating it, thus transforming a feminine expression of emotion into a masculine assessment of fact. "They can't, of course, be allowed to start scattering like this. They provide necessary labor."

"Why is it that Shanty-Towners do almost all the farming?"

"Because they're good for nothing else. Get that slop out of the way, Michael."

"Hardly any of our people know how to farm," Luz observed. She was thinking. She had dark, strongly arched eyebrows, as her father did, and when she was thinking they lay in a straight line above her eyes. This straight line displeased her father. It did not suit the face of a pretty girl of twenty. It gave her a hard, unwomanly look. He had often told her this, but she had never broken the bad habit.

"My dear, we are City people, not peasants."

"But who did the farming before the Shanty-Towners came? The Colony was sixty years old when they came."

"The working people did the manual work, of course. But even our working people were never peasants. We are City people."

"And we starved, didn't we? There were the

Famines." Luz spoke dreamily, as if recalling an old history recitation, but her eyebrows were still down in that straight black line. "In the first ten years of the Colony, and other times . . . lots of people starved. They didn't know how to cultivate bog-rice or raise sugar-root, until the Shanty-Towners came."

Her father's black brows were now a straight line too. He dismissed Michael, the maid, and the subject of conversation with one wave of the hand. "It's a mistake," he said in his dry voice, "to send peasants and women to school. The peasants become insolent, the women become boring."

It would have made her cry, two or three years ago. She would have wilted, and crept off to her room to weep, and been miserable until her father said something kind to her. But these days he could not make her cry. She didn't know why it was, and it seemed very strange to her. Certainly she feared and admired him as much as ever; but she always knew what he was going to say. It was never anything new. Nothing was ever new.

She turned and looked out through the thick, whorled glass again at Songe Bay, the farther curve of the shore veiled by unending rain. She stood straight, a vivid figure in the dull light, in her long red homespun skirt and ruffled shirt. She looked indifferent, and alone, standing there in the center of the high, long room; and she felt so. Also she felt her father's gaze on her. And knew what he was going to say.

"It's time you were married, Luz Marina."

She waited for the next sentence.

"Since your mother died. . . ." And the sigh.

Enough, enough, enough!

She turned to face him. "I read that book," she said.

"Book?"

"Doctor Martin must have left it. What does it mean, 'penal colony'?"

"You had no business to touch that!"

He was surprised. That at least made things interesting.

"I thought it was a box of dried fruits," she said, and laughed. "But what does it mean, 'penal colony'? A colony of criminals, a prison?"

"That is nothing you need to know."

"Our ancestors were sent here as prisoners, is that right? That's what the Shanty-Towners in school said." Falco's face was getting white, but the danger exhilarated Luz; her mind raced, and she spoke her mind. "They said the First Generation were all criminals. The Earth Government used Victoria for a jail. The Shanty-Towners said *they* were sent because they believed in peace or something, but *we* were sent because we were all thieves and murderers. And most of them, the First Generation, were men, their women couldn't come unless they were married to them, and that's why there were so few women to start with. That always seemed stupid, not to send enough women for a colony. And it explains why the ships were made only to come, not to go back. And why the Earth people never come here. We're locked out. It's true, isn't it? We call ourselves Victoria Colony. But we're a jail."

Falco had risen. He came forward; she stood still,

poised on her feet. "No," she said, lightly, as if indifferent. "No, don't, Papa."

Her voice stopped the man in his anger; he too stood still, and looked at her. For a moment he saw her. She saw in his eyes that he saw her, and that he was afraid. For a moment, only a moment.

He turned away. He went to the table and picked up the book Dr. Martin had left. "What does all that matter, Luz Marina?" he said at last.

"I'd like to know."

"It was a hundred years ago. And Earth is lost. And we are what we are."

She nodded. When he spoke that way, dry and quiet, she saw the strength she admired and loved in him.

"What angers me," he said, but not with anger, "is that you listened to that talk from those vermin. They put everything backward. What do they know? You let them tell you that Luis Firmin Falco, my great-grandfather, the founder of our House, was a thief, a jailbird. What do they know about it! I know, and I can tell you, what our ancestors were. They were men. Men too strong for Earth. The Government on Earth sent them here because they were afraid of them. The best, the bravest, the strongest—all the thousands of little weak people on Earth were afraid of them, and trapped them, and sent them off in the one-way ships, so that they could do as they liked with Earth, you see. Well, when that was done, when the real men were gone, the Earth people were left so weak and womanish that they began to be afraid even of rabble like the Shanty-Towners. So they sent them here for us to keep in order. Which we have done. You see? That's how it was."

Luz nodded. She accepted her father's evident intent to placate her, though she did not know why for the first time he had spoken to her placatingly, explaining something as if she were his equal. Whatever the reason, his explanation sounded well; and she was used to hearing what sounded well, and figuring out later what it might really mean. Indeed, until she had met Lev at school, it had not occurred to her that anyone might prefer to speak a plain fact rather than a lie that sounded well. People said what suited their purposes, when they were serious; and when they weren't serious, they talked without meaning anything at all. Talking to girls, they were hardly ever serious. Ugly truths were to be kept from girls, so that their pure souls did not become coarse and soiled. And anyhow, she had asked about the penal colony mostly to get her father off the subject of her marriage; and the trick had worked.

But the trouble with such tricks, she thought when she was in her own room alone, is that they trick you too. She had tricked herself into arguing with her father, and winning the argument. He would not forgive her that.

All the girls of her age and class in the City had been married for two or three years now. She had evaded marriage only because Falco, whether he knew it or not, didn't want to let her go from his house. He was used to having her there. They were alike, very much alike; they enjoyed each other's company more, perhaps, than anyone else's. But he had looked at her this evening as if seeing someone different, someone he wasn't used to. If he began noticing her as a person different from himself, if she began winning battles with him, if she was no longer his little girl pet, he might begin thinking about what else she was—what use she was.

And what use was she, what was she good for? The continuation of the house of Falco, of course. And then what? Either Herman Marquez or Herman Macmilan. And nothing whatever she could do about it. She would be a wife. She would be a daughter-in-law. She would wear her hair in a bun, and scold the servants, and listen to the men carousing in the hall after supper, and have babies. One a year. Little Marquez Falcos. Little Macmilan Falcos. Eva, her old playmate, married at sixteen, had three babies and was expecting the fourth. Eva's husband, the Councillor's son Aldo Di Giulio Hertz, beat her; and she was proud of it. She showed the bruises and murmured, "Aldito has such a temper, he's so wild, like a little boy in a tantrum."

Luz made a face, and spat. She spat on the tiled floor of her room, and let the spittle lie. She stared at the small grayish blob and wished she could drown Herman Marquez in it, and then Herman Macmilan. She felt dirty. Her room was close, dirty: a prison cell. She fled the thought, and the room. She darted out into the hall, gathered up her skirts, and climbed the ladder to the place under the roof, where nobody else ever came. She sat on the dusty floor there—the roof, loud with rain, was too low to stand up under —and let her mind go free.

It went straight out, away from the house and the hour, back to a wider time.

On the playing field by the schoolhouse, an afternoon of spring, two boys were playing catch, Shanty-Towners, Lev and his friend Timmo. She stood on the porch of the schoolhouse watching them, wondering at what she saw, the reach and stretch of back and arm, the lithe swing of the body, the leap of the ball through light. It was as if they played a silent music, the music of moving. The light came under storm clouds, from the west, over Songe Bay, level and golden; the earth was brighter than the sky. The bank of raw earth behind the field was golden, the weeds above it burned. The earth burned. Lev stood waiting to catch a long throw, his head back, his hands poised, and she stood watching, amazed by beauty.

A group of City boys came around the schoolhouse to play football. They yelled at Lev to hand over the ball, just as he leaped, his arm at full stretch, to catch Timmo's high throw. He caught it, and laughed, and tossed the ball over to the others.

As the two came by the porch, she ran down the steps. "Lev!"

The west blazed behind him, he stood black between her and the sun.

"Why did you give them the ball like that?"

She could not see his face against the light. Timmo, a tall, handsome boy, held back a little and did not look into her face.

"Why do you let them push you around?"

Lev answered at last. "I don't," he said. As she came closer to him she saw him looking straight at her.

"They say 'Give it here!' And you just give it—"

"They want to play a game; we were just fooling around. We had our turn."

"But they don't ask you for it, they order you. Don't you have any pride?"

Lev's eyes were dark, his face was dark and rough, unfinished; he smiled, a sweet, startled smile. "Pride? Sure. If I didn't, I'd hang onto it when it's their turn."

"Why are you always so full of answers?"

"Because life's so full of questions."

He laughed, but he kept looking at her as if she were a question herself, a sudden question with no answer. And he was right, for she had no idea why she was challenging him like this.

Timmo stood by, a little uncomfortable. Some of the boys on the playing field were already looking at them: two Shanty-boys talking to a senhorita.

Without a word said, the three walked away from the schoolhouse, down to the street below it, where they could not be seen from the field.

"If any of them talked to each other like that, the way they yelled at you," Luz said, "there'd have been a fight. Why don't you fight?"

"For a football?"

"For anything!"

"We do."

"When? How? You just walk away."

"We walk into the City, to school, every day," Lev said. He was not looking at her now as they walked along side by side, and his face looked as usual, an ordinary boy's face, stubborn, sullen. She did not understand what he meant at first, and when she did, she did not know what to say.

"Fists and knives are the least of it," he said, and perhaps heard pomposity in his own voice, a certain boastfulness, for he turned to Luz with a laugh and shrug—"and words aren't much good either!"

They came out from the shadow of a house into the level golden light. The sun lay, a molten blur, between the dark sea and the dark clouds, and the roofs of the City burned with unearthly fire. The three young people stopped, looking into that tremendous brightness and darkness of the west. The sea wind, smelling of salt and space and wood smoke, blew cold in their faces. "Don't you see," Lev said, "you can see it—you can see what it should be, what it is."

She saw it, with his eyes, she saw the glory, the City that should be, and was.

The moment broke. The haze of glory still burned between sea and storm, the City still stood golden and endangered on the eternal shore; but people came down the street behind them, talking and calling. They were Shanty-girls, who had stayed in school to help the mistresses clean up the classrooms. They joined Timmo and Lev, greeting Luz gently but, like Timmo, warily. Her way home lay to the left, down into the City; theirs to the right, up over the bluffs and onto the Town Road.

As she went down the steep street she glanced back at them going up it. The girls wore work suits of bright, soft colors. City girls sneered at Shanty girls for wearing trousers; but they made their own skirts of Shanty cloth if they could get it, for it was finer and better dyed than any the City made. The boys' trousers and long-sleeved, high-necked jackets were the creamy white of the natural silkweed fiber. Lev's head of thick, soft hair looked very black above that whiteness. He was walking behind the others, with Southwind, a beautiful, low-voiced girl. Luz could tell from the way his head was turned that he was listening to that low voice, and smiling.

"Screw!" said Luz, and strode down the street, her long skirts whipping at her ankles. She had been too well brought up to know swearwords. She knew "Hell!" because her father said it, even in front of women, when he was annoyed. She never said "Hell!" —it was her father's property. But Eva had told her, years ago, that "screw" was a very bad word, and so, when alone, she used it.

And there, materializing like a wotsit out of nothing, and like a wotsit humpbacked, beady-eyed, and vaguely feathery, there was her duenna, Cousin Lores, who she thought had given up and gone home half an hour ago. "Luz Marina! Luz Marina! Where were you? I waited and waited—I ran all the way to Casa Falco and back to the school—where were you? Why are you walking all by yourself? Slow down, Luz Marina, I'm dying, I'm dying."

But Luz would not slow down for the poor squawking woman. She strode on, fighting tears that had come upon her unawares: tears of anger because she could never walk alone, never do anything by herself, never. Because the men ran everything. They had it all their way. And the older women were all on their side. So that a girl couldn't walk in the streets of the City alone, because some drunken working man might insult her, and what if he did get put in jail or get his ears cut off for it afterward? A lot of good that would do. The girl's reputation would be ruined. Because her reputation was what the men thought of her. The men thought everything, did everything, ran everything, made everything, made the laws, broke the laws, punished the lawbreakers; and there was no room left for the women, no City for the women. Nowhere, nowhere, but in their own rooms, alone.

Even a Shanty-Towner was freer than she was. Even Lev, who wouldn't fight for a football, but who challenged the night as it came up over the edge of the world, and laughed at the laws. Even Southwind, who was so quiet and mild—Southwind could walk home with anyone she liked, hand in hand across the open fields in the wind of evening, running before the rain.

The rain drummed on the tile roof of the attic, where she had taken refuge that day three years ago when she got home at last, Cousin Lores puffing and squawking behind her all the way.

The rain drummed on the tile roof of the attic, where she had taken refuge today.

Three years, since that evening in the golden light. And nothing to show for it. Less now than there had been then. Three years ago she had still gone to school; she had believed that when school was over she would magically be free.

A prison. All Victoria was a prison, a jailhouse. And no way out. Nowhere else to go.

Only Lev had gone away, and found a new place somewhere far in the north, in the wilderness, a place to go. . . . And he had come back from it, and had stood up and said "No" to the Boss Falco.

But Lev was free, he had always been free. That was why there was no other time in her life, before or since, like the time when she had stood with him on the heights of her City in the golden light before the storm, and seen with him what freedom was. For one moment. A gust of the sea wind, a meeting of the eyes.

It was more than a year since she had even seen him. He was gone, back to Shanty Town, off to the new settlement, gone free, forgetting her. Why should he remember her? Why should she remember him? She had other things to think about. She was a grown woman. She had to face life. Even if all life had to show her was a locked door, and behind the locked door, no room.

3

The two human settlements on the planet Victoria were six kilometers apart. There were, so far as the inhabitants of Shantih Town and Victoria City knew, no others.

A good many people had work, hauling produce or drying fish, which took them from one settlement to the other frequently, but there were many more who lived in the City and never went to the Town, or who lived in one of the farm-villages near the Town and never from year's end to year's end went to the City.

As a small group, four men and a woman, came down the Town Road to the edge of the bluffs, several of them looked with lively curiosity and considerable awe at the City spread out beneath them on the hilly shore of Songe Bay; they stopped just under the Monument Tower—the ceramic shell of one of the ships that had brought the first settlers to Victoria—but did not spend much time looking up at it; it was a familiar sight, impressive by its size, but skeletal and rather pitiful set up there on the cliff-top, pointing bravely at the stars but serving merely as a guide to fishing boats out at sea. It was dead; the City was alive. "Look at that," said Hari, the eldest of the group. "You couldn't count all those houses if you sat here for an hour! Hundreds of them!"

"Just like a city on Earth," another, a more frequent visitor, said with proprietary pride.

"My mother was born in Moskva, in Russia the Black," a third man said. "She said the City would only be a little town, there on Earth." But this was rather farfetched, to people whose lives had been spent between the wet fields and the huddled villages, in a close continuous bind of hard work and human companionship, outside which lay the immense, indifferent wilderness. "Surely," one of them said with mild disbelief, "she meant a big town?" And they stood beneath the hollow shell of the space ship, looking at the bright rust color of the tiled and thatched roofs, and the smoking chimneys, and the geometrical lines of walls and streets, and not looking at the vast landscape of beaches and bay and ocean, empty valleys, empty hills, empty sky, that surrounded the City with a tremendous desolation.

Once they came down past the schoolhouse into the streets they could entirely forget the presence of the wilderness. They were surrounded on all sides by the works of mankind. The houses, mostly row-built, lined the way on both sides with high walls and little windows. The streets were narrow, and a foot deep in mud. In places walkways of planking were laid over the mud, but these were in bad repair, and slippery with rain. Few people passed, but an open door might give a glimpse into the swarming interior courtyard of a house, full of women, washing, children, smoke, and voices. Then again the cramped, sinister silence of the street.

"Wonderful! Wonderful!" sighed Hari.

They passed the factory where iron from the Government mines and foundry was made into tools, kitchenware, door latches, and so on. The doorway was wide open, and they stopped and peered into the sulfurous darkness lit with sparking fires and loud with banging and hammering, but a workman yelled at them to move on. So they went on down to Bay Street, and looking at the length and width and straightness of Bay Street, Hari said again, "Wonderful!" They followed Vera, who knew her way about the City, up Bay Street to the Capitol. At the sight of the Capitol, Hari had no words left, but merely stared.

It was the biggest building in the world—four times the height of any common house—and built of solid stone. Its high porch was supported by four columns, each a single huge ringtree trunk, grooved and whitewashed, the heavy capitals carved and gilt. The visitors felt small passing between these columns, small entering the portals that gaped so wide and tall. The entry hall, narrow but also very high, had plastered walls, and these had been decorated years ago with frescoes that stretched from floor to ceiling. At the sight of these the people from Shantih stopped again and gazed, silent; for they were pictures of the Earth.

There were still people in Shantih who remembered Earth and would tell about it, but the memories, fifty-five years old, were mostly of things seen by children. Few were left who had been adults at the time of the exile. Some had spent years of their lives in writing down the history of the People of the Peace and the sayings of its leaders and heroes, and descriptions of the Earth, and sketches of its remote, appalling history. Others had seldom spoken of the Earth; at most they had sung to their children born in exile, or to their children's children, an old song with strange names and words in it, or told them tales about the children and the witch, the three bears, the king who rode on a tiger. The children listened round-eyed. "What is a bear? Does a king have stripes too?"

The first generation of the City, on the other hand, sent to Victoria fifty years before the People of the Peace, had mostly come from the cities, Buenos Aires, Rio, Brasilia, and the other great centers of Brasil-America; and some of them had been powerful men, familiar with stranger things even than witches and bears. So the fresco painter had painted scenes that were entirely marvelous to the people now looking at them: towers full of windows, streets full of wheeled machines, skies full of winged machines; women with shimmering, bejeweled clothes and blood-red mouths; men, tall heroic figures, doing incredible things— sitting on huge four-legged beasts or behind big shiny blocks of wood, shouting with arms upraised at vast crowds of people, advancing among dead bodies and pools of blood at the head of rows of men all dressed alike, under a sky full of smoke and bursting fire. . . . The visitors from Shantih must either stand there gazing for a week in order to see it all, or hurry on past at once, because they should not be late to the Council meeting. But they all stopped once more at the last panel, which was different from the others. Instead of being filled with faces and fire and blood and machines, it was black. Low in the left corner was a little blue-green disk, and high in the right corner was another; between and around them, nothing—black. Only if you looked close at the blackness did you see that it was flecked with a countless minute glittering of stars; and at last you saw the finely drawn silver space ship, no longer than a fingernail-paring, poised in the void between the worlds.

At the doorway beyond the black fresco two guards stood, imposing figures, dressed alike in wide trousers, jerkins, boots, belts. They carried not only coiled whips stuck in their belts, but guns: long muskets, with hand-carved stocks and heavy barrels. Most of the Shantih people had heard of guns but never seen one, and they stared with curiosity at them.

"Halt!" said one of the guards.

"What?" said Hari. The people of Shantih had early adopted the language spoken in Victoria City, since they had been people of many different tongues and needed a common language among themselves and with the City; but some of the older ones had not learned some of the City usages. Hari had never heard the word "Halt."

"Stop there," the guard said.

"All right," Hari said. "We're to wait here," he explained to the others.

The sound of voices making speeches came from behind the closed doors of the Council Room. The Shantih people presently began to wander back down the hall to look at the frescoes while they waited; the guards ordered them to wait in a group, and they came wandering back. At last the doors were opened, and the delegation from Shantih was escorted by the guards into the Council Hall of the Government of Victoria: a big room, filled with grayish light from windows set up high in the wall. At the far end was a raised platform on which ten chairs stood in a half-circle; on the wall behind them hung a sheet of red cloth, with a blue disk in the middle, and ten yellow stars around the disk. A couple of dozen men sat here and there on the rows of benches, facing the dais. Of the ten chairs on the dais, only three were occupied.

A curly-headed man who sat by a little table just below the dais stood up and announced that a delegation from Shanty Town had asked permission to address the Supreme Plenum of the Congress and Council of Victoria.

"Permission granted," said one of the men on the dais.

"Come forward—no, not there, along the side—" The curly man whispered and fussed till he got the delegation where he wanted them, near the platform. "Who is the spokesman?"

"Her," said Hari, nodding at Vera.

"State your name as listed in the National Registry. You are to address the Congressmen as 'Gentlemen' and the Councillors as 'Your Excellencies,' " the clerk whispered, frowning with agitation. Hari watched him with benign amusement, as if he were a pouchbat. "Go on, go on!" the clerk whispered, sweating.

Vera took a step forward from the group. "I'm Vera Adelson. We came to discuss with you our plans for sending a group north to start a new settlement. We hadn't had time the other day to talk the matter over, and so there was some misunderstanding and disagreement. That's all settled. Jan has the map that Councillor Falco asked for, we're happy to give you this copy for the Archives. The explorers warn us that it's not very accurate, but it does give a general idea of the country north and east of Songe Bay, including some passable routes and fords. We cordially hope that it may be of use to our community." One of the men held out a roll of leafpaper, and the worried clerk took it, glancing up at the Councillors for permission.

Vera, in her trouser-suit of white treesilk, stood quiet as a statue in the gray light; her voice was tranquil.

"One hundred and eleven years ago, the Government of Brasil-America sent several thousand people to this world. Fifty-six years ago, the Government of Canamerica sent two thousand more. The two groups have not merged, but have cooperated; and by now the City and the Town, though still distinct, are deeply interdependent.

"The first decades, for each group, were very hard; there were many deaths. There have been fewer, as we learned how to live here. The Registry has been discontinued for years, but we estimate the population of the City as about eight thousand, and the population of Shantih, at our last count, was four thousand three hundred and twenty."

There was a movement of surprise on the benches.

"Twelve thousand in the Songe Bay region is all the area can feed, we think, without over-intensive farming and a constant risk of famine. So we think it's time for some of us to move out and start a new settlement. There is, after all, a good deal of room."

Falco, up on his Councillor's chair, smiled faintly.

"Because the Town and City haven't merged, but still form two separate groups, we feel that a joint attempt to make a new settlement would be unwise. The pioneers will have to live together, work together, depend on one another, and, of course, intermarry. The strain of trying to keep up two social castes, in such a situation, would be intolerable. Anyhow, those who want to start a new settlement are all Shantih people.

"About two hundred and fifty families, some thousand people, are considering going north. They won't go all at once, but a couple of hundred at a time. As they go, their places on the farms will be filled by young people who stay here, and also, since the City is getting rather full, some City families may want to move out onto the land. They will be welcome. Even though a fifth of our farmers go north, there should be no drop in food production; and of course there'll be a thousand less mouths to feed.

"This is our plan. We trust that by discussion, criticism, and mutual striving toward truth, we may arrive together at full agreement on a matter which concerns us all."

There was a brief silence.

A man on one of the benches got up to speak, but sat down hastily when he saw Councillor Falco was about to speak.

"Thank you, Senhora Adelson," Falco said. "You will be informed of the Council's decision concerning this proposal. Senhor Brown, what is the next item on the agenda?"

The curly clerk made frantic gestures at the Shantih people with one hand while trying to find his place among the papers on his desk with the other. The two guards came forward briskly and flanked the five townspeople. "Come on!" one of them ordered.

"Excuse me," Vera said to them, gently. "Councillor Falco, I'm afraid we're misunderstanding one another again. We have made a decision, a tentative one. We wish now, in cooperation with you, to make a definite one. Neither we, nor you, can decide alone upon a matter which concerns us all."

"You misunderstand," Falco said, looking at the air above Vera's head. "You have made a proposal. The decision is up to the Government of Victoria."

Vera smiled. "I know you're not used to women speaking at your meetings, maybe it would go better if Jan Serov speaks for us." She stepped back, and a big, fair-skinned man replaced her. "You see," he said, as if continuing Vera's sentence, "first we have to settle what we want and how to do it, and then when we've agreed on that, we do it."

"The topic is closed," said bald Councillor Helder, at Falco's left on the dais. "If you continue to obstruct the business of the Plenum you must be forcibly removed."

"We aren't obstructing business, we're trying to get it done," Jan said. He didn't know what to do with his big hands, which hung uneasily at his sides, half-closed, wanting the handle of an absent hoe. "We have to talk this business over."

Falco said very quietly, "Guards."

As the guards pressed forward again, Jan looked in perplexity at Vera, and Hari spoke up: "Oh, now, calm down, Councillor, all we want is a bit of sensible talk, you can see that."

"Your Excellency! Have these people taken out!" shouted a man from the benches, and others started calling out, as if they wanted to be heard doing so by the Councillors on the dais. The Shantih people stood quiet, though Jan Serov and young King stared rather wide-eyed at the angry, shouting faces turned toward them. Falco conferred a moment with Helder, then signaled one of the guards, who left the hall at a run. Falco raised his hand for silence.

"You people," he said quite gently, "must understand that you aren't members of the Government, but subjects of the Government. To 'decide' upon some 'plan' contrary to the Government's decision is an act of rebellion. To make this clear to you, and the rest of your people, you'll be detained here until we are certain that normal order is restored."

"What's 'detained'?" Hari whispered to Vera, who said, "Prison." Hari nodded. He had been born in a prison, in Canamerica; he didn't remember it, but he was proud of it.

Eight guards now came shoving in and began to hustle the Shantih people to the door. "Single file! Hurry up now! Don't run or I'll shoot!" their officer commanded. None of the five showed the least sign of trying to run, resist, or protest. King, shoved by an impatient guard, said, "Oh, sorry," as if he had got in the way of someone in a rush.

The guards bundled the group out past the frescoes, under the columns, into the street. There they stopped. "Where to?" one asked the officer.

"Jail."

"Her too?"

They all looked at Vera, neat and delicate in her white silk. She looked back at them with tranquil interest.

"The boss said jail," the officer said, scowling.

"Hesumeria, sir, we can't stick her in there," said a little, sharp-eyed, scar-faced guard.

"That's what the boss said."

"But look, she's a lady."

"Take her to Boss Falco's house and let him decide when he gets home," suggested another, Scarface's twin, but scarless.

"I'll give you my word to stay wherever you decide, but I'd rather stay with my friends," said Vera.

"Please shut up, lady!" the officer said, clutching his head. "All right. You two take her to Casa Falco."

"The others will give their word too, if—" Vera began, but the officer turned his back on her and shouted, "All right! Get going! Single file!"

"This way, senhora," said Scarface.

At the turning Vera paused and held up her hand to salute her four companions, now far down the street. "Peace! Peace!" Hari shouted back, enthusiastically. Scarface muttered something and spat thickly aside. The two guards were men Vera would have been afraid of if she had passed them in a City street alone, but as they walked now, flanking her, their protectiveness of her was evident even in their gait. She realized that they felt themselves to be her rescuers.

"Is the jail very disagreeable?" she asked.

"Drunks, fights, stink," Scarface replied, and his twin added with grave propriety, "No place for a lady, senhora."

"Is it any better place for a man?" she inquired, but neither answered.

Casa Falco stood only three streets from the Capitol:

a big, low, white building with a red tile roof. The plump housemaid who came to the door was flustered by the presence of two soldiers and an unknown senhora on the doorstep; she curtseyed and panted and whispered, "Oh, hesumeria! Oh, hesumeria!" —and fled, leaving them on the doorstep. After a long pause, during which Vera conversed with her guards and found that they were indeed twin brothers, named Emiliano and Anibal, and that they liked their work as guards because they got good pay and didn't have to take any lip off anybody, but Anibal—Scarface— didn't like standing around so much because it made his feet hurt and his ankles swell—after this, a girl entered the front hall, a straight-backed, red-cheeked girl in sweeping full skirts. "I am Senhorita Falco," she said, with a quick glance at the guards, but speaking to Vera. Then her face changed. "Senhora Adelson, I didn't recognize you. I'm sorry. Please come in!"

"This is embarrassing, my dear, you see, I'm not a visitor, I'm a prisoner. These gentlemen have been very kind. They thought the jail had no place for women, so they brought me here. I think they have to come in too, if I come in, to guard me."

Luz Marina's eyebrows had come down in a fine, straight line. She stood silent for a moment. "They can wait in the entrance here," she said. "Sit on those chests," she said to Anibal and Emiliano. "Senhora Adelson will be with me."

The twins edged stiffly through the door after Vera.

"Please come in," Luz said, standing aside with formal courtesy, and Vera entered the hall of Casa

Falco, with its cushioned wooden chairs and settees, its inlaid tables and patterned stone floor, its thick glass windows and huge cold fireplaces, her prison. "Please sit down," said her jailer, and went to an inner door to order a fire laid and lighted, and coffee brought.

Vera did not sit down. As Luz returned toward her she looked at the girl with admiration. "My dear, you are kind and courteous. But I really am under arrest—by your father's order."

"This is my house," Luz said. Her voice was as dry as Falco's. "It is a house hospitable to guests."

Vera gave a docile little sigh, and sat down. Her gray hair had been blown about by the wind in the streets; she smoothed it back, then clasped her thin, brown hands in her lap.

"Why did he arrest you?" The question had been suppressed, and shot out under pressure. "What did you do?"

"Well, we came and tried to talk with the Council about plans for the new settlement."

"Did you know they'd arrest you?"

"We discussed it as one possibility."

"But what is it all about?"

"About the new settlement—about freedom, I suppose. But really, my dear, I mustn't talk about it with you. I've promised to be a prisoner, and prisoners aren't supposed to preach their crime."

"Why not?" said Luz disdainfully. "Is it catching, like a cold?"

Vera laughed. "Yes! —I know we've met, I don't know where it was."

The flustered maid hurried in with a tray, set it

on the table, and hurried out again, panting. Luz poured the black, hot drink—called coffee, made from the roasted root of a native plant—into cups of fine red earthenware.

"I was at the festival in Shanty Town a year ago," she said. The authoritative dryness was gone from her voice; she sounded shy. "To see the dancing. And there were a couple of times you spoke at school."

"Of course! You and Lev and all that lot were in school together! You knew Timmo, then. You know he died, on the journey north?"

"No. I didn't. In the wilderness," the girl said, and a brief silence followed the word. "Was Lev— Is Lev in jail now?"

"He didn't come with us. You know, in a war, you don't put all your soldiers in the same place at once." Vera, with recovered cheerfulness, sipped her coffee, and winced very slightly at the taste.

"A war?"

"Well, a war without fighting, of course. Maybe a rebellion, as your father says. Maybe, I hope, just a disagreement." Luz still looked blank. "You know what a war is?"

"Oh, yes. Hundreds of people killing each other. History of Earth at school was full of them. But I thought . . . your people wouldn't fight?"

"No," Vera agreed. "We don't fight. Not with knives and guns. But when we've agreed that something ought to be done, or not done, we get very stubborn. And when that meets up with another stubbornness, it can make a kind of war, a struggle of ideas, the only kind of war anybody ever wins. You see?"

Luz evidently did not.

"Well," Vera said comfortably, "you will see."

4

The ringtree of Victoria led a double life. It began as a single, fast-growing seedling with serrated red leaves. When it matured it flowered lavishly with large, honey-colored blossoms. Wotsits and other small flying creatures, attracted by the sweet-tasting petals, ate them, and while doing so fertilized the bitter-flavored heart of the flower with pollen caught on their fur, scales, wings, or vanes. The fertilized remnant of the flower curled itself up into a hard-shelled seed. There might be hundreds of these on the tree, but they dried up and dropped off, one after another, leaving at last one single seed on a high central branch. This seed, hard and ill-flavored, grew and grew while its tree weakened and withered, until the leafless branches drooped sadly beneath the big, heavy, black ball of the seed. Then, some afternoon when the autumn sun shone through gaps in the rainclouds, the seed performed its extraordinary feat: time-ripened and sun-warmed, it exploded. It went off with a bang that could be heard for miles. A cloud of dust and fragments rose and drifted slowly off across the hills. All was over, apparently, with the ringtree.

But in a circle around the central stem, several hundred seedlets, exploded from the shell, were burrowing themselves with energy down into the damp rich dirt. A year later the shoots were already competing for root-room; the less hardy ones died. Ten years later, and for a century or two after that, from twenty to sixty copper-leaved trees stood in a perfect ring about the long-vanished central stem. Branch and root, they stood apart, yet touching, forty ringtrees, one tree-ring. Once every eight or ten years they flowered and bore a small edible fruit, the seeds of which were excreted by wotsits, pouchbats, far-fallies, tree-coneys, and other fruit lovers. Dropped in the right spot, a seed germinated and produced the single tree; and it the single seed; and the cycle was repeated, from ringtree to tree-ring, timelessly.

Where the soil was favorable the rings grew inter-locking, but otherwise no large plants grew in the central circle of each ring, only grasses, moss, and ferns. Very old rings so exhausted their central ground that it might sink and form a hollow, which filled with ground seepage and with rain, and the circle of high, old dark-red trees was then mirrored in the still water of a central pool. The center of a tree-ring was always a quiet place. The ancient, pool-centered rings were the most quiet, the most strange.

The Meeting House of Shantih stood outside town in a vale which contained such a ring: forty-six trees rearing their columnar trunks and bronze crowns around a silent circle of water, rough with rain, or cloud-gray, or bright with sunlight flashing through red foliage from a sky briefly clear. Roots of the trees grew gnarled at the water's edge, making seats for the solitary contemplater. A single pair of herons lived in the Meeting-House Ring. The Victorian heron was not a heron; it was not even a bird. To describe their new world the exiles had had only words from their old world. The creatures that lived by the pools, one pair to a pool, were stilt-legged, pale-gray fish eaters: so they were herons. The first generation had known that they were not really herons, that they were not birds, nor reptiles, nor mammals. The following generations did not know what they were not, but did, in a way, know what they were. They were herons.

They seemed to live as long as the trees. Nobody had ever seen a baby heron, or an egg. Sometimes they danced, but if a mating followed the dance it was in the secrecy of the wilderness night, unseen. Silent, angular, elegant, they nested in the drifts of red leaves among the roots, and fished for water creatures in the shallows, and gazed across the pool at human beings with large, round eyes as colorless as water. They showed no fear of man, but never allowed a close approach.

The settlers of Victoria had never yet come upon any large land animal. The biggest herbivore was the coney, a fat slow rabbity beast with fine waterproof scales all over it; the biggest predator was the larva, red-eyed and shark-toothed, half a meter long. In captivity the larvas bit and screeched in insane frenzy till they died; the coneys refused to eat, lay down quietly, and died. There were big creatures in the sea; "whales" came into Songe Bay and were caught for food every summer; out at sea beasts huger than the whales had been seen, enormous, like writhing islands. The whales were not whales, but what the monsters were or were not, nobody knew. They never came near fishing boats. And the beasts of the plains and forests never came near, either. They did not run away. They simply kept their distance. They watched for a while, with clear eyes, and then moved away, ignoring the stranger.

Only the bright-winged farfallies and the wotsits ever consented to come near. Caged, a farfallie folded its wings and died; but if you put out honey for it, it might set up housekeeping on your roof, constructing there the little nest-like rain-cup in which, being semiaquatic, it slept. Wotsits evidently trusted in their peculiar ability to look like something else every few minutes. Occasionally they showed a positive desire to fly round and round a human being, or even to sit on him. Their shape-changing had in it an element of eye-fooling, perhaps of hypnosis, and Lev had sometimes wondered if the wotsits liked to use human beings to practice their tricks on. In any case, if you caged a wotsit, it turned into a shapeless brown lump like a clod of dirt, and after two or three hours, died.

None of the creatures of Victoria would be tamed, would live with man. None of them would approach him. They evaded; they slipped away, into the rain-shadowed, sweet-scented forests, or into the deep sea, or into death. They had nothing to do with man. He was a stranger. He did not belong.

"I had a cat," Lev's grandmother used to tell him, long ago. "A fat, gray cat with fur like the softest, softest treesilk. He had black stripes on his legs, and green eyes. He'd jump up on my lap, and put his nose under my ear, so I could hear him, and purr, and purr—like this!" The old lady would make a deep, soft, rumbling noise, to which the little boy listened with intense delight.

"What did he say when he was hungry, Nana?" He held his breath.

"PRRREEOWW! PRRREEOWW!"

She laughed, and he laughed.

There was only one another. The voices, the faces, the hands, the holding arms, of one's own kind. The other people, the other aliens.

Outside the doors, beyond the small plowed fields, lay the wilderness, the endless world of hills and red leaves and mist, where no voice spoke. To speak, there, no matter what you said, was to say, "I am a stranger."

"Some day," the child said, "I'll go and explore the whole world."

It was a new idea he had had, and he was full of it. He was going to make maps, and everything. But Nana wasn't listening. She had the sad look. He knew what to do about that. He came up quietly next to her and nuzzled in her neck below the ear, saying, "Prrrrr. . . ."

"Is that my cat Mino? Hello, Mino! Why," she said, "it isn't Mino, it's Levuchka! What a surprise!"

He sat on her lap. Her large, old, brown arms were around him. On each wrist she wore a bangle of fine red soapstone. Her son Alexander, Sasha, Lev's father, had carved them for her. "Manacles," he had said when he gave them to her on her birthday. "Victoria manacles, Mama." And all the grown-ups had laughed, but Nana had had the sad look while she laughed.

"Nana. Was Mino Mino's name?"

"Of course, silly."

"But why?"

"Because I named him Mino."

"But animals don't have names."

"No. Not here."

"Why don't they?"

"Because we don't know their names," the grand-mother said, looking out over the small plowed fields.

"Nana."

"Well?" said the soft voice in the soft bosom against which his ear was pressed.

"Why didn't you bring Mino here?"

"We couldn't bring anything on the space ship. Nothing of our own. There wasn't room. But anyhow, Mino was dead long before we came. I was a child when he was a kitten, and I was still a child when he was old and died. Cats don't live long, just a few years."

"But people live a long time."

"Oh, yes. A very long time."

Lev sat still on her lap, pretending he was a cat, with gray fur like the down of the cottonwool, only warm. "Prrr," he said softly, while the old woman sitting on the doorstep held him and gazed over his head at the land of her exile.

As he sat now on the hard broad root of a ringtree at the edge of the Meeting Pool, he thought of Nana, of the cat, of the silver water of Lake Serene, of the mountains above it which he longed to climb, of climbing the mountains out of the mist and rain into the ice and brightness of the summits; he thought of many things, too many things. He sat still, but his

mind would not be still. He had come here for stillness, but his mind raced, raced from past to future
and back again. Only for a moment did he find quiet.
One of the herons walked silently out into the water
from the far side of the pool. Lifting its narrow head
it gazed at Lev. He gazed back, and for an instant
was caught in that round transparent eye, as depthless
as the sky clear of clouds; and the moment was round,
transparent, silent, a moment at the center of all
moments, the eternal present moment of the silent
animal.

The heron turned away, bent its head, searching
the dark water for fish.

Lev stood up, trying to move as quietly and deftly
as the heron itself, and left the circle of the trees,
passing between two of the massive red trunks. It was
like going through a door into a different place entirely. The shallow valley was bright with sunlight,
the sky windy and alive; sun gilt the red-painted
timber roof of the Meeting House, which stood on the
south-facing slope. A good many people were at the
Meeting House already, standing on the steps and
porch talking, and Lev quickened his pace. He
wanted to run, to shout. This was no time for stillness. This was the first morning of the battle, the
beginning of victory.

Andre hailed him: "Come on! Everybody's waiting
for Boss Lev!"

He laughed, and ran; he came up the six steps of
the porch in two strides. "All right, all right, all right,"
he said, "what kind of discipline is this, where are
your boots, do you consider that a respectful position,

Sam?" Sam, a brown, stocky man wearing only white trousers, was standing calmly on his head near the porch railing.

Elia took charge of the meeting. They did not go inside, but sat around on the porch to talk, for the sunlight was very pleasant. Elia was in a serious mood, as usual, but Lev's arrival had cheered the others up, and the discussion was lively but brief. The sense of the meeting was clear almost at once. Elia wanted another delegation to go to the City to talk with the Bosses, but no one else did; they wanted a general meeting of the people of Shantih. They arranged that it would take place before sundown, and the younger people undertook to notify outlying villages and farms. As Lev was about to leave, Sam, who had serenely stood on his head throughout the discussion, came upright in a single graceful motion and said to Lev, smiling, "Arjuna, it will be a great battle."

Lev, his mind busy with a hundred things, smiled at Sam and strode off.

The campaign which the people of Shantih were undertaking was a new thing to them, and yet a familiar one. All of them, in the Town school and the Meeting House, had learned its principles and tactics; they knew the lives of the hero-philosophers Gandhi and King, and the history of the People of the Peace, and the ideas that had inspired those lives, that history. In exile, the People of the Peace had continued to live by those ideas; and so far had done so with success. They had at least kept themselves independent, while taking over the whole farming enterprise of the community, and sharing the produce fully and freely with the City. In exchange, the City provided them tools and machinery made by the Government ironworks, fish caught by the City fleet, and various other products which the older-established colony could more easily provide. It had been an arrangement satisfactory to both.

But gradually the terms of the bargain had grown more unequal. Shantih raised the cottonwool plants and the silktrees, and took the raw stuff to the City mills to be spun and woven. But the mills were very slow; if the townsfolk needed clothes, they did better to spin and weave the cloth themselves. The fresh and dried fish they expected did not arrive. Bad catches, the Council explained. Tools were not replaced. The City had furnished the farmers tools; if the farmers were careless with them it was up to them to replace them, said the Council. So it went on, gradually enough that no crisis arose. The people of Shantih compromised, adjusted, made do. The children and grandchildren of the exiles, now grown men and women, had never seen the technique of conflict and resistance, which was the binding force of their community, in action.

But they had been taught it: the spirit, the reasons, and the rules. They had learned it, and practiced it in the minor conflicts that arose within the Town itself. They had watched their elders arrive, sometimes by passionate debate and sometimes by almost wordless consent, at solutions to problems and disagreements. They had learned how to listen for the sense of the meeting, not the voice of the loudest. They had learned that they must judge each time whether obedience was necessary and right, or misplaced and wrong. They had learned that the act of violence is the act of weakness, and that the spirit's strength lies in holding fast to the truth.

At least they believed all that, and believed that they had learned it beyond any shadow of a doubt. Not one of them, under any provocation, would resort to violence. They were certain, and they were strong.

"It won't be easy, this time," Vera had said to them, before she and the others left for the City. "You know, it won't be easy."

They nodded, smiling, and cheered her. Of course it wouldn't be easy. Easy victories aren't worth winning.

As he went from farm to farm southwest of Shantih, Lev asked people to come to the big meeting, and answered their questions about Vera and the other hostages. Some of them were afraid of what the City men might do next, and Lev said, "Yes, they may do worse than take a few hostages. We can't expect them simply to agree with us, when we don't agree with them. We're in for a fight."

"But when they fight they use knives—and there's that—that whipping place, you know," said a woman, lowering her voice. "Where they punish their thieves and. . . ." She did not finish. Everyone else looked ashamed and uneasy.

"They're caught in the circle of violence that brought them here," said Lev. "We aren't. If we stand firm, all of us together, then they'll see our strength; they'll see it's greater than theirs. They'll begin to listen to us. And to win free, themselves." His face and voice were so cheerful as he spoke that the farmers could see that he was speaking the simple truth, and began to look forward to the next confrontation with the City instead of dreading it. Two brothers with names taken from the Long March, Lyons and Pamplona, got especially worked up; Pamplona, who was rather simple, followed Lev around from farm to farm the rest of the morning so he could hear the Resistance Plans ten times over.

In the afternoon Lev worked with his father and the other three families that farmed their bog-rice paddy, for the last harvest was ripe and must be got in no matter what else was going on. His father went on with one of these families for supper; Lev went to eat with Southwind. She had left her mother's house and was living alone in the little house west of town which she and Timmo had built when they married. It stood by itself in the fields, though within sight of the nearest group of houses outlying from the town. Lev, or Andre, or Martin's wife Italia, or all three of them, often came there for supper, bringing something to share with Southwind. She and Lev ate together, sitting on the doorstep, for it was a mild, golden autumn afternoon, and then went on together to the Meeting House, where two or three hundred people were already gathered, and more coming every minute.

Everyone knew what they were there for: to reassure one another that they were all together, and to discuss what was to be done next. The spirit of the gathering was festive and a little excited. People stood up on the porch and spoke, all saying in one way or another, "We're not going to give in, we're not going to let our hostages down!" When Lev spoke he was cheered: grandson of the great Shults who led the Long March, explorer of the wilderness, and a general favorite anyhow. The cheering was interrupted, there was a commotion in the crowd, which now numbered over a thousand. Night had come on, and the electric lights on the Meeting House porch, powered by the town generator, were feeble, so it was hard to see what was going on at the edge of the crowd. A squat, massive, black object seemed to be pushing through the people. When it got nearer the porch it could be seen as a mass of men, a troop of guards from the City, moving as a solid block. The block had a voice: "Meetings . . . order . . . pain," was all anyone could hear, because everyone was asking indignant questions. Lev, standing under the light, called for quiet, and as the crowd fell silent the loud voice could be heard:

"Mass meetings are forbidden, the crowd is to disperse. Public meetings are forbidden by order of the Supreme Council upon pain of imprisonment and punishment. Disperse at once and go to your homes!"

"No," people said, "why should we?"—"What right have they got?"—"Go to your own homes!"

"Come on, quiet!" Andre roared, in a voice nobody knew he possessed. As they grew quiet again he said to Lev in his usual mumble, "Go on, talk."

"This delegation from the City has a right to speak," Lev said, loud and clear. "And to be heard. And when we've heard what they say, we may disregard it, but remember that we are resolved not to threaten by act or word. We do not offer anger or injury to these men who come amongst us. What we offer them is friendship and the love of truth!"

He looked at the guards, and the officer at once repeated the order to disperse the meeting in a flat, hurried voice. When he was through, there was silence. The silence continued. Nobody said anything. Nobody moved.

"All right now," the officer shouted, forcing his voice, "get moving, disperse, go to your homes!"

Lev and Andre looked at each other, folded their arms, and sat down. Holdfast, who was also up on the porch, sat down too; then Southwind, Elia, Sam, Jewel, and the others. The people on the meeting ground began to sit down. It was a queer sight in the shadows and the yellowish, shadow-streaked light: the many, many dark forms all seeming to shrink to half their height, with a faint rustling sound, a few murmurs. Some children giggled. Within half a minute they were all sitting down. No one remained afoot but the troop of guards, twenty men standing close together.

"You've been warned," the officer shouted, and his voice was both vindictive and embarrassed. He was evidently not sure what to do with these people who now sat silently on the ground, looking at him with expressions of peaceable curiosity, as if they were children at a puppet show and he was the puppet. "Get up and disperse, or I'll begin the arrests!"

Nobody said anything.

"All right, arrest the thir—the twenty nearest. Get up. You, get up!"

The people spoken to or laid hands on by the guardsmen got up, and stood quietly. "Can my wife come too?" a man asked the guard in a low voice, not wanting to break the great, deep stillness of the crowd.

"There will be no further mass meetings of any kind. By order of the Council!" the officer bawled, and led his troop off, herding a group of about twenty-five townsfolk. They disappeared into the darkness outside the reach of the electric lights.

Behind them the crowd was silent.

A voice rose from it, singing. Other voices joined in, softly at first. It was an old song, from the days of the Long March on Earth.

> O when we come,
> O when we come to the Free Land
> Then we will build the City,
> O when we come. . . .

As the group of guards and prisoners went on into the darkness the singing did not sound fainter behind them but stronger and clearer, as all the hundreds of voices joined and sent the music ringing over the dark quiet lands between Shantih and the City of Victoria.

The twenty-four people who had been arrested by the guards, or had voluntarily gone off with them, returned to Shantih late the following day. They had been put into a warehouse for the night, perhaps because the City Jail had no room for so many, and sixteen of them women and children. There had been a trial in the afternoon, they said, and when it was done they were told to go home. "But we're supposed to pay a fine," old Pamplona said importantly.

Pamplona's brother Lyons was a thriving orcharder, but Pamplona, slow and sickly, had never amounted to much. This was his moment of glory. He had gone to prison, just like Gandhi, just like Shults, just like on Earth. He was a hero, and delighted.

"A fine?" Andre asked, incredulous. "Money? They know we don't use their coins—"

"A fine," Pamplona explained, tolerant of Andre's ignorance, "is that we have to work for twenty days on the new farm."

"What new farm?"

"Some kind of new farm the Bosses are going to make."

"The Bosses are going in for farming?" Everybody laughed.

"They'd better, if they want to eat," a woman said.

"What if you don't go work on this new farm?"

"I don't know," Pamplona said, getting confused. "Nobody said. We weren't supposed to talk. It was a court, with a judge. The judge talked."

"Who was the judge?"

"Macmilan."

"Young Macmilan?"

"No, the old one, the Councillor. The young one was there, though. A big fellow he is! Like a tree! And he smiles all the time. A fine young man."

Lev came, at a run, having just got news of the prisoners' return. He hugged the first ones he came to, in the excited group that had gathered in the street to welcome them. "You're back, you're back— All of you?"

"Yes, yes, they're all back, you can go eat supper now!"

"The others, Hari and Vera—"

"No, not them. They didn't see them."

"But all of you— They didn't hurt you?"

"Lev said he couldn't eat anything till you got back, he's been fasting."

"We're all right, go eat some dinner, what a stupid thing to do!"

"They treated you well?"

"Like guests, like guests," old Pamplona asserted. "We're all brothers. Isn't that so? A good big breakfast they gave us, too!"

"Our own rice we grew, that's what they gave us. Fine hosts! to lock their guests up in a barn as black as night and as cold as last night's porridge, I have an ache in every bone and I want a bath, every one of those guard people was crawling with lice, I saw one right on his neck, the one that arrested me, a louse the size of your fingernail, ugh, I want a bath!" This was Kira, a buxom woman who lisped because she had lost her two front teeth; she said she didn't miss the teeth, they got in the way of her talking anyhow. "Who'll put me up for the night? I'm not going to walk home to East Village with every bone aching and a dozen lice creeping up and down my backbone!" Five or six people at once offered her a bath, a bed, hot food. All the freed prisoners were looked after and made much of. Lev and Andre went off down the little side street that led to Lev's home. They walked in silence for a while.

"Thank God!" said Lev.

"Yes. Thank God. They're back; it worked. If only Vera and Jan and the others had come back with them."

"They're all right. But this lot—none of them was ready, they hadn't thought about it, they hadn't prepared themselves. I was afraid they'd be hurt, I was afraid they'd be frightened, get angry. It was our responsibility, we led the sit-down. We got them arrested. But they held out. They weren't frightened, they didn't fight, they held fast!" Lev's voice shook. "It was my responsibility."

"Ours," Andre said. "We didn't send them, you didn't send them; they went. They chose to go. You're worn out, you ought to eat. Sasha!" They were at the door of the house. "Make this man eat. They fed his prisoners, now you feed him."

Sasha, sitting by the hearth sanding down a hoe handle, looked up; his mustache bristled, his eyebrows bristled over his deep-set eyes. "Who can make my son do what he doesn't want to do?" he said. "If he wants to eat, he knows where the soup bowl is."

5

The Senhor Councillor Falco gave a dinner party. During most of it, he wished sincerely that he had not given a dinner party.

It was to be a party in the old style, the Old World style, with five courses, and fine clothes, and conversation, and music after dinner. The old men arrived at the hour, each accompanied by his wife and an unmarried daughter or two. Some of the younger men, such as young Helder, also arrived on time, with their wives. The women stood about the fireplace at one end of the hall of Casa Falco in their long gowns and jewelry, and chattered; the men stood about the fireplace at the other end of the hall in their best black suits, and talked. All seemed to be going well, just as it had gone when Councillor Falco's grandfather Don Ramon had given dinner parties, just like dinner parties back on Earth, as Don Ramon had often said with satisfaction and conviction, for after all his father Don Luis had been born on Earth and had been the greatest man in Rio de Janeiro.

But some of the guests had not come on time. It got later, and still they did not come. Councillor Falco was summoned by his daughter to the kitchen: the cooks' faces were tragic, the superb dinner would be ruined. At his command the long table was carried into the hall and set, the guests sat down, the first course was served, eaten, cleared away, the second course was served, and then, only then, in came young Macmilan, young Marquez, young Weiler, free and easy, without an apology and, what was worse, with a whole rabble of their friends, uninvited: seven or eight big bucks with whips in their belts and broad-brimmed hats which they didn't know enough to take off indoors, and dirty boots, and a lot of loud dirty talk. New places had to be set, crowded in

among the others. The young men had been drinking
before they came, and went on swilling Falco's best
ale. They pinched the maidservants, but ignored the
ladies. They shouted across the table, and blew
their noses in the embroidered napkins. When the
supreme moment of the dinner arrived, the meat
course, roast coney—Falco had hired ten trappers
for a week to supply this luxury—the latecomers piled
their plates so greedily that there was not enough to
go round, and no one at the foot of the table got
meat. The same thing happened with the dessert, a
molded pudding made with root starch, boiled fruits,
and nectar. Several of the young men scooped it
out of the bowls with their fingers.

Falco signaled his daughter, at the foot of the table,
and she led a retreat of the ladies to the garden sitting
room at the back of the house. This left the young
toughs all the more freedom to lounge, spit, belch,
swear, and get drunker. Small cups of the brandy
for which the stillrooms of Casa Falco were famous
got tossed off like water, and the young men yelled
at the bewildered servants to refill. Some of the other
young men, and some of the older ones, liked this
crude behavior, or perhaps thought it was how one
was expected to behave at a dinner party, and joined
in it. Old Helder got so drunk he went and vomited
in the corner, but he came back to table and started
drinking again.

Falco and some close friends, the elder Marquez,
Burnier, and the doctor, withdrew to the hearth and
tried to talk; but the noise around the long table was
deafening. Some were dancing, some quarreling; the

musicians hired to play after dinner had mixed in with the guests and were drinking like fish; young Marquez had a serving girl on his lap, where she sat white-faced and cringing, muttering, "Oh hesumeria! Oh hesumeria!"

"A very merry party, Luis," old Burnier said, after a particularly painful outburst of song and screeching.

Falco had remained calm throughout; his face was calm as he replied, "A proof of our degeneration."

"The young fellows aren't used to such feasts. Only Casa Falco knows how to give a party in the old style, the real Earth style."

"They are degenerates," Falco said.

His brother-in-law Cooper, a man of sixty, nodded. "We have lost the style of Earth."

"Not at all," said a man behind them. They all turned. It was Herman Macmilan, one of the late-comers; he had been guzzling and shouting with the rest, but showed no signs of drunkenness now, except perhaps the heightened color of his handsome young face. "It seems to me, gentlemen, that we're redis-covering the style of Earth. After all, who were our ancestors that came from the Old World? Not weak, meek men, were they? Brave men, bold, strong men, who knew how to live. Now we're learning again how to live. Plans, laws, rules, manners, what's that got to do with us? Are we slaves, women? What are we afraid of? We're men, free men, masters of a whole world. It's time we came into our inheritance; that's how it is, gentlemen." He smiled, deferential, yet perfectly self-confident.

Falco was impressed. Perhaps this wreck of a dinner

party might serve some purpose after all. This young Macmilan, who had never seemed anything but a fine muscular animal, a likely future match for Luz Marina, was showing both willpower and brains, the makings of a man. "I agree with you, Don Herman," he said. "But I'm able to agree with you only because you and I are still able to talk. Unlike most of our friends there. A man must be able to drink and think. Since only you of the young men seem able to do both, tell me: what do you think of my idea of making latifundia?"

"Big farms, that means?"

"Yes. Big farms; large fields, planted in one crop, for efficiency. My idea is to pick managers from among our best young men; to give each a large region to run, an estate, and enough peasants to work it; and let him run it as he wishes. Thus more food will be produced. The excess population in Shanty Town will be put to work, and kept under control, to prevent any more talk about independence and new colonies. And the next generation of City Men will include a number of great estate owners. We've kept close together for strength long enough. It's time, as you said, that we spread out, use our freedom, make ourselves masters of this rich world of ours."

Herman Macmilan listened, smiling. His finely cut lips had an almost constant smile.

"Not a bad idea," he said. "Not a bad idea at all, Senhor Councillor."

Falco bore with his patronizing tone, because he had decided that Herman Macmilan was a man he could make use of.

"Consider it," he said. "Consider it for yourself."
He knew young Macmilan was doing just that. "How
would you like to own such an estate, Don Herman?
A little—what's the word, an old word—"

"Kingdom," old Burnier supplied.

"Yes. A little kingdom for yourself. How does it
strike you?" He spoke flatteringly, and Herman Macmilan preened himself. In the self-important, Falco
reflected, there is always room for a little more self-
importance.

"Not bad," Macmilan said, nodding judiciously.

"To carry out the plan, we'll need the vigor of you
young men, and the brains. Opening up new farmland
has always been a slow business. Forced labor is the
only way to clear large areas quickly. If this unrest in
Shanty Town goes on, we can have plenty of peasant
rebels to sentence to forced labor. But, since they're
all words and no actions, they may have to be pushed,
we may have to crack the whip to make them fight, we
may have to drive them to rebellion, you understand?
How does that kind of action strike you?"

"A pleasure, senhor. Life's boring here. Action is
what we want."

Action, Falco thought, is also what I want. I should
like to knock this condescending young man's teeth
out. But he is going to be useful, and I shall use
him, and smile.

"That's what I hoped to hear! Listen, Don Herman.
You have influence among the young men—a natural
gift of leadership. Now tell me what you think of this.
Our regular guards are loyal enough, but they're
commoners, stupid men, easily confused by the Shanty-

Towners' tricks. What we need to lead them is a troop of elite soldiers, young aristocrats, brave, intelligent, and properly commanded. Men who love fighting, like our brave ancestors of Earth. Do you think such a troop could be brought together and trained? How would you suggest we go about it?"

"All you need is a leader," Herman Macmilan said without hesitation. "I could train up a group like that in a week or two."

After that night, young Macmilan became a frequent visitor at Casa Falco, coming in at least once a day to talk with the Councillor. Whenever Luz was in the front part of the house it seemed Macmilan was there; and she took to spending more and more time in her own room, or the attic, or the garden sitting room. She had always avoided Herman Macmilan, not because she disliked him, it was impossible to dislike anyone so handsome, but because it was humiliating to know that everybody, seeing Luz and Herman say a word to each other, was thinking and saying, "Ah, they'll be married soon." Whether he wanted to or not he brought the idea of marriage with him, constraining her too to think about it; and not wanting to think about it, she had always been very shy with him. Nowadays it was the same, except that, seeing him daily as a familiar of the house, she had decided that—although it was wasteful and a pity—you could dislike even a very handsome man.

He came into the back sitting room without knocking at the door, and stood in the doorway, a graceful and powerful figure in his tightly belted tunic. He surveyed the room, which faced inward on the large central garden around which the back part of the house was built. The garden doors stood open and the sound of fine mild rain falling on the paths and shrubs of the garden filled the room with quietness. "So this is where you hide away," he said.

Luz had risen when he appeared. She wore a dark homespun skirt and a white shirt that glimmered in the dim light. Behind her in the shadows another woman sat spinning with a drop spindle.

"Always hiding away here, eh?" Herman repeated. He came no farther into the room, perhaps waiting to be invited in, perhaps also conscious of his dramatic presence framed in the doorway.

"Good afternoon, Don Herman. Are you looking for my father?"

"I've just been talking to him."

Luz nodded. Though she was curious to know what Herman and her father talked about so much lately, she certainly wasn't going to ask. The young man came on into the room and stood in front of Luz, looking at her with his good-humored smile. He reached out and took her hand, raised it to his lips, and kissed it. Luz pulled away in a spasm of annoyance. "That is a stupid custom," she said, turning away.

"All customs are stupid. But the old folks can't get on without them, eh? They think the world would fall apart. Hand-kissing, bowing, senhor this and senhora that, how it was done on the Old World, history, books, rubbish. . . . Well!"

Luz laughed in spite of herself. It was fine to hear

Herman simply brush away as nonsense the things that loomed so large and worrisome in her life.

"The Black Guards are coming on very well," he said. "You must come see us train. Come tomorrow morning."

"What 'Black Guards'?" she asked disdainfully, sitting down and taking up her work, a bit of fine sewing for Eva's expected fourth child. That was the trouble with Herman, if you once smiled or said something natural or felt like admiring him, he pushed in, pushed his advantage, and you had to snub him at once.

"My little army," he replied. "What's that?" He sat down beside her on the wicker settee. There was not enough room for his big body and her slight one. She tugged her skirt out from under his thigh. "A bonnet," she said, trying to control her temper, which was rising. "For Evita's baby."

"Oh, God, yes, what a breeder that girl is! Aldo has his quiver full. We don't take married men in the Guards. A fine bunch they are. You have to come see them."

Luz made a microscopic embroidery knot, and no reply.

"I've been out looking over my land. That's why I wasn't here yesterday."

"I didn't notice," said Luz.

"Choosing my property. A valley down on Mill River. Fine country that is, once it's cleared. My house will be built up on a hill. I saw the site for it at once. A big house, like this one, but bigger, two stories, with porches all round. And barns and a smithy and so on.

Then, down in the valley near the river, the peasants' huts, where I can look down on them. Bog-rice in the marshes where the river spreads out in the valley bottom. Orchards on the hillsides—treesilk and fruit. I'll lumber some of the forests and save some for coney hunting. A beautiful place it'll be, a kingdom. Come and see it with me next time I go down there. I'll send the pedicab from Casa Macmilan. It's too far for a girl to walk. You should see it."

"What for?"

"You'll like it," Herman said with absolute confidence. "How would you like to have a place like that yourself? Own everything in sight. A big house, lots of servants. Your own kingdom."

"Women aren't kings," Luz said. She bent her head over a stitch. The light was really too dim now for sewing, but it gave her the excuse not to look at Herman. He kept looking at her, staring, his face intent and expressionless; his eyes seemed darker than usual and he had stopped smiling. But all at once his mouth opened and he laughed, "Ha, ha!"—a small laugh for so big a man. "No. All the same, women have a way of getting what they want, don't they, my little Luz?"

She sewed on and did not answer.

Herman put his face close to hers and whispered, "Get rid of the old woman."

"What did you say?" Luz inquired in a normal speaking voice.

"Get rid of her," Herman repeated, with a slight nod.

Luz stuck her needle carefully into its case, folded

her sewing, and stood up. "Excuse me, Don Herman. I must go speak to the cook," she said, and went out. The other woman sat still, spinning. Herman sat for a minute sucking his lips; he smiled, got up, and sauntered out, his thumbs in his belt.

After a quarter-hour Luz looked in the doorway by which she had left, and seeing no Herman Macmilan, came back in. "That clod," she said, and spat on the floor.

"He's very good-looking," said Vera, teasing out a last shred of treesilk, twirling it into a fine even thread, and bringing the full spindle back to her lap.

"Very," said Luz. She picked up the neatly folded baby bonnet on which she had been working, looked at it, squashed it into a ball and threw it across the room. "Screw!" she said.

"The way he talked to you makes you angry," Vera said, half questioningly.

"The way he talks, the way he looks, the way he sits, the way he is. . . . Ugh! My little army, my big house, my servants, my peasants, my little Luz. If I were a man I'd knock his head on the wall till his big teeth fell out."

Vera laughed. She did not laugh often, usually only when she was startled. "No, you wouldn't!"

"I would. I'd kill him."

"Oh, no. No. You wouldn't. Because if you were a man, you'd know you were as strong as he, or stronger, and so you wouldn't have to prove it. The trouble is, being a woman, here, where they always tell you you're weak, you believe them. That was funny, when

he said the South Valleys are too far for a girl to walk!
About twelve kilometers!".

"I've never walked that far. Probably not half that
far."

"Well, that's what I mean. They tell you you're
weak and helpless. And if you believe it, you get mad
and want to hurt people."

"Yes, I do," Luz said, facing around to Vera. "I
want to hurt people. I want to and I probably will."

Vera sat still, looking up at the girl. "Yes." She
spoke more gravely. "If you marry a man like that and
live his life, then I agree. You may not really want to
hurt people, but you will."

Luz stared back at her. "That is hateful," she said
at last. "Hateful! To say it that way. That I haven't
any choice, that I have to hurt people, that it doesn't
even matter what I want."

"Of course it matters, what you want."

"It doesn't. That's the whole point."

"It does. And that's the whole point. *You* choose.
You choose whether or not to make choices."

Luz stood there a minute longer, still staring at her.
Her cheeks were still burning red with temper, but
her eyebrows were not drawn down level; they were
raised as if in surprise or fright, as if something altogether unexpected had risen up before her.

She moved indecisively, then went out the open
door into the garden that lay at the heart of the house.

The touch of the sparse rain on her face was gentle.
Raindrops falling into the little fountain basin in
the center of the garden made delicate interlocking

rings, each ring gone in an instant of urgent outward motion, a ceaseless tremor of clear fleeting circles on the surface of the water in the round basin of gray stone.

House walls and shuttered windows stood all round the garden, silent. The garden was like an inner room of the house, shut in, protected. But a room with the roof taken off. A room into which rain fell.

Luz's arms were wet and cold. She shuddered. She returned to the door, the dim room where Vera sat.

She stood between Vera and the light and said in a rough, low voice, "What kind of man is my father?"

There was a pause. "Is it fair of you to ask me that? Or of me to answer? . . . Well, I suppose so. So what can I say? He's strong. He's a king, a real one."

"It's just a word, I don't know what it means."

"We have old stories—the king's son who rode on the tiger. . . . Well, I mean he's strong of soul, he has grandeur of heart. But when a man is shut up inside walls that he's been building stronger and higher all his life, then maybe no strength is enough. He can't get out."

Luz crossed the room, stooped to pick up the baby bonnet she had flung under a chair, and stood with her face turned from Vera, smoothing out the little scrap of half-embroidered cloth.

"Neither can I," she said.

"Oh, no, no," the older woman said energetically. "You're not inside the walls with him! He doesn't protect you—you protect him. When the wind blows, it doesn't blow on him, but on the roof and walls of this City that his fathers built as a fortress against the unknown, a protection. And you're part of that City, part of his roofs and walls, his house, Casa Falco. So is his title, Senhor, Councillor, Boss. So are all his servants and his guards, all the men and women he can give orders to. They're all part of his house, the walls to keep the wind off him. Do you see what I mean? I say it so foolishly. I don't know how to say it. What I mean is, I think your father is a man who should be a great man, but he's made a bad mistake. He has never come outside into the rain."

Vera began to wind the thread she had spun off the spindle into a skein, peering at it in the dim light. "And so, because he won't let himself be hurt, he does wrong to those he loves best. And then he sees that, and after all, it hurts him."

"Hurts *him*?" the girl said fiercely.

"Oh, that's the last thing we learn about our parents. The last thing, because after we learn it, they aren't our parents any longer, but just other people like us. . . ."

Luz sat down on the wicker settee and put the baby bonnet on her knee, continuing to smoothe it out carefully with two fingers. After quite a while she said, "I'm glad you came here, Vera."

Vera smiled and went on winding off the thread.

"I'll help with that."

On her knees, feeding the thread off the spindle so that Vera could wind it in even loops, she said, "It was stupid of me to say that. You want to go back to your family, you're in jail here."

"A very pleasant jail! And I have no family. Of course I want to go back. To come and go as I like."

"You never married?"

"There was so much else to do," Vera said, smiling and placid.

"So much else to do! There's nothing else to do, for us."

"No?"

"If you don't marry, you're an old maid. You make bonnets for other women's babies. You order the cook to make fish soup. You get laughed at."

"Are you afraid of that, being laughed at?"

"Yes. Very much." Luz spent some while untangling a length of thread that had snagged on the shank of the spindle. "I don't care if stupid people laugh," she said more quietly. "But I don't like to be scorned. And the scorn would be deserved. Because it takes courage to really be a woman, just as much as to be a man. It takes courage to really be married, and to bear children, and to bring them up."

Vera watched her face. "Yes. It does. Great courage. But, again, is that your only choice—marriage and motherhood, or nothing?"

"What else is there, for a woman? What else that really counts?"

Vera turned a little to look out the open doors into the gray garden. She sighed, a deep involuntary drawing of breath.

"I wanted a child very much," she said. "But you see, there were other things . . . that counted." She smiled faintly. "Oh, yes, it's a choice. But not the only one. One can be a mother and a great deal else besides. One can do more than one thing. With the will, and the luck. . . . My luck wasn't good, or maybe I was wrongheaded, made the wrong choice. I don't like compromise, you see. I set my heart on a man who . . . had his heart set on somebody else. That was Sasha—Alexander Shults, Lev's father. Oh, a long long time ago, before you were born. So he married, and I went on with the work I was good at, because it always interested me, but there weren't any other men who did. But even if I'd married did I have to sit in the back room all my life? You know, if we sit in the back room, with babies or without babies, and leave all the rest of the world to the men, then of course the men will do everything and be everything. Why should they? They're only half the human race. It's not fair to leave them all the work to do. Not fair to them or us. Besides," and she smiled more broadly, "I like men very much, but sometimes . . . they're so stupid, so stuffed with theories. . . . They go in straight lines only, and won't stop. It's dangerous to do that. It's dangerous to leave everything up to the men, you know. That's one reason why I'd like to go home, at least for a visit. To see what Elia with his theories, and my dear young Lev with his ideals, are up to. I get worried they'll go too fast and too straight and get us into a place we can't get out of, a trap. You see it seems to me that where men are weak and dangerous is in their vanity. A woman has a center, is a center. But a man isn't, he's a reaching out. So he reaches out and grabs things and piles them up around him and says, I'm this, I'm that, this is me, that's me, I'll prove that I am me! And he can wreck a lot of things, trying to prove it. That's what I was trying to say about your father. If he'd only be Luis Falco. That is quite enough. But no, he has to be the Boss, the Councillor, the Father, and so on. What a waste! And Lev, he's terribly vain too, maybe in the same way. A great heart, but not sure where the center is. Oh, I wish I could talk with him, just for ten minutes, and make sure. . . ." Vera had long since forgotten to wind her thread; she shook her head sadly and looked down at the skein with a faraway gaze.

"Go on, then," Luz said in a low voice.

Vera looked mildly puzzled.

"Go back to the Town. Tonight. I'll let you out. And I'll tell my father, tomorrow, that I did so. I can do something—something besides sit here and sew and swear and listen to that stupid Macmilan!"

Lithe, robust, and commanding, the girl had leapt to her feet and stood over Vera, who sat still, looking shrunken.

"I've given my word, Luz Marina."

"What does that matter?"

"If I don't speak truth I can't seek truth," Vera answered in a hard voice.

They stared at each other, their faces set.

"I have no child," Vera said, "and you have no mother. If I could help you, child, I would. But not that way. I keep my promises."

"I make no promises," Luz said.

She cleared a strand of thread from the spindle, Vera wound it onto the skein.

6

Whip butts rattled on doors. Men's voices rang out; down by River Farm somebody was shouting or screaming. Villagers huddled together in a group in the cold, smoke-scented fog; it was not daybreak yet, houses and faces were lost in the fog and dark. Inside the little houses children, frightened by their parents' fear and confusion, screamed aloud. People tried to get lamps lighted, to find their clothes, to hush the children. The City guards, excited, armed among the weaponless and clothed among the unclothed, flung open doors, shouldered into warm dark interiors of houses, shouted orders at the villagers and each other, pushed men one way and women another; their officer could have no control over them, dispersed as they were in the dark, among houses, and in the growing crowd in the one street of the village; only the docility of the villagers prevented the excitement of brutality from becoming the ecstasy of murder and rape. They protested, argued, and questioned verbally, but since most of them thought they were being arrested, and all had agreed at the Meeting House not to resist arrest, they obeyed the guards' orders as promptly as they could; when they understood the orders, they passed the information on readily and clearly—grown men out onto the street, women and children stay indoors—as the best means of self-protection; so the frantic officer found his prisoners rounding themselves up. As soon as there was a group of twenty or so, he told off four guards, one armed with a musket, to march them out of the village. Two such groups had been marched off from Tableland Village; the fourth from South Village was being brought together when Lev arrived. Lyons's wife Rosa had run from Tableland to Shantih, and, exhausted, had hammered at the Shultses' door, gasping, "They're taking off the men, the guards, they're taking off all the men." Lev had set off at once, alone, leaving Sasha to rouse the rest of the Town. As he came up, panting from the three-kilometer run, the fog was thinning, growing luminous; the figures of villagers and guards on the South Road bulked strangely in the half-light, as he cut across the fields to the head of the group. He stopped in front of the man at the head of the half-bunched, half-straggling line. "What's going on?"

"Labor draft. Get in line with the others."

Lev knew the guard, a tall fellow named Angel; they had been at school together for a year. Southwind and the other girls from Shantih had been afraid of Angel, because he cornered them in the hallway when he could and tried to handle them.

"Get in line," Angel repeated, and swung up his musket, resting the end of the barrel on Lev's chest. He was breathing almost as hard as Lev, and his eyes were widely dilated; he gave a kind of gasping laugh, watching how Lev's winded breathing made the gun barrel rise and fall. "You ever hear one of these go off, boy? Loud, loud, like a ringtree seed—" He pushed the musket harder against Lev's breastbone, then swung the gun up suddenly pointing at the sky, and fired.

Dazed by the terrific noise, Lev staggered back and stood staring. Angel's face had gone dead gray; he also stood blank for some seconds, shaken by the recoil of the crudely made gun.

The villagers behind Lev, thinking he had been shot, came surging forward, and the other guards ran with them, yelling and cursing; the long whips uncoiled and cracked, flickering weirdly in the fog. "I'm all right," Lev said. His voice sounded faint and distant inside his head. "I'm all right!" he shouted as loud as he could. He heard Angel also shouting, saw a villager take a whiplash straight across his face. "Get back in line!" He joined the group of villagers, and they huddled together, then, obeying the guards, strung out by twos and threes, and started to walk southward down the rough track.

"Why are we going south? This isn't the City Road, why are we going south?" the one next to him, a boy of eighteen or so, said in a ragged whisper.

"It's a labor draft," Lev said. "Some kind of work. How many have they taken?" He shook his head to rid it of a buzzing dizziness.

"All the men in our valley. Why do we have to go?"

"To bring the others back. When we're all together we can act together. It'll be all right. Nobody got hurt?"

"I don't know."

"It'll be all right. Hold fast," Lev whispered, not knowing what he was saying. He began to drop back through the others until he came alongside the man who had been whipped. He was walking with his arm across his eyes, another man was holding his shoulder to guide him; they were last in line; barely visible in the ground mist, a guard followed behind.

"Can you see?"

"I don't know," the man said, pressing his arm across his face. His gray hair stood up ruffled and tufted; he was wearing a nightshirt and trousers, and was barefoot; his broad bare feet looked curiously childlike, shuffling and stubbing on the rocks and mud of the road.

"Take your arm away, Pamplona," the other man said anxiously. "So we can have a look."

The guard following behind shouted something, a threat or an order to move along faster.

Pamplona lowered his arm. Both his eyes were shut; one was untouched, the other was lost in an open bleeding slash where the whipthong had cut from the corner of the brow to the bridge of the nose. "It hurts," he said. "What was it? I can't see, there's something in my eye. Lyons? Is that you? I want to go home."

More than a hundred men were taken from the villages and outlying farms south and west of Shantih to begin work on the new estates in South Valley. They got there in mid-morning, as the fog was lifting off Mill River in writhing banners. Several guards were posted out on the South Road to prevent trouble-makers from Shantih joining the forced-labor group. Tools were distributed, hoes, mattocks, brush-knives; and they were put to work in groups of four or five, each watched over by a guard armed with whip or musket. No barracks or shelters had been set up for them or for the thirty guards. When evening came, they built campfires of wet wood and slept on the wet ground. Food had been provided, but the bread had got rain-soaked so that most of it was a mass of dough. The guards grumbled bitterly among themselves. The villagers talked, persistently. At first the officer in charge of the operation, Captain Eden, tried to forbid them from talking, fearing conspiracy; then, when he realized that one group among them was arguing with another lot who were for running off during the night, he let them talk. He had no way to prevent them from sneaking off by ones and twos in the darkness; guards were stationed about with muskets, but they couldn't see in the dark, there was no possibility of keeping bright fires going in the rain, and they had not been able to build a "compound area" as ordered. The villagers had worked hard at ground-clearing, but had proved inept and stupid at constructing any kind of fence or palisade out of the cut shrubs and brambles, and his own men would not lay down their weapons to do such work.

Captain Eden set his men on watch and watch; he himself did not sleep that night.

In the morning the whole lot of them, his men and the villagers, still seemed to be there; everyone was

slow-moving in the misty cold, and it took hours to get
fires lighted and some kind of breakfast cooked and
served out. Then the tools must be distributed again,
the long hoes, the wicked steel brush-knives, mattocks,
machetes. A hundred and twenty men armed with
those, against thirty with whips and muskets. Didn't
they see what they could so easily do? Under Captain
Eden's disbelieving gaze the villagers filed past the
heap of tools, just as they had done yesterday, took
what they needed, and set to work again clearing the
brush and undergrowth off the slope down to the river.
They worked hard and well; they knew this kind of
work; without paying much heed to the guards' com-
mands, they divided themselves into teams, rotating
the hardest labor. Most of the guards both looked and
felt bored, cold, and superfluous; their mood was
sullen, as it had been ever since the brief and unful-
filled excitement of raiding the villages and rounding
up the men.

The sun came out late in the morning, but by
midday the clouds had thickened and the rain was
beginning again. Captain Eden ordered a break for a
meal—another ration of ruined bread—and was talking with two guards he was sending back to the City
to request fresh supplies and some canvas to use for
tents and groundcloths, when Lev came over to him.

"One of our people needs a doctor, and two of
them are too old for this kind of work." He pointed
to Pamplona, who sat, his head bandaged with a torn
shirt, talking with Lyons and two gray-headed men.
"They should be sent back to their village."

Lev's manner, though not that of an inferior addressing an officer, was perfectly civil. The captain looked at him appraisingly, but not with prejudice. Angel had pointed out this wiry little fellow last night as one of the Shanty Town ringleaders, and it was evident that the villagers tended to look at Lev whenever an order was given or a threat made, as if for direction. How they got it the captain did not know, for he had not seen Lev giving them any orders himself; but if the boy was, in some fashion, a leader, Captain Eden was willing to deal with him as such. The most unnerving element in the situation to the captain was its lack of structure. He was in charge, yet he had no authority beyond what these men, and his own men, were willing to allow him. His men were rough customers at best, and now felt frustrated and ill-used; the Shanty people were an unknown quantity. In the last analysis he had nothing completely dependable except his musket; and nine of his men were also armed.

Whether the odds were thirty against a hundred and twenty, or one against a hundred and forty-nine, the wise course was evidently reasonable firmness without bullying. "It's just a whip cut," he said quietly to the young man. "He can lay off work for a couple of days. The old men can look after the food, dry out this bread, keep the fires going. No one is allowed to leave until the work is done."

"The cut's deep. He'll lose his eye if it isn't looked after. And he's in pain. He has got to go home."

The captain considered. "All right," he said. "If he can't work, he can go. Alone."

"It's too far for him to walk without help."

"Then he stays."

"He'll have to be carried. It'll take four men to carry a stretcher."

Captain Eden shrugged and turned away.

"Senhor, we've agreed not to work until Pamplona's taken care of."

The captain turned to face Lev again, not impatiently, but with a steady gaze. " 'Agreed'—?"

"When he and the old men are sent home, we'll get back to work."

"My orders are from the Council," the captain said, "and your orders are from me. You must make that clear to these men."

"Look," the young man said, with a little warmth but no anger, "we've decided to go ahead, at least temporarily. The work's worth doing, the community does need new farmlands; this is a good location for a village. But we're not obeying orders. We're yielding to your threat of force, in order to spare ourselves, and you, injury or murder. But right now the man whose life's at stake is Pamplona there, and if you won't act to save him, then we have to. The two old men, too; they can't stay here with no shelter. Old Sun has arthritis. Until they're sent home, we can't go on with the work."

Captain Eden's round, swarthy face had gone rather pale. Young Boss Macmilan had told him, "Round up a couple of hundred peasants and get them clearing the west bank of Mill River below the ford," and that had sounded straightforward, not an easy job but a man's job, a real responsibility with reward to follow. But he seemed to be the only one responsible. His men were barely under control, and these Shanty-Towners were incomprehensible. First they were frightened and incredibly meek, now they were trying to give orders to him. If in fact they weren't afraid of his guards, why did they waste time talking? If he was one of them he'd say the hell with it, and make sure he had a machete; they were four to one, and ten at most would be shot before they pulled down and pitchforked the guards who had muskets. There was no sense to their behavior, but it was shameful, unmanly. Where was he to find his own self-respect, in this damned wilderness? The gray river smoking with rain, the tangled, soggy valley, the moldy porridge that was supposed to be bread, the cold down his back where his soaked tunic clung to him, the sullen faces of his men, the voice of this queer boy telling him what to do, it was all too much. He shifted his musket around into his hands. "Listen," he said. "You, and the rest, get back to work. Now. Or I'll have you tied and taken back to the City, to jail. Take your pick."

He had not spoken loudly, but all the others, guards and villagers, were aware of the confrontation. Many stood up from the campfires, knots and clumps of men, mud-blackened, wet hair lank on their foreheads. A while passed, a few seconds, half a minute at most, very long, silent, except for the sound of rain on the raw dirt around them and on the tangled brush sloping down to the river and the leaves of the cotton-wool trees by the river, a fine, soft, vast pattering.

The captain's eyes, trying to watch everything at

once, his men, the villagers, the pile of tools, met Lev's eyes and were held.

"We're stuck, senhor," the young man said almost in a whisper. "What now?"

"Tell them to get to work."

"All right!" Lev said, and turning, "Rolf, Adi, will you start making a stretcher? You and two of the City men will carry Pamplona back to Shantih. Thomas and Sun will go with them. The rest of us back to the job, right?" He and the rest of them went to the pile of hoes and mattocks, picked up their tools, and unhurriedly strung out across the slope again, chopping at the mats of bramble, digging at the roots of shrubs.

Captain Eden, with a cold feeling in the pit of his stomach, turned to his men. The two to whom he had been giving orders stood nearest. "You'll escort the sick ones to their village, before going to the City. And be back with the two able-bodied ones by nightfall. Understand?" He saw Angel, musket in hand, looking at him. "You'll go with them, lieutenant," he said crisply. The two guards, looking blank, saluted; Angel's gaze was openly insolent, jeering.

That evening, by the cooking fire, Lev and three other villagers came to the captain again. "Senhor," said one of the older men, "we've decided, see, that we'll work here for a week, as community labor, if you City men work along with us. It won't do, see, twenty or thirty of you just standing around doing nothing while we work."

"Get these men back where they belong, Martin!" the captain said to a guard on watch duty. The guard lounged forward, hand on whip butt; the villagers looked at one another, shrugged, and returned to their campfire. The important thing, Captain Eden said to himself, was not to talk, not to let them talk. Night came on, black and pouring. It never rained like this in the City; there were roofs there. The noise of the rain was terrible in the darkness, all around, on miles, miles, miles of black wilderness. The fires sputtered, drowned. The guards huddled wretchedly under trees, dropped their musket muzzles in squelching mud, crouched and cursed and shivered. When dawn came, there were no villagers; they had melted off in the night, in the rain. Fourteen guards were also missing.

White-faced, hoarse, defeated, defiant, Captain Eden got his bone-soaked remnant of a troop together and set off back to the City. He would lose his captaincy, perhaps be whipped or mutilated in punishment for his failure, but at the moment he did not care. He did not care for anything they did to him unless it was exile. Surely they would see that it wasn't his fault, nobody could have done this job. Exile was rare, only for the worst crimes, treason, assassination of a Boss; for that men had been driven out of the City, taken by boat far up the coast, marooned there alone in the wilderness, utterly alone, to be tortured and shot if they ever returned to the City, but none ever had; they had died alone, lost, in the terrible uncaring emptiness, the silence. Captain Eden breathed hard as he walked, his eyes searching ahead for the first sight of the roofs of the City.

In the darkness and the heavy rain the villagers had had to keep to the South Road; they would have got lost at once if they had tried to scatter out over the hills. It was difficult enough to keep to the road, which was no more than a track worn by the feet of fishermen and rutted in places by the wheels of lumber carts. They had to go very slowly, groping their way, until the rain thinned and then the light began to grow. Most of them had crept off in the hours after midnight, and by first light they were still little more than halfway home. Despite their fear of pursuit, most stayed on the road, in order to go faster. Lev had gone with the last group to go, and now deliberately held back behind the others. If he saw the guards coming he could shout warning, and the others could scatter off the road into the underbrush. There was no real need for him to do this, all of them were keeping a sharp lookout behind them; but it was an excuse for him to be alone. He didn't want to be with the others, or to talk. He wanted to be by himself, as the wet silver sunrise lifted over the eastern hills; he wanted to walk alone with victory.

They had won. It had worked. They had won their battle without violence. No deaths; one injury. The "slaves" freed without making a threat or striking a blow; the Bosses running back to their Bosses to report failure, and perhaps to wonder why they had failed, and to begin to understand, to see the truth. . . . They were decent enough men, the captain and the others; when they finally got a glimpse of freedom, they would come to it. The City would join the Town, in the end. When their guards deserted them, the Bosses would give up their miserable playing at government, their pretense of power over other men. They too would come, more slowly than the working people, but even they would come to understand that to be free they must put their weapons and defenses down and come outside, equal among equals, brothers. And then indeed the sun would rise over the community of Mankind on Victoria, as now, beneath the heavy masses of the clouds over the hills the silver light broke clear, and every shadow leaped black across the narrow road, and every puddle of last night's rain flashed like a child's laugh.

And it was I, Lev thought with incredulous delight, it was I who spoke for them, I whom they turned to, and I didn't let them down. We held fast! Oh, my God, when he fired that gun in the air, and I thought I was dead, and then I thought I was deaf! But yesterday, with the captain, I never thought "What if he fired?" because I knew he never could have raised the gun, he knew it, the gun wasn't any use. . . . If there's something you must do, you can do it. You can hold fast. I came through, we all came through. Oh, my God, how I love them, love all of them. I didn't know, I didn't know there was such happiness in the world!

He strode on through the bright air toward home, and the fallen rain broke in its quick, cold laughter round his feet.

7

"We need more hostages—especially their leaders, their chiefs. We must anger them into defiance, but not frighten them so much that they're afraid to act. Do you understand? Their defense is passivity and talk, talk, talk. We want them to strike back, while we have their leaders, so their defiance will be disorganized and easily broken. Then they'll be demoralized, easy to work with. You must try to take the boy, what's his name, Shults; the man Elia; anyone else who acts as spokesman. You must provoke them, but stop short of terrifying them. Can you count on your men to stop when you say stop?"

Luz could hear no reply from Herman Macmilan but a careless, grudging mumble. Clearly he did not like being told that he "must" do this and that, nor being asked if he understood.

"Be sure you get Lev Shults. His grandfather was one of their great leaders. We can threaten execution. And carry it out if need be. But it would be better not to. If we frighten them too much they'll fall back on these ideas of theirs, and cling to them because they have nothing else. What we want to do, and it will take restraint on our part, is to force them to betray their ideas—to lose faith in their leaders and their arguments and their talk about peace."

Luz stood outside her father's study, just beneath the window, which was wide open to the windless, rainy air. Herman Macmilan had come stomping into the house a few minutes ago with some news; she had heard his voice, loud in anger and accusation— "We should have used my men in the first place! I told you so!" She was curious to know what had happened, and curious to hear anybody speak in such a tone to her father. But Herman's tirade did not last long. By the time she got outside and under the window where she could eavesdrop, Falco was in full control and Herman was grumbling, "Yes, yes." So much for Bigmouth Macmilan. He had learned who gave the orders in Casa Falco, and in the City. But the orders. . . .

She touched her cheeks, wet with fine rain, and then shook her hands quickly as if she had touched something slimy. Her silver bracelets clinked, and she froze like a coney, pressed up close to the house wall beneath the window so that if Herman or her father looked out they would not see her. Once while Falco was speaking he came and leaned his hands on the sill; his voice was directly above her, and she imagined she could feel the warmth of his body in the air. She felt a tremendous impulse to jump up and shout "Boo!" and at the same time was wildly planning excuses, explanations—"I was looking for a thimble I dropped—" She wanted to laugh aloud, and was listening, listening, with a sense of bewilderment that made tears rise in her throat. Was that her father, her father saying such hideous things? Vera had said that he had a great soul. Would a great soul talk so about tricking people, frightening them, killing them, using them?

That's what he's doing with Herman Macmilan, Luz thought. Using him.

Why not, why not? What else was Herman Macmilan good for?

And what was she good for? To be used, and he had used her—for his vanity, for his comfort, as his pet, all her life; and these days, he used her to keep

Herman Macmilan docile. Last night he had ordered her to entertain Herman with courtesy, whenever he wanted to speak with her. Herman had no doubt complained about her running away from him. Great, whining, complaining bully. Bullies, both of them, all of them, with their big chests and their big boasts and their orders and their cheating plans.

Luz was no longer listening to what the two men were saying. She stepped away from the house wall, standing straight, as if indifferent to any eye that saw her. She walked on around the house to the back entrance, went in through the peaceful, dirty kitchens of siesta time, and to the room that had been given to Vera Adelson.

Vera had been taking siesta too, and received her sleepily.

"I've been eavesdropping on my father and Herman Macmilan," Luz said, standing in the middle of the room, while Vera, sitting on the bed, blinked at her. "They're planning a raid on the Town. They're going to take Lev and all the other leaders prisoner, and then try to make your people get angry and fight, so they can beat them up and send a lot of them to work on the new farms as punishment. They already sent some of them down there, but they all ran away, or the guards ran away—I didn't hear that part clearly. So now Macmilan is going with his 'little army' and my father tells him to force the people to fight back, then they'll betray their ideas and then he can use them as he likes."

Vera sat staring. She said nothing.

"You know what he means. If you don't, Herman does. He means let Herman's men go for the women." Luz' voice was cold, though she spoke very quickly. "You should go warn them."

Vera still said nothing. She gazed at her own bare feet with a remote stare, either dazed or thinking as fast as Luz had been talking.

"Do you still refuse to go? Does your promise still hold you? After that?"

"Yes," the older woman said, faintly, as if absentmindedly, then more strongly, "yes."

"Then I'm going to go."

"Go where?"

She knew; she asked merely to gain time.

"To warn them," Luz said.

"When is this attack to be?"

"Tomorrow night, I think. In the night, but I wasn't sure which night they meant."

There was a pause.

"Maybe it's tonight. They said, 'It's better if they're in bed.'" It was her father who had said that, it was Herman Macmilan who had laughed.

"And if you go . . . then what will you do?"

Vera still spoke as if sleepy, in a low voice, pausing often.

"I'll tell them, and then come back."

"Here?"

"No one will know. I'll leave word I'm visiting with Eva. That doesn't matter. —If I tell the Town people what I heard, what will they do?"

"I don't know."

"But it would help if they knew, and could plan ahead? You told me how you have to plan what you're going to do, get everybody ready—"

"Yes. It would help. But—"

"Then I'll go. Now."

"Luz. Listen. Think what you're doing. Can you go in broad daylight, and nobody notice you leaving the City? Can you come back? Think—"

"I don't care if I can't come back. This house is full of lies," the girl said in the same cold, quick voice; and she went.

Going was easy. Keeping on going was hard.

To take up an old black shawl as she went out, and wrap herself in it as a raincoat and a disguise; to slip out the back door and up the back street, trotting along like a servant in a hurry to be home; to leave Casa Falco, to leave the City, that was easy. That was exciting. She was not afraid of being stopped; she was not afraid of anybody. If they stopped her all she need say was, "I am the daughter of Councillor Falco!" and they wouldn't dare say a word. No one stopped her. She was quite sure that no one recognized her, for she went by back alleys, the shortest way out of the City, up past the school; the black shawl was over her head, and the rainy sea wind that seemed to blow her on her way blew in the eyes of anyone coming against her. Within a few minutes she was out of the streets, cutting across the back of the Macmilans' lumberyards, among the stacks of logs and planks; then up the bluffs, and she was on the road to Shanty Town.

That was when it began to be hard, when she set her feet on that road. She had only been on it once in her life, when she had gone with a group of her friends, suitably escorted by aunts, duennas, and guards from Casa Marquez, to see the dancing at the Meeting House. It had been summer, they had chattered and laughed all the way, Eva's Aunt Caterina's pedicab had lost a wheel and plumped her down in the dust and all afternoon Aunt Caterina had watched the dancing with a great circle of white dust on the rear of her black dress, so that they couldn't stop giggling. . . . But they had not even gone through the Town. What was it like there? Whom should she ask for, in Shanty Town, and what should she say to them? She should have talked it over with Vera first, instead of rushing out in such a hurry. What would they say to her? Would they even let her in, coming from the City? Would they stare at her, jeer at her, try to hurt her? They were not supposed to hurt anybody. Probably they simply would not talk to her. The wind at her back felt cold now. Rain had soaked through shawl and dress down her back, and the hem of her skirt was heavy with mud and moisture. The fields were empty, gray with autumn. When she looked back there was nothing to be seen but the Monument Tower, pallid and derelict, pointing meaninglessly at the sky; everything she knew now lay hidden behind that marking point. To the left sometimes she glimpsed the river, wide and gray, rain blowing across it in vague gusts.

She would give her message to the first person she

met, let them do what they liked about it; she would turn straight round and come back home. She would be back within an hour at most, long before supper-time.

She saw a small farmhouse off to the left of the road among orchard trees, and a woman out in the yard. Luz checked her rapid walk. She would turn aside to the farm, give the woman her message, then the woman could go on and tell the people in Shanty Town, and she could turn back right here and go home. She hesitated, started toward the farm, then turned and strode back through the rain-soaked grasses onto the road again. "I'll just go on and get it done and come back," she whispered to herself. "Go on, get it done, come back." She walked faster than ever, almost running. Her cheeks were burning; she was out of breath. She had not walked far or fast for months, years. She must not come in among strangers all red and gasping. She forced herself to slow her pace, to walk steadily, erect. Her mouth and throat were dry. She would have liked to stop and drink the rain off the leaves of roadside bushes, curling her tongue to get at the cool drops that beaded every blade of wild grass. But that would be like a child. It was a longer road than she had thought. Was she on the Shanty Town road at all? Had she mistaken the way and got on some loggers' road, some track with no end, leading out into the wilderness?

At the word—the wilderness—a cold jolt of terror went right through her body, stopping her in mid-step.

She looked back to see the City, the dear narrow

warm crowded beautiful City of walls and roofs and
streets and faces and voices, her house, her home, her
life, but there was nothing, even the Tower had
dropped behind the long rise of the road and was
gone. The fields and hills were empty. The vast, soft
wind blew from the empty sea.

There's nothing to be afraid of, Luz told herself.
Why are you such a coward? You can't get lost, you're
on a road, if it's not the Town Road all you have to
do is turn back and you'll get home. You won't be
climbing so you won't come on a rock scorpion, you
won't be in the woods so you won't get into poison
rose, what are you so afraid of, there's nothing to hurt
you, you're perfectly safe, on the road.

But she walked in terror, her eyes on every stone
and shrub and clump of trees, until over the crest of
a stony rise she saw red-thatched roofs, and smelled
hearth smoke. She came walking into Shanty Town.
Her face was set, her back straight; she held the shawl
wrapped tight around her.

The small houses stood straggled about among
trees and vegetable gardens. There were a lot of
houses, but the place wasn't gathered in, walled,
protective, like the City. It was all straggling, damp,
humble-looking in the quiet, rainy afternoon. There
were no people nearby. Luz came slowly down the
wandering street, trying to decide—should I call to that
man over there? should I knock at this door?

A small child appeared from nowhere in particular
and stared at her. He was fair-skinned, but coated
with brown mud from toes to knees and fingertips to
elbows, with more mud in splotches here and there,

so that he seemed to be a variegated or piebald child. What clothes he wore were also ringstraked and spotted with an interesting variety of tones of mud. "Hello," he said after a long pause, "who are you?"

"Luz Marina. Who are you?"

"Marius," he said, and began to sidle away.

"Do you know where—where Lev Shults lives?" She did not want to ask for Lev, she would rather face a stranger; but she could not remember any other name. Vera had told her about many of them, she had heard her father mention the "ringleaders'" names, but she could not remember them now.

"Lev what?" said Marius, scratching his ear and thus adding a rich deposit to the mudbank there. Shanty-Towners, she knew, never seemed to use last names among themselves, only in the City.

"He's young, and he . . ." She didn't know what Lev was, a leader? a captain? a boss?

"Sasha's house is down there," said the variegated child, pointing down a muddy, overgrown lane, and sidled away so effectively that he seemed simply to become part of the general mist and mud.

Luz set her teeth and walked to the house he had pointed out. There was nothing to be afraid of. It was just a dirty little place. The children were dirty and the people were peasants. She would give her message to whoever opened the door, then it would be done and she could go home to the high, clean rooms of Casa Falco.

She knocked. Lev opened the door.

She knew him, though she had not seen him for two years. He was half-dressed and disheveled, having been roused from siesta, staring at her with the luminous, childish stupidity of the half-awake. "Oh," he said, yawning, "where's Andre?"

"I am Luz Marina Falco. From the City."

The luminous stare changed, deepened, he woke up.

"Luz Marina Falco," he said. His dark, thin face flashed into life; he looked at her, past her for her companions, at her again, his eyes charged with feelings—alert, wary, amused, incredulous. "Are you here—with—"

"I came alone. I have a—I have to tell you—"

"Vera," he said. No smile on that flashing face now, but tension, passion.

"Vera is all right. So are the others. It's about you, about the Town. Something happened last night, I don't know what—you know about it—"

He nodded, watching her.

"They're angry, and they're going to come here, I think it's tomorrow night, the men young Macmilan has been training, the bullies, and try and take you and the other leaders prisoner, and then—outrage the others so that they'll fight back, and then they can beat them and make them work on the latifundia for punishment for rebelling. They're coming after dark, tomorrow I think but I'm not sure of that, and he has about forty of them, I think, but all with muskets."

Lev still watched her. He said nothing. Only then, in his silence, did she hear the question she had not asked herself.

And the question took her so off guard, she was so far from the merest beginning of an answer to it, that she stood there and stared back at him, her face growing dull red with bewilderment and fear, and could not say another word.

"Who sent you, Luz?" he asked at last, gently.

It was natural that this should be his answer to the question, that he should think she was lying, or was being used for some kind of trick or spying by Falco. It was natural that he should think that, that he should imagine she was serving her father, and not imagine that she was betraying her father. All she could do was shake her head. Her legs and arms tingled, and there were flashes of light in her eyes; she felt that she was going to be sick. "I have to go back now," she said, but did not move, because her knees would not work.

"Are you all right? Come in, sit down. For a minute."

"I'm dizzy," she said. Her voice sounded thin and whiny, she was ashamed of it. He brought her inside and she sat down in a wicker chair by a table in a dark, long, low-beamed room. She pulled the shawl off her head to get rid of the heat and weight of it; that helped; her cheeks began to cool, and the lights stopped flashing in her eyes as she got used to the dusk of the room. Lev stood near her, at the end of the table. He was barefoot, wearing only trousers; he stood quietly; she could not look at his face, but she sensed in his stance and his quietness no threat, no anger, no contempt.

"I hurried," she said. "I wanted to get back quickly, it's a long way, it made me dizzy." Then she got hold of herself, finding that there was, under the fluster and the fear, a place inside her, a silent corner where her mind could crouch down and think. She thought, and finally spoke again.

"Vera has been living with us. In Casa Falco. You knew that? She and I have been together every day. We talk. I tell her what I hear that's going on, she tells me . . . all kinds of things. . . . I tried to make her come back here. To warn you. She won't, she says she promised not to run away, so she has to keep the promise. So I came. I heard them talking, Herman Macmilan and my father. I listened, I went and stood under the window to listen. What they said made me angry. It made me sick. So when Vera wouldn't come, I came. Do you know about these new guards, Macmilan's guards?"

Lev shook his head, watching, intent.

"I'm not lying," she said coldly. "Nobody is using me. Nobody but Vera even knows I left the house. I came because I'm sick of being used and sick of lies and sick of doing nothing. You can believe me or not. I don't care."

Lev shook his head again, blinking, as if dazzled. "No, I don't— But slow down a little—"

"There isn't time. I have to go back before anybody notices. All right, my father got young Macmilan to train up a troop of other men, Bosses' sons, as a special army, to use against you people. They haven't talked about anything else for two weeks. They're coming here because of whatever it was that happened down in South Valley, and they're supposed to catch you and the other leaders, and then force your people into fighting so you'll betray your idea of peace, of what do you call it, nonviolence. And then you'll fight and you'll lose, because we're better fighters, and anyway we have guns. Do you know Herman Macmilan?"

"By sight, I think," Lev said. He was so utterly different from the man whose name she had just said and whose image filled her mind—the splendid face and muscular body, broad chest, long legs, strong hands, heavy clothing, tunic, trousers, boots, belt, coat, gun, whip, knife. . . . This man was barefoot; she could see the ribs and breastbone under the dark, fine skin of his chest.

"I hate Herman Macmilan," Luz said, less hurriedly, speaking from the small cool place inside her where she could think. "His soul is about the size of a toenail. You should be afraid of him. I am. He likes to hurt people. Don't try to talk to him, the way you people do. He won't listen. He fills up his whole world. All you can do with that kind of man is hit him, or run away from him. I ran away from him.—Do you believe me?" She could ask that, now.

Lev nodded.

She looked at his hands on the chair back; he was gripping the wooden bar tightly; his hands were nerve and bone under the dark skin, strong, fragile.

"All right. I have to go back," she said, and stood up.

"Wait. You should tell this to the others."

"I can't. You tell them."

"But you said you ran away from Macmilan. Now you're going back to him?"

"No! To my father—to my house—"

But he was right. It was the same thing.

"I came to warn you," she said coldly, "because Macmilan was going to trick you, and deserves to be tricked himself. That's all."

But it wasn't enough.

She looked out the open door and saw the lane she would have to walk on, beyond it the street, then the road, then the City and its streets and her house and her father—

"I don't understand," she said. She sat down again, abruptly, because she was shaky again, though not with fear, now, but with anger. "I didn't think. Vera said—"

"What did she say?"

"She said to stop and think."

"Has she—"

"Wait. I have to think. I didn't then, I have to now."

She sat still in the chair for some minutes, her hands clenched in her lap.

"All right," she said. "This is a war, Vera said. I should be— I have betrayed my father's side. Vera is a hostage to the City. I'll have to be a hostage to the Town. If she can't come and go, neither can I. I have to go through with it." Her breath stuck in her throat, making a catching sound at the end of the sentences.

"We don't take hostages, make prisoners, Luz—"

"I didn't say you did. I said I have to stay here. I *choose* to stay here. Will you let me?"

Lev strode off down the room, ducking automatically as he came under the low crossbeam. His shirt had been drying on a chair before the fire; he

put it on, went into the back room, came out with
his shoes in his hand, sat down at a chair by the table
to put them on. "Look," he said, stooping down to
get his shoe on, "you can stay here. Anybody can. We
don't make anybody go, we don't make anybody stay."
He straightened up, looking directly at her. "But
what is your father going to think? Even if he believed you were staying here by choice—"

"He wouldn't allow it. He'd come to get me."

"By force."

"Yes, by force. With Macmilan and his little army,
no doubt."

"Then you become the pretext for violence they
seek. You must go home, Luz."

"For your sake," she said.

She was simply thinking it out, seeing what she had
done and what consequences must follow. But Lev
sat motionless, a shoe—a muddy, battered, low boot,
she noticed—in his hand.

"Yes," he said. "For our sake. You came here for
our sake. Now you go back for our sake. And if they
find out you've been here—?" There was a pause.
"No," he said. "You can't go back. You'd be caught
in the lie—yours and theirs. You came *here*. Because
of Vera, because of us. You're with us."

"No, I'm not," Luz said, angrily; but the light and
warmth in Lev's face bewildered her mind. He spoke
so plainly, with such certainty; he was smiling now.
"Luz," he said, "remember, when we were in school?
You were always—I always wanted to talk to you, I
never got up the courage— We did talk once, at
sunset, you asked why I wouldn't fight Angel and his

crowd. You never were like the other City girls, you didn't fit, you didn't belong. You belong here. The truth matters to you. Do you remember when you got mad at the teacher once, when he said coneys don't hibernate and Timmo tried to tell how he'd found a whole cave of them hibernating and the teacher was going to whip him for being insolent, do you remember?"

"I said I'd tell my father," Luz said in a low voice. She had turned very white.

"You stood up in the class, you said the teacher didn't know the truth and was going to whip Timmo for telling it—you were only about fourteen. Luz, listen, come with me now, we'll go to Elia's house. You can tell them what you told me and we can settle what to do. You can't go back now and be punished, be ashamed! Listen, you can stay with Southwind, she lives outside of town, you can be quiet there. But come with me now, we can't lose time." He reached out his hand to her across the table, that fine, warm hand full of life; she took it, and met his eyes; her eyes filled up with tears. "I don't know what to do," she said, in tears. "You only have one shoe on, Lev."

Short as the time was, the entire community must be rallied, brought together, to stand firm together, to hold fast. Indeed haste was in their favor, for, under no pressure, the timorous and halfhearted might fall away; under threat of imminent attack, all were eager to find and keep the center, the strength of the group.

A center there was, and he was in it—was the center, himself, with Andre, Southwind, Martin, Italia, Santha, and all the others, the young, the determined. Vera was not there, and yet was there, in all their decisions, her gentleness and unshakable firmness. Elia was not there; he and Jewel and several others, mostly older people, stood aside, must stand aside, because their will was not the will of the community. Elia had never been strong for the plan of emigration, and now he argued that they had gone too far, the girl must be sent back to her father at once, with a delegation who would "sit down with the Council and talk—if we'll only sit down and talk to each other, there's no need for all this distrust and defiance. . . ."

"Armed men don't sit down and talk, Elia," said old Lyons, wearily.

It was not to Elia that they turned, but to "Vera's people," the young ones. Lev felt the strength of his friends and the whole community, supporting and upholding. It was as if he were not Lev alone, but Lev times a thousand—himself, but himself immensely increased, enlarged, a boundless self mingled with all the other selves, set free, as no man alone could ever be free.

There was scarcely need to take counsel, to explain to people what must be done, the massive, patient resistance which they must set against the City's violence. They knew already, they thought for him and he for them; his word spoke their will.

The girl Luz, the stranger, self-exiled: her presence in Shantih sharpened this sense of perfect community by contrast, and edged it with compassion. They knew why she had come, and they tried to be kind to her. She was alone among them, scared and suspicious, drawing herself up in her pride and her Boss's-daughter arrogance whenever she did not understand. But she did understand, Lev thought, however much her reason might confuse her; she understood with the heart, for she had come to them, trusting.

When he told her that, told her that she was and always had been, in spirit, one of them, one of the People of the Peace, she put on her disdainful look. "I don't even know what these ideas of yours are," she said. But she had, in fact, learned a great deal from Vera; and during these strange, tense, inactive days of waiting for word or attack from the City, while ordinary work was suspended and "Vera's people" were much together, Lev talked with her as often as he could, longing to bring her fully among them, into the center where so much peace and strength was and where one was not alone.

"It's very dull, really," he explained, "a kind of list of rules, just like school. First you do this, next you do that. First you try negotiation and arbitration of the problem, whatever it is, by existing means and institutions. You try to talk it out, the way Elia keeps saying. That step was Vera's group going to talk with the Council, you see. It didn't work. So you go on to step two: noncooperation. A kind of settling down and holding still, so they know you mean what you said. That's where we are now. Then step three, which we're now preparing: issue of an ultimatum. A final appeal, offering a constructive solution, and a clear explanation of what will be done if that solution isn't agreed upon now."

"And what will be done, if they don't happen to agree?"

"Move on to step four. Civil disobedience."

"What's that?"

"A refusal to obey any orders or laws, no matter what, issued by the authority being challenged. We set up our own, parallel, independent authority, and follow our own course."

"Just like that?"

"Just like that," he said smiling. "It worked, you know, over and over again, on Earth. Against all kinds of threats and imprisonments, tortures, attacks. You can read about it, you should read Mirovskaya's *History*—"

"I can't read books," the girl said with her disdainful air. "I tried one once. —If it worked so well, why did you get sent away from Earth?"

"There weren't enough of us. The governments were too big and too powerful. But they wouldn't have sent us off into exile, would they, if they hadn't been afraid of us?"

"That's what my father says about *his* ancestors," Luz remarked. Her eyebrows were drawn down level above her eyes, dark pondering eyes. Lev watched her, stilled for a moment by her stillness, caught by her strangeness. For despite his insistence that she was one of them, she was not; she was not like Southwind, not like Vera, not like any woman he knew. She was different, alien to him. Like the gray heron of the Meeting Pool, there was a silence in her, a silence that drew him, drew him aside, toward a different center.

He was so caught, so held in watching her, that though Southwind said something he did not hear it, and when Luz herself spoke again he was startled, and for a moment the familiar room of Southwind's house seemed strange, an alien place.

"I wish we could forget about all that," she said. "Earth—it's a hundred years ago, a different world, a different sun, what does it matter to us here? We're here, now. Why can't we do things our way? I'm not from Earth. You're not from Earth. This is our world. . . . It ought to have its own name. 'Victoria,' that's stupid, it's an Earth word. We ought to give it its own name."

"What name?"

"One that doesn't mean anything. Ooboo, or Baba. Or call it Mud. It's all mud—if Earth's called 'earth' why can't this one be called 'mud'?" She sounded angry, as she often did, but when Lev laughed she laughed too. Southwind only smiled, but said in her soft voice, "Yes, that's right. And then we could make a world of our own, instead of always imitating what they did on Earth. If there wasn't any violence there wouldn't have to be any nonviolence. . . ."

"Start with mud and build a world," said Lev. "But don't you see, that's what we're doing?"

"Making mudpies," said Luz.

"Building a new world."

"Out of bits of the old one."

"If people forget what happened in the past, they have to do it all over again, they never get on into the future. That's why they kept fighting wars, on Earth. They forgot what the last one was like. We *are* starting fresh. Because we remember the old mistakes, and won't make them."

"Sometimes it seems to me," said Andre, who was sitting on the hearth mending a sandal for South-wind—his side-trade was cobbling—"if you don't mind my saying so, Luz, that in the City they remember all the old mistakes so they can make them all over again."

"I don't know," she said with indifference. She stood up, and went to the window. It was closed, for the rain had not stopped and the weather was colder, with a wind from the east. The small fire in the hearth kept the room warm and bright. Luz stood with her back to that snugness, looking out through the tiny, cloudy panes of the window at the dark fields and the windy clouds.

On the morning after she came to Shantih, after talking with Lev and the others, she had written a letter to her father. A short letter, though it had taken her all morning to write it. She had shown it first to Southwind, then to Lev. When he looked at her now, the straight strong figure outlined black against the

light, he saw again the writing of her letter, straight
black stiff strokes. She had written:

Honored Sir!
I have left our House. I will stay in Shanty
Town because I do not approve of Your plans. I
decided to leave and I decided to stay. No body
is holding me prisoner or hostage. These people
are my Hosts. If you mis treat them I am not on
Your side. I had to make this choice. You have
made a mistake about H. Macmilan. Senhora
Adelson had nothing to do with my coming here.
It was my Choice.
Your respectful Daughter
Luz Marina Falco Cooper

No word of affection; no plea for forgiveness.

And no answer. The letter had been taken by a
runner at once, young Welcome; he had shoved it
under the door of Casa Falco and trotted right on.
As soon as he got safe back to Shantih, Luz had
begun to wait for her father's response, to dread it
but also, visibly, to expect it. That was two full days
ago. No answer had come; no attack or assault at
night; nothing. They all discussed what change in
Falco's plans Luz's defection might have caused, but
they did not discuss it in front of her, unless she
brought it up.

She said now, "I don't understand your ideas, really.
All the steps, all the rules, all the talk."

"They are our weapons," Lev replied.

"But why fight?"

"There's no other choice."

"Yes, there is. To go."

"Go?"

"Yes! Go north, to the valley you found. Just go. Leave. It's what I did," she added, looking imperiously at him when he did not answer at once. "I left."

"And they'll come after you," he said gently.

She shrugged. "They haven't. They don't care."

Southwind made a little noise of warning, protest, sympathy; it really said all that needed saying, but Lev translated it—"But they do, and they will, Luz. Your father—"

"If he comes after me, I'll run farther. I'll go on."

"Where?"

She turned away again and said nothing. They all thought of the same thing: of the wilderness. It was as if the wilderness came into the cabin, as if the walls fell down, leaving no shelter. Lev had been there, Andre had been there, months of the endless, voiceless solitude; it was in their souls now and they could never wholly leave it. Southwind had not been in the wilderness, but her love lay buried in it. Even Luz who had never seen or known it, the child of those who for a hundred years had built up their walls against it and denied it, knew it and feared it, knew it was foolishness to talk of leaving the Colony, alone. Lev watched her in silence. He pitied her, sharp pity, as for a hurt, stubborn child who refuses comfort, holds aloof, will not weep. But she was not a child. It was a woman he saw standing there, a woman standing alone in a place without help or shelter, a woman in the wilderness; and pity was lost in admiration and in fear. He was afraid of her. There was a strength in her that was not drawn from love or trust or community, did not rise from any source that should give strength, any source he recognized. He feared that strength, and craved it. These three days he had been with her, he had thought of her constantly, had seen everything in terms of her: as if all their struggle made sense only if she could be made to understand it, as if her choice outweighed their plans and the ideals they lived by. —She was pitiable, admirable, precious as any human soul was precious, but she must not take over his mind. She must be one of them, acting with him, supporting him, not filling and confusing his thoughts like this. Later, there would be time to think about her and understand her, when the confrontation was over, when they had won through to peace. Later, there would be all the time in the world.

"We can't go north now," he said patiently, a little coldly. "If a group left now, it would weaken the unity of those who must stay behind. And the City would track settlers down. We have to establish our freedom to go—here, now. Then we will go."

"Why did you give them the maps, show them the way!" Luz said, impatiently and hotly. "That was stupid. You could have just *gone*."

"We are a community," Lev said, "the City and the Town." And left it at that.

Andre rather spoiled his point by adding, "Anyhow, we couldn't just sneak off. A big lot of people migrating leave a very easy trail to follow."

"So if they did follow you all the way north there to your mountains—you're there already, and you say, Too bad, this is ours, go find yourselves another valley, there's plenty of room!"

"And they would use force. The principle of equality and free choice must be established first. Here."

"But they use force here! Vera's already a prisoner, and the others in the Jail, and the old man lost his eye, and the bullies are coming to beat you up or shoot you—all to establish a 'principle,' when you could have gone, got out, gone free!"

"Freedom's won by sacrifice," Southwind said. Lev looked at her, then quickly at Luz; he was not sure if Luz knew of Timmo's death on the journey to the north. Probably, here alone with Southwind the last three nights, she did. In any case, the quietness of Southwind's voice quieted her. "I know," Luz said. "You have to take risks. But sacrifice. . . . I hate that idea, sacrifice!"

Lev grinned in spite of himself. "And what have you done?"

"Not sacrificed myself for any idea! I just ran away —don't you understand? And that's what you all ought to do!" Luz spoke in challenge, defiance, self-defense, not conviction; but Southwind's response startled Lev. "You may be right," she said. "So long as we stand and fight, even though we fight with our weapons, we fight their war."

Luz Falco was an outsider, a stranger, she did not know how the People of the Peace thought and felt,

but to hear Southwind say something irresponsible
was shocking, an affront to their perfect unity.

"To run away and hide in the forest—that's a
choice?" Lev said. "For coneys, yes. Not for human
beings. Standing upright and having two hands
doesn't make us human. Standing up and having ideas
and ideals does! And holding fast to those ideals. Together. We can't live alone. Or we die alone—like
animals."

Southwind nodded sadly, but Luz frowned straight
back at him. "Death is death, does it matter whether
it's in bed in the house or outside in the forest? We
are animals. That's why we die at all."

"But to live and die for—for the sake of the spirit
—that's different, that's different from running and
hiding, all separate, selfish, scratching for food, cower-
ing, hating, each alone—" Lev stammered, he felt his
face hot. He met Luz's eyes, and stammered again,
and was silent. Praise was in her look, praise such as
he had never earned, never dreamed of earning, praise
and rejoicing, so that he knew himself confirmed, in
that same moment of anger and argument, confirmed
totally, in his words, his life, his being.

This is the true center, he thought. The words went
quick and clear across his mind. He did not think of
them again, but nothing, on the far side of those
words, was the same; nothing would ever be the same.
He had come up into the mountains.

His right hand was half held out toward Luz in a
gesture of urgent pleading. He saw it, she saw it,
that unfinished gesture. Suddenly self-conscious, he

dropped his hand; the gesture was unfinished. She moved abruptly, turning away, and said with anger and despair, "Oh, I don't understand, it's all so strange, I'll never understand, you know everything and I've never even thought about anything. . . ." She looked physically smaller as she spoke, small, furious, surrendering. "I just wish—" She stopped short.

"It will come, Luz," he said. "You don't have to run to it. It comes, it will come—I promise—"

She did not ask what he promised. Nor could he have said.

When he left the house the rainy wind struck him in the face, taking his breath away. He gasped; tears filled his eyes, but not from the wind. He thought of that bright morning, the silver sunrise and his great happiness, only three days ago. Today it was gray, no sky, little light, a lot of rain and mud. Mud, the world's name is Mud, he thought, and wanted to laugh, but his eyes were still full of tears. She had renamed the world. That morning on the road, he thought, that was happiness, but this is—and he had no word for it, only her name, Luz. Everything was contained in that, the silver sunrise, the great burning sunset over the City years ago, all the past, and all that was to come, even their work now, the talking and the planning, the confrontation, and their certain victory, the victory of the light. "I promise, I promise," he whispered into the wind. "All my life, all the years of my life."

He wanted to walk slower, to stop, to hold the moment. But the very wind that blew in his face forced him forward. There was so much to do, so little time now. Later, later! Tonight might be the night Macmilan's gang came; there was no knowing. Evidently, guessing that Luz had betrayed their plan, they had changed it. There was nothing to do, until their own plans were complete, but wait and be ready. Readiness was all. There would be no panic. No matter whether City or Town made the first move, the People of the Peace would know what to do, how to act. He strode on, almost running, into Shantih. The taste of the rain was sweet on his lips.

He was at home, late in the dark afternoon, when the message came. His father brought it from the Meeting House. "A scar-faced fellow, a guard," Sasha said in his soft ironic voice. "Came strolling up, asked for Shults. I think he meant you, not me."

It was a note on the thick, coarse paper they made in the City. For a moment Lev thought Luz had written the stiff black words—

> Shults: I will be at the smelting ring at
> sundown today. Bring as many as you like.
> I will be alone.
>   Luis Burnier Falco

A trick, an obvious trick. Too obvious? There was just time to get back to Southwind's house and show Luz the note.

"If he says he'll be there alone, he'll be alone," she said.

"You heard him planning to trick us, with Macmilan," Andre said.

She glanced past Andre with contempt. "This is his name," she said. "He wouldn't put his name to a lie. He'll be there alone."

"Why?"

She shrugged.

"I'm going," Lev said. "Yes! With you, Andre! And as many as you think necessary. But you'll have to round them up pretty quick. There's only an hour or so of daylight left."

"You know they want you as a hostage," Andre said. "Are you going to walk right into their hands?"

Lev nodded energetically. "Like a wotsit," he said, and laughed. "In—and out! Come on, let's get a bunch together, Andre. Luz—do you want to come?"

She stood indecisive.

"No," she said; she winced. "I can't. I'm afraid."

"You're wise."

"I should go. To tell him myself that you're not keeping me here, that I chose. He doesn't believe it."

"What you choose, and whether he believes it, doesn't really matter," Andre said. "You're still a pretext: their property. Better not come, Luz. If you're there they'll probably use force to get you back."

She nodded, but still hesitated. Finally she said, "I should come." She said it with such desperate resolution that Lev broke in, "No—" but she went on: "I have to. I won't stand aside and be talked about, fought over, handed back and forth."

"You will not be handed back," Lev said. "You belong to yourself. Come with us if you choose."

She nodded.

The smelting ring was an ancient ringtree site, south

of the Road halfway between Town and City, and centuries older than either; the trees had long ago fallen and decayed, leaving only the round central pond. The City's first iron-smelting works had been set up there; it too had decayed, when richer ore was found in the South Hills forty years ago. The chimneys and machinery were gone, the old sheds, rotten-planked and crazy, overgrown with bindweed and poison rose, crouched abandoned by the flat shore of the pond.

Andre and Lev had got together a group of twenty as they came. Andre led them around by the old sheds, to make sure no party of guards was hiding in or behind them. They were empty, and there was no other place for a gang to conceal themselves within several hundred meters; it was a flat place, treeless, desolate and miserable-looking in the gloomy end of the daylight. Fine rain fell onto the round gray water that lay unsheltered, defenseless, like a blind, open eye. On the far side of the pond Falco stood waiting for them. They saw him move away from a thicket where he had taken some shelter from the rain, and come walking around the shore to them, alone.

Lev started forward from the others. Andre let him go ahead, but followed a couple of meters behind him, with Sasha, Martin, Luz, and several others. The rest of their group stayed scattered out along the gray pond's edge and on the slope that led up to the Road, on guard.

Falco stopped, facing Lev. They stood right on the shore of the pond, where the walking was easier. Between them lay a tiny muddy inlet of the water, a bay no wider than the length of a man's arm, with shores of fine sand, a harbor for a child's toy boat. In the intense vividness of his perceptions Lev was as aware of that bit of water and sand, and of how a child might play there, as he was of Falco's erect figure, his handsome face that was Luz's face and yet wholly different, his belted coat darkened by rain on the shoulders and sleeves.

Falco certainly saw his daughter in the group behind Lev, but he did not look at her nor speak to her; he spoke to Lev, in a soft dry voice, a little hard to hear over the vast whisper of the rain.

"I'm alone, as you see, and unarmed. I speak for myself alone. Not as Councillor."

Lev nodded. He felt a desire to call this man by his name, not Senhor or Falco, but his own name, Luis; he did not understand the impulse, and did not speak.

"I wish my daughter to come home."

Lev indicated, with a slight open gesture, that she was there behind him. "Speak to her, Senhor Falco," he said.

"I came to speak to you. If you speak for the rebels."

"Rebels? Against what, senhor? I, or any of us, will speak for Shantih, if you like. But Luz Marina can speak for herself."

"I did not come to argue," Falco said. His manner was perfectly controlled and polite, his face rigid. The quietness, the stiffness were those of a man in pain. "Listen. There is to be an attack on the Town. You know that, now. I could not prevent it, now, if I wanted to, though I have delayed it. But I want my daughter out of it. Safe. If you'll send her home with me, I'll send Senhora Adelson and the other hostages, under guard, to you tonight. I'll come with them, if you like; let her go back with me then. This is between us alone. The rest of it, the fighting—you started it by your disobedience, I cannot stop it, neither can you, now. This is all we can do. Trade our hostages, and so save them."

"Senhor, I respect your candor—but I didn't take Luz Marina from you, and I can't give her back."

As he spoke, Luz came up beside him, wrapped in her black shawl. "Father," she said in a clear, hard voice, not softly as he and Falco had spoken, "you can stop Macmilan's bullies if you want to."

Falco's face did not change; could not change, perhaps, without going to pieces. There was a long silence, full of the sound of rain. The light was heavy, bright only low and far away in the west.

"I can't, Luz," he said in that painful quiet voice. "Herman is—he is determined to take you back."

"And if I came back with you, so that he had no pretext, would you order him not to attack Shantih?"

Falco stood still. He swallowed, hard, as if his throat were very dry. Lev clenched his hands, seeing that, seeing the man stand there in his pride that could endure no humiliation and was humiliated, his strength that must admit to impotence.

"I can't. Things have gone too far." Falco swallowed again, and tried again. "Come home with me, Luz Marina," he said. "I will send the hostages back at once. I give my word." He glanced at Lev, and his white face said for him what he could not say, that he asked Lev's help.

"Send them!" Luz said. "You have no right to keep them prisoner."

"And you'll come—" It was not quite a question.

She shook her head. "You have no right to keep me prisoner."

"Not a prisoner, Luz, you are my daughter—" He stepped forward. She stepped back.

"No!" she said. "I will *not* come when you bargain for me. I will never come back so long as you attack and, and p-persecute people!" She stammered and groped for words. "I'll never marry Herman Macmilan, or look at him, I de—I detest him! I'll come when I'm free to come and do what I choose to do and so long as he comes to Casa Falco I will never come home!"

"Macmilan?" the father said in agony. "You don't have to marry Macmilan—" He stopped, and looked from Luz to Lev, a little wildly. "Come home," he said. His voice shook, but he struggled for control. "I will stop the attack if I can. We—we'll talk, with you," he said to Lev. "We'll talk."

"We'll talk now, later, whenever you want," Lev said. "It's all we ever asked, senhor. But you must not ask your daughter to trade her freedom for Vera's, or for your goodwill, or for our safety. That is wrong. You can't do it; we won't accept it."

Again Falco stood still, but it was a different stillness: defeat, or his final refusal of defeat? His face, white and wet with rain or sweat, was set, inexpressive.

"Then you will not let her go," he said.

"I will not come," Luz answered.

Falco nodded once, turned, and walked slowly away

along the curving shore of the pond. He passed the thickets that stood blurred and shapeless in the late twilight, and set off up the slight slope to the road that led back to the City. His straight, short, dark figure was quickly lost to sight.

9

One of the servant girls tapped at Vera's door, opened it, and said in the half-impertinent, half-timid voice the maids used when "following orders," "Senhora Vera, Don Luis will see you in the big room, please!"

"Oh dear, oh dear," Vera sighed. "Is he still in a bad mood?"

"Terrible," the girl, Teresa, said, at once dropping her "following orders" manner and stooping to scratch a callus on her hard, bare, plump foot. Vera was by now considered a friend, a kind of good luck aunt or elder sister, by all the house girls; even the stern middle-aged cook Silvia had come to Vera's room the day after Luz's disappearance, and had discussed it with her, apparently not caring in the least that she was seeking reassurance from the enemy. "Have you seen Michael's face?" Teresa went on. "Don Luis knocked two of his teeth loose yesterday because Michael was slow taking off his boots, he was grunting and groaning, you know how he does everything, and Don Luis just went whack! with his foot with the boot still on. Now Michael's all swelled up like a pouchbat, he does look funny. Linda says that Don Luis went to

Shanty Town yesterday evening all by himself,
Marquez's Thomas saw him, he was going right up
the road. What do you think happened? Was he
trying to steal poor Senhorita Luz back, do you think?"

"Oh dear," Vera sighed again. "Well, I'd better not
keep him waiting." She smoothed her hair, straightened her clothes, and said to Teresa, "What pretty
earrings you have on. Come on!" And she followed
the girl to the hall of Casa Falco.

Luis Falco was sitting in the deep window seat,
gazing out over Songe Bay. A restless morning light
lay on the sea; the clouds were big, turbulent, their
crests dazzling white as the sun flashed out on them,
dark when the wind flawed and higher clouds veiled
the light. Falco stood up to meet Vera. His face looked
hard and very weary. He did not look at her as he
spoke. "Senhora, if you have any belongings here you
wish to take with you, please get them."

"I have nothing," Vera said slowly. Falco had never
frightened her before; indeed, in her month in his
house, she had come to like him very much, to honor
him. There was a change in him now; not the pain
and rage that had been visible, and understandable,
since Luz's flight; not an emotion, but a change in
the man, an evidence of destruction, as in one deathly
ill or injured. She sought somehow to reach him, and
did not know how. "You gave me clothes, Don Luis,
and all the rest," she said. The clothes she wore now
had been his wife's, she knew that; he had had a chest
of clothing brought to her room, beautiful fine-woven
skirts and blouses and shawls, all folded away care-

fully, leaves of the sweet lavender scattered among them so long ago that all their scent was gone. "Shall I go change to my own things?" she asked.

"No. —Yes, if you wish. As you like. —Come back here as quickly as possible, please."

When she returned in five minutes, in her own suit of white treesilk, he was again sitting motionless in the window seat, gazing out over the great silver cloud-hung bay.

Again he rose when she approached him, again he did not look at her. "Come with me, please, senhora."

"Where are you going?" Vera asked, not moving.

"To the Town." He added, as if he had forgotten to mention it, thinking of something entirely different, "I hope it will be possible for you to rejoin your people there."

"I hope so too. What would make it impossible, Don Luis?"

He did not answer. She felt that he was not evading her question, only that the labor of answering it was beyond him. He stood aside for her to precede him. She looked around the big room that she had come to know so well, and at his face. "I will thank you now for your kindness to me, Don Luis," she said with formality. "I will remember the true hospitality, that made a prisoner a guest."

His tired face did not change; he shook his head, and waited for her.

She passed him, and he followed her through the hall and out onto the street. She had not set foot across that doorway since the day she was brought to the house.

She had hoped that Jan and Hari and the others might be there, but there was no sign of them. A dozen men, whom she recognized as Falco's personal guards and servants, were waiting in a group, and there was another group of middle-aged men, among them Councillor Marquez and Falco's brother-in-law Cooper, with some of their retinue, perhaps thirty in all. Falco looked them all over with a rapid glance, then, still with mechanical deference to Vera, letting her precede him by a step, set off down the steep street, with a gesture to the others to follow him.

As they walked she heard old Marquez talking to Falco, but did not hear what they said. Scarface, Anibal, gave her the faintest shadow of a wink as he stepped smartly by with his brother. The force and brightness of the wind and sunlight, after so long indoors or in the walled garden of the house, bewildered her; she felt unsteady walking, as if she had been sick in bed a long time.

In front of the Capitol a larger group was waiting, about forty men, perhaps fifty, all of them fairly young, all of them wearing the same kind of coat, a heavy blackish-brown material; the cottonwool mills must have worked overtime to make so much cloth all the same, Vera thought. The coats were belted and had big metal buttons, so that they all looked pretty much alike. All the men had both whips and muskets. They looked like one of the murals inside the Capitol. Herman Macmilan stepped forward from among them, tall, broad-shouldered, smiling. "At your service, Don Luis!"

"Good morning, Don Herman. All ready?" Falco said in his stifled voice.

"All ready, senhor. To the Town, men!" And he swung round and led the column of men straight up Seaward Street, not waiting for Falco, who took Vera by the arm and hurried forward with her among the dark-coated men to join Macmilan at the head of the troop. His own followers tried to press in behind him. Vera was jostled among the men, their guns and whipstocks, their hard arms, their faces glancing down at her, young and hostile. The street was narrow and Falco shoved his way by main force, pulling Vera along with him. But the instant he came out abreast of Macmilan at the head of the troop he let go Vera's arm and walked sedately, as if he had been there at the head all along.

Macmilan glanced at him and smiled, his usual tight, pleased smile. He then pantomimed surprise at the sight of Vera. "Who is that, Don Luis? Have you brought a duenna along?"

"Any more reports of the Town this last hour?"

"Still gathering; not on the move yet, at last report."

"The City Guard will meet us at the Monument?"

The young man nodded. "With some reinforcements Angel rounded up. High time we got moving! These men have been kept waiting too long."

"They're your men, I expect you to keep them in order," Falco said.

"They're so keen for action," Macmilan said with pretended confidentiality. Vera saw Falco shoot him one quick, black glance.

"Listen, Don Herman. If your men won't take orders—if you won't take orders—then we stop here: now." Falco stopped, and the force of his personality was such that Vera, Macmilan, and the men behind them stopped with him, as if they were all tied to him on one string.

Macmilan's smile was gone. "You are in command, Councillor," he said, with a flourish that did not hide the sullenness beneath.

Falco nodded and strode on. It was now he who set the pace, Vera noticed.

As they approached the bluffs she saw at the top, near the Monument, a still larger body of men waiting for them; and when they reached the top and passed under the shadow of the spectral, dingy space ship, this troop joined in behind Falco's men and Macmilan's browncoats, so that as they went on along the Road there were two hundred or more of them.

But what are they doing? Vera thought. Is this the attack on Shantih? But why would they bring me? What are they going to do? Falco is mad with pain and Macmilan is mad with envy, and then these men, all these men, all so big, with their guns and their coats and striding along like this, I can't keep up, if only Hari and the others were here so I could see a human face! Why have they brought only me, where are the other hostages, have they killed them? They're all mad, you can smell them, they smell like blood— Do they know they're coming, in Shantih? Do they know? What will they do? Elia! Andre! Lev my dear! What are you going to do, what are you going to do?

Can you hold fast? I can't keep up, they walk so fast, I can't keep up.

Though the people of Shantih and the villages had begun gathering—for the Short March, as Sasha unsmilingly described it—early in the morning, they did not get under way until nearly noon; and being a large crowd, unwieldy, and rendered somewhat chaotic by the presence of many children and by the constant arrival of stragglers seeking for friends to walk with, they did not move very quickly down the road toward the City.

Falco and Macmilan, on the contrary, had moved very quickly when they were brought word of a great massing of Shanty-Towners on the road. They had their troop—Macmilan's army, City Guards, the private bodyguards of several Bosses, and a mixed lot of volunteers—out on the Road by noon, and moving fast.

So the two groups met on the road at Rocktop Hill, closer to the Town than to the City. The vanguard of the People of the Peace came over the low crest of the hill and saw the City men just starting up the rise toward them. They halted at once. They had the advantage of superior height where they stood, but a disadvantage too, in that most of them were still on the eastern side of the hill, and so could not see what was going on, nor be seen. Elia suggested to Andre and Lev that they withdraw a hundred meters or so, to meet the City on equal footing at the hilltop; and though this withdrawal might be construed as yielding

or weakness, they decided it was best. It was worth it
to see Herman Macmilan's face when he swaggered
up to the hilltop and saw for the first time what he
was facing: some four thousand people massed along
the road down the whole slope of the hill and far back
along the flat, children and women and men, the
greatest gathering of human beings ever to take place
on that world; and they were singing. Macmilan's
ruddy face lost its color. He gave some order to his
men, the ones in brown coats, and they all did something with their guns, and then held them ready in
their hands. Many of the guards and volunteers
began yelling and shouting to drown out the singing,
and it was some while before they could be brought to
silence so that the leaders of the two groups could
speak.

Falco had begun speaking, but there was still a lot
of noise, and his dry voice did not carry. Lev stepped
forward and took the word from him. His voice
silenced all others, ringing out in the silvery, windy
air of the hilltop, jubilant.

"The People of the Peace greet the representatives
of the City in comradeship! We have come to explain
to you what we intend to do, what we ask you to do,
and what will happen if you reject our decisions.
Listen to what we say, people of Victoria, for all our
hope lies in this! First, our hostages must be set free.
Second, there will be no further forced-work drafts.
Third, representatives from Town and City will meet
to set up a fairer trade agreement. Finally, the Town's
plan to found a colony in the north will proceed
without interference from the City, as the City's plan

to open South Valley along the Mill River to settlement will proceed without interference from the Town. These four points have been discussed and agreed upon by all the people of Shantih, and they are not subject to negotiation. If they are not accepted by the Council, the people of Shantih must warn the people of the City that all cooperation in work, all trade, all furnishing of food, wood, cloth, ores, and products will cease and will not be resumed until the four points are accepted and acted upon. This resolve is not open to compromise. We will in no case use violence against you; but until our demands are met we will in no way cooperate with you. Nor will we bargain with you, or compromise. I speak the conscience of my people. We will hold fast."

So surrounded by the big brown-coated men that she could see nothing but shoulders and backs and gun stocks, Vera stood trembling, still badly out of breath from the hurried march, and blinking back tears. The clear, courageous, strong, young voice, speaking without anger or uncertainty, singing the words of reason and of peace, singing Lev's soul, her soul, their soul, the challenge and the hope—

"There is no question," said the dark dry voice, Falco's voice, "of bargaining or compromise. On that we agree. Your show of numbers is impressive. But bear in mind, all of you, that we stand for the law, and that we are armed. I do not wish there to be violence. It is unnecessary. It is you who have forced it on us, by bringing out so large a crowd to force your demands on us. This is intolerable. If your people attempt to advance one step farther toward the City, our men will be ordered to stop them. The responsibility for injuries or deaths will be yours. You have forced us to take extreme measures in defense of the Community of Man on Victoria. We will not hesitate to take them. I will presently give the order to this crowd to disperse and go home. If they do not obey at once, I will order my men to use their weapons at will. Before that, I wish to exchange hostages, as we agreed. The two women, Vera Adelson and Luz Marina Falco, are here? Let them cross the line between us in safety."

"We agreed to no exchange!" Lev said, and now there was anger in his voice.

Herman Macmilan had forced his way among his men and seized Vera by the arm, as if to prevent her escape, or perhaps to escort her forward. That heavy grip on her arm shocked and enraged her, and she trembled again, but she did not pull away, or say anything to Macmilan. She could see both Lev and Falco now, and she stood still.

Lev stood facing her, some ten meters away on the level hilltop. His face looked extraordinarily bright in the restless, flashing sunlight. Elia stood beside him, and was saying something to him hurriedly. Lev shook his head and faced Falco again. "No agreement was made, none will be made. Let Vera and the others free. Your daughter is already free. We do not make bargains, do you understand? And we do not heed threats."

There was no sound now among the thousands of people standing back along the road. Though they could not all hear what was said, the silence had swept back among them; only there was, here and there, a little babbling and whimpering of babies, fretting at being held so tight. The wind on the hilltop gusted hard and ceased. The clouds above Songe Bay were massing heavier, but had not yet hidden the high sun.

Still Falco did not answer.

He turned at last, abruptly. Vera saw his face, rigid as iron. He gestured towards her, to her, unmistakably, to come forward—to come free. Macmilan let go her arm. Incredulous, she took a step forward, a second step. Her eyes sought Lev's eyes; he was smiling. Is it so easy, victory? so easy?

The explosion of Macmilan's gun directly beside her head jerked her whole body backward as if with the recoil of the gun itself. Off balance, she was knocked sideways by the rush of the brown-coated men, then knocked down on hands and knees. There was a crackling, snapping noise and a roaring and high hissing screaming like a big fire, but all far away, where could a fire be burning, here there were only men crushing and crowding and trampling and stumbling; she crawled and cowered, trying to hide, but there was no hiding place, there was nothing left but the hiss of fire, the trampling feet and legs, the crowding bodies, and the sodden stony dirt.

There was a silence, but not a real silence. A stupid meaningless silence inside her own head, inside her right ear. She shook her head to shake the silence out of it. There was not enough light. The sunlight had gone. It was cold, the wind was blowing cold, but it made no sound blowing. She shivered as she sat up, and held her arms against her belly. What a stupid place to fall down, to lie down; it made her angry. Her good suit of treesilk was muddy and blood-soaked, clammy against her breasts and arms. A man was lying down next to her. He wasn't a big man at all. They had all looked so big when they were standing up and crowding her along, but lying down he was quite thin, and he was trampled into the ground as if he was trying to become part of it, half gone back to mud already. Not a man at all anymore, just mud and hair and a dirty brown coat. Not a man at all anymore. Nobody left. She was cold sitting there, and it was a stupid place to sit; she tried to crawl a little. There was nobody left to knock her down, but she still could not get up and walk. From now on she would always have to crawl. Nobody could stand up anymore. There was nothing to hold onto. Nobody could walk. Not anymore. They all lay down on the ground, the few that were left. She found Lev after she had crawled for a while. He was not so trampled into the mud and dirt as the brown-coated man; his face was there, the dark eyes open looking up at the sky; but not looking. There was not enough light left. No light at all anymore, and the wind made no sound. It was going to rain soon, the clouds were heavy overhead like a roof. One of Lev's hands had been trampled, and the bones were broken and showing white. She dragged herself a little farther to a place where she did not have to see that, and took his other hand in her own. It was unhurt, only cold. "So," she said, trying to find some words to comfort him. "So, there, Lev my dear." She could barely hear the words she said, way off in the silence. "It will be all right soon, Lev."

10

"It's all right," Luz said. "Everything is going well. Don't worry." She had to speak loudly, and she felt foolish, always saying the same thing; but it always worked, for a while. Vera would lie back and be quiet. But presently she would be trying to sit up again, asking what was happening, anxious and frightened. She would ask about Lev: "Is Lev all right? His hand was hurt." Then she would say she had to go back to the City, to Casa Falco. She should never have come with those men with the guns, it was her fault, for wanting so badly to come home. If she went back to being a hostage again things would go better, wouldn't they? "Everything is all right, don't worry," Luz said, loudly, for Vera's hearing had been damaged. "Everything is going well."

And indeed people went to bed at night and got up in the morning, did the work, cooked meals and ate them, talked together; everything went on. Luz went on. She went to bed at night. It was hard to get to sleep, and when she slept she woke up in the black dark from a horrible crowd of pushing, screaming people; but none of that was happening. It had happened. The room was dark and silent. It had happened, it was over, and everything went on.

The funeral of the seventeen who had been killed was held two days after the march to the City; some were to be buried in their own villages, but the meeting and service for all of them was held at the Meeting House. Luz felt that she did not belong there, and that Andre and Southwind and the others would find it easier if she did not come with them. She said she would stay with Vera, and they left her. But when a long time had passed in the utter silence of the house in the rainswept fields, Vera asleep, Luz picking the seeds from silktree fiber to be doing something with her hands, a man came to the door, a slight, gray-haired man; she did not recognize him at first. "I am Alexander Shults," he said. "Is she asleep? Come on. They shouldn't have left you here." And he took her back with him to the Meeting House, to the end of the service for the dead, and on to the burial ground, in the silent procession that bore the twelve coffins of the dead from Shantih. So she stood in her black shawl in the rain at the graveside by Lev's father. She was grateful to him for that, though she said nothing to him, nor he to her.

She and Southwind worked daily in Southwind's potato field, for the crop had to be got in; another few days and it would begin to rot in the wet ground. They worked together when Vera was asleep, and took turns, one in the field and one in the house, when she was wakeful and needed someone with her. Southwind's mother was often there, and the big, silent, competent Italia, Southwind's friend; and Andre came by once a day, though he too had field-work and also had to spend time daily at the Meeting

House with Elia and the others. Elia was in charge, it was Elia who talked with the City men now. Andre told Luz and Southwind what had been done and said; he expressed no opinion; Luz did not know if he approved or disapproved. All the opinions, beliefs, theories, principles, all that was gone, swept away, dead. The heavy, defeated grief of the great crowd at the funeral service was all that was left. Seventeen people of Shantih dead, there on the Road; eight people of the City. They had died in the name of peace, but they had also killed in the name of peace. It had all fallen apart. Andre's eyes were dark as coals. He joked to cheer up Southwind (and Luz saw, as she saw everything now, dispassionately, that he had been in love with Southwind for a long time), and both girls smiled at his jokes, and tried to make him rest for a while, there with them and Vera. Luz and Southwind worked together, afternoons in the fields. The potatoes were small, firm, and clean, pulling up out of the mud on their fine-tangled tracery of roots. There was a pleasure in the fieldwork; not much in anything else.

From time to time Luz thought, "None of this is happening," for it seemed to her that what did happen was only a kind of picture or screen, like a shadow-play, behind which lay whatever was real. This was a puppet show. It was all so strange, after all. What was she doing in a field in the late afternoon in a misty dark drizzle, wearing patched trousers, mud to the thighs and elbows, pulling potatoes for Shanty Town? All she had to do was get up and walk home. Her blue skirt and the embroidered blouse would be hanging clean and pressed in the closet in her dressing room; Teresa would bring hot water for a bath. There would be big logs in the fireplace at the west end of the hall of Casa Falco, in this weather, and a clear fire burning. Outside the thick glass of the windows the evening would darken bluer and bluer over the Bay. The doctor might drop in for a chat, with his crony Valera, or old Councillor Di Giulio hoping for a game of chess with her father—

No. Those were the puppets, little bright mind-puppets. That was nowhere; this was here: the potatoes, the mud, Southwind's soft voice, Vera's swollen, discolored face, the creaking of the straw mattress in the loft of this hut in Shanty Town in the black dark and stillness of the night. It was strange, it was all wrong, but it was all that was left.

Vera was improving. The physician, Jewel, said the effect of the concussion had worn off; she must stay in bed at least a week longer, but she would be all right. She asked for something to do. Southwind gave her a great basket of cottonwool, gathered from wild trees over in Red Valley, to spin.

Elia came to the door. The three women had just had their noon dinner. Southwind was washing up, Luz was straightening the table, Vera was sitting up against her pillow tying a starter-thread on the spindle. Elia looked clean, like the little potatoes, Luz thought, with his firm round face and blue eyes. His voice was unexpectedly deep, but very gentle. He sat at the cleared table and talked, mostly to Vera. "Everything is going well," he told her. "Everything is all right."

Vera said little. The left side of her face was still misshapen and bruised where she had been kicked or clubbed, but she tilted that side forward in order to hear; her right eardrum had been broken. She sat up against her pillow, set her spindle whirling, and nodded as Elia talked. Luz did not pay much heed to what he said. Andre had told them already: the hostages had been freed; terms of cooperation between City and Town agreed upon, and a fairer exchange in tools and dried fish for the food supplied by the Town; now they were discussing a plan for the joint settlement of the South Valley—work parties from the City opening up the land, then volunteer colonists from the Town moving there to farm.

"And the northern colony?" Vera asked in her quiet thin voice.

Elia looked down at his hands. Finally he said, "It was a dream."

"Was it all a dream, Elia?"

Vera's voice had changed; Luz, putting away the bowls, listened.

"No," the man said. "No! But too much, too soon—too fast, Vera. Too much staked rashly on an act of open defiance."

"Would covert defiance have been better?"

"No. But confrontation was wrong. Cooperation, talking together—reasoning—*reason*. I told Lev— All along, I tried to say—"

There were tears in Elia's blue eyes, Luz noticed. She stacked the bowls neatly in the cupboard and sat down by the hearth.

"Councillor Marquez is a reasonable man. If only he

had been Chief of the Council—" Elia checked himself. Vera said nothing.

"It's Marquez you mostly talk with now, Andre says," said Luz. "Is he Chief of the Council now?"

"Yes."

"Is my father in jail?"

"Under house arrest, they call it," Elia replied, with extreme embarrassment. Luz nodded, but Vera was staring at them. "Don Luis? Alive? I thought—Arrest? What for?"

Elia's embarrassment was painful to see. Luz answered, "For killing Herman Macmilan."

Vera stared; the pulse of her heart throbbed in her swollen temple.

"I didn't see it," Luz said in her dry calm voice. "I was back in the crowd with Southwind. Andre was up front with Lev and Elia, he saw it and told me. It was after Macmilan shot Lev. Before any of us knew what was happening. Macmilan's men were just beginning to shoot at us. My father took a gun out of one of the men's hands and used it like a club. He didn't shoot it, Andre said. I suppose it was hard to tell, after the fighting there, and people trampling back and forth over them, but Andre said they thought the blow must have killed Macmilan. Anyway he was dead when they came back."

"I saw it too," Elia said, thickly. "It was— I suppose it was what—what kept some of the City men from shooting, they were confused—"

"No order was ever given," Luz said. "So there was time for the marchers to rush in on them. Andre thinks that if my father hadn't turned on Macmilan, there would have been no fighting at all. Just them shooting and the marchers running."

"And no betrayal of our principles," said Southwind, clearly and steadily. "Perhaps, if we hadn't rushed forward, the City men wouldn't have fired in self-defense."

"And only Lev would have been killed?" Luz said, equally clearly. "But Macmilan would have ordered them all to fire, Southwind. He'd started it. If the marchers had run away sooner, yes, maybe fewer would have been shot. And no City men beaten to death. Your principles would be all right. But Lev would still be dead. And Macmilan would be alive."

Elia was looking at her with an expression she had not seen before; she did not know what it meant—detestation, perhaps, or fear.

"Why," Vera said in a pitiful dry whisper.

"I don't know!" Luz said, and because it was such a relief to be saying these things, talking about them, instead of hiding them and saying everything was all right, she actually laughed. "Do I understand what my father does, what he thinks, what he is? Maybe he went insane. That's what old Marquez told Andre, last week. I know if I'd been where he was, I would have killed Macmilan too. But that doesn't explain why *he* did it. There is no explanation. It's easiest to say he was insane. You see, that's what's wrong with your ideas, Southwind, you people. They're all true, all right and true, violence gains nothing, killing wins nothing—only sometimes nothing is what people want. Death is what they want. And they get it."

There was a silence.

"Councillor Falco saw the folly of Macmilan's act," Elia said. "He was trying to prevent—"

"No," Luz said, "he wasn't. He wasn't trying to prevent more shooting, more killing, and he wasn't on your side. Don't you have anything in your head but reason, Senhor Elia? My father killed Macmilan for the same 'reason' that Lev stood up there facing the men with guns and defying them and got killed. Because he was a man, that's what men do. The reasons come afterward."

Elia's hands were clenched; his face was pale, so that his blue eyes stood out unnaturally bright. He looked straight at Luz and said, gently enough, "Why do you stay here, Luz Marina?"

"Where else should I go?" she asked, almost jeering.

"To your father."

"Yes, that's what women do. . . ."

"He is in distress, in disgrace; he needs you."

"And you don't."

"Yes, we do," Vera said, with desperation. "Elia, are you insane too? Are you trying to drive her out?"

"It was because of her— If she hadn't come here, Lev— It was her fault—" Elia was in the grip of emotion he could not master, his voice going high, his eyes wide. "It was her fault!"

"What are you saying?" Vera whispered, and South-wind, fiercely, "It was not! None of it!"

Luz said nothing.

Elia, shaking, put his hands over his face. No one said anything for a long time.

"I'm sorry," he said, looking up. His eyes were dry and bright, his mouth worked strangely as he spoke.

"Forgive me, Luz Marina. There was no meaning in what I said. You came to us, you're welcome here among us. I get—I get very tired, trying to see what ought to be done, what's right—it's hard to see what's right—"

The three women were silent.

"I compromise, yes, I compromise with Marquez, what else can I do? Then you say, Elia is betraying our ideals, selling us into permanent bondage to the City, losing all we struggled for. What do you want, then? More deaths? You want another confrontation, you want to see the People of the Peace being shot again, fighting, beating—beating men to death again —we who—who believe in peace, in nonviolence—"

"Nobody is saying that of you, Elia," Vera said.

"We have to go slowly. We must be reasonable. We can't do it all at once, rashly, violently. It's not easy—not easy!"

"No," Vera said. "It's not easy."

"We came from all over the world," the old man said. "From great cities and from little villages, the people came. When the March began in the City of Moskva there were four thousand, and when they reached the edge of the place called Russia already there were seven thousand. And they walked across the great place called Europe, and always hundreds and hundreds of people joined the March, families and single souls, young and old. They came from towns nearby, they came from great lands far away over the oceans, India, Africa. They all brought what they could bring of food and precious money to buy

food, for so many marchers always needed food. The
people of the towns stood along the side of the road
to watch the marchers pass, and sometimes children
ran out with presents of food or precious money.
The armies of the great countries stood along the
roadside too, and watched, and protected the
marchers, and made sure they did no damage to the
fields and trees and towns, by being so many. And
the marchers sang, and sometimes the armies sang
with them, and sometimes the men of the armies
threw away their guns and joined the March in the
darkness of the night. They walked, they walked. At
night they camped and it was like a great town growing up all at once in the open fields, all the people.
They walked, they walked, they walked, across the
fields of France and across the fields of Germany and
across the high mountains of Spain, weeks they walked
and months they walked, singing the songs of peace,
and so they came at last, ten thousand strong, to the
end of the land and the beginning of the sea, to the
City Lisboa, where the ships had been promised
them. And there the ships lay in harbor.

"So that was the Long March. But it wasn't over,
the journey! They went into the ships, to sail to the
Free Land, where they would be welcomed. But there
were too many of them now. The ships would hold
only two thousand, and their numbers had grown
and grown as they marched, there were ten thousand
of them now. What were they to do? They crowded,
they crowded; they built more beds, they crowded
ten to a room of the great ships, a room that was

meant to hold two. The ships' masters said, Stop, you can't crowd the ships any more, there isn't enough water for the long voyage, you can't all come aboard the ships. So they bought boats, fishing boats, boats with sails and with engines; and people, grand rich people, with boats of their own, came and said, Use my boat, I'll take fifty souls to the Free Land. Fishermen came from the city called England and said, Use my boat, I'll take fifty souls. Some were afraid of the small boats, to cross so great a sea; some went back home then, and left the Long March. But always new people came to join them, so their numbers grew. And so at last they all sailed from the harbor of Lisboa, and music played and there were ribbons in the wind and all the people in the great ships and the little boats sailed out together singing.

"They couldn't stay together on the sea. The ships were fast, the boats were slow. In eight days the big ships sailed into the harbor of Montral, in the land of Canamerica. The other boats came after, strung out all across the ocean, some days behind, some weeks behind. My parents were on one of the boats, a beautiful white boat named *Anita*, that a noble lady had lent to the People of the Peace so that they could come to the Free Land. There were forty on that boat. Those were good days, my mother said. The weather was good and they sat on the deck in the sun and planned how they would build the City of Peace in the land they had been promised, the land between the mountains, in the northern part of Canamerica.

"But when they came to Montral, they were met by

men with guns, and taken, and put into prisons; and there were all the others, from the big ships, all the people, waiting, in the prison camps.

"There were too many of them, the leaders of that land said. There were to have been two thousand, and there were ten thousand. There was no land or place for so many. They were dangerous, being so many. People from all over the Earth kept coming there to join them, and camping outside the city and outside the prison camps, and singing the songs of peace. Even from Brasil they were coming, they had begun their own Long March northward up the length of the great continents. The rulers of Canamerica were frightened. They said there was no way to keep order, or to feed so many. They said this was an invasion. They said the Peace was a lie, not the truth, because they didn't understand it and didn't want it. They said their own people were leaving them and joining the Peace, and this could not be allowed, because they must all fight the Long War with the Republic, that had been fought for twenty years and still was being fought. They said the People of the Peace were traitors, and spies from the Republic! And so they put us into the prison camps, instead of giving that land between the mountains they had promised us. There I was born, in the prison camp of Montral.

"At last the rulers said: Very well, we'll keep our promise, we'll give you land to live on, but there's no place for you on Earth. We'll give you the ship that was built in Brasil long ago, to send thieves and murderers away. Three ships they built, two they sent out to the world called Victoria, the third they never used because their law was changed. No one wants the ship because it was made to make only the one voyage, it cannot come back to Earth. Brasil has given us that ship. Two thousand of you are to go in it, that is all it can hold. And the rest of you must either find your way back to your own land across the ocean, back to Russia the Black, or live here in the prison camps making weapons for the War with the Republic. All your leaders must go on the ship, Mehta and Adelson, Kaminskaya and Wicewska and Shults; we will not have those men and women on the Earth, because they do not love the War. They must take the Peace to another world.

"So the two thousand were chosen by lot. And the choosing was bitter, the bitterest day of all the bitter days. For those that went, there was hope, but at what risk—going out unpiloted across the stars to an unknown world, never to return? And for those that must stay, there was no hope left. For there was no place left for the Peace on Earth.

"So the choice was made, and the tears were wept, and the ship was sent. And so, for those two thousand, and for their children and the children of their children, the Long March has ended. Here in the place we named Shantih, in the valleys of Victoria. But we do not forget the Long March and the great voyage and those we left behind, their arms stretched out to us. We do not forget the Earth."

The children listened: fair faces and dark, black hair and brown; eyes intent, drowsy; enjoying the story, moved by it, bored by it. . . . They had all heard it before, young as some of them were. It was part of the world to them. Only to Luz was it new.

There were a hundred questions in her mind, too many; she let the children ask their questions. "Is Amity black because her grandmother came from Russia the Black?"—"Tell about the space ship! about how they went to sleep on the space ship!"—"Tell about the animals on Earth!"— Some of the questions were asked for her; they wanted her, the outsider, the big girl who didn't know, to hear their favorite parts of the saga of their people. "Tell Luz about the flying-air-planes!" cried a little girl, very excited, and turning to Luz began to gabble the old man's story for him: "His mother and father were on the boat in the middle of the sea and a flying ship went over them in the air, and went boom and fell in the sea and blew up and that was the Republic, and they saw it. And they tried to pick people up out of the water but there weren't any and the water was poisonous and they had to go on."—"Tell about the people that came from Afferca!" a boy demanded. But Hari was tired. "Enough now," he said. "Let's sing one of the songs of the Long March. Meria?"

A girl of twelve stood up, smiling, and faced the others. "O when we come," she began in a sweet ringing voice, and the others joined in—

O when we come,
O when we come to Lisboa,
The white ships will be waiting
O when we come. . . .

* * *

The clouds were moving away, heavy and ragged-fringed, over the river and the northern hills. To the south a streak of the outer Bay lay silver and remote. Drops from the last rainfall fell heavy now and then from the leaves of the big cottonwool trees on the summit of this hill that stood east of Southwind's house; there was no other sound. A silent world, a gray world. Luz stood alone under the trees, looking out over the empty land. She had not been alone for a long time. She had not known, when she set off toward the hill, where she was going, what she was looking for. This place, this silence, this solitude. Her feet had borne her toward herself.

The ground was muddy, the weeds heavy with wet, but the poncho-coat Italia had given her was thick; she sat down on the springy leaf mold under the trees, and with arms around knees beneath the poncho sat still, gazing westward over the bend of the river. She sat so for a long time, seeing nothing but the moveless land, the slow-moving clouds and river.

Alone, alone. She was alone. She had not had time to know that she was alone, working with Southwind, nursing Vera, talking with Andre, joining little by little in the life of Shantih; helping to set up the new Town school, for the City school was closed henceforth to the people of Shantih; drawn in as guest to this house and that, this family and that; drawn in, made welcome, for they were gentle people, inexpert in resentment or distrust. Only at night, on the straw mattress in the dark of the loft, had it come to her, her loneliness, wearing a white and bitter face. She had been frightened, then. What shall I do? she had cried in her mind, and turning over to escape the bitter face of her solitude, had taken refuge in her weariness, in sleep.

It came to her now, walking softly along the gray hilltop. Its face now was Lev's face. She had no wish to turn away.

It was time to look at what she had lost. To look at it and see it all. The sunset of spring over the roofs of the City, long ago, and his face lit by that glory— "There, there, you can see what it should be, what it is. . . ." The dusk of the room in Southwind's house, and his face, his eyes. "To live and die for the sake of the spirit—" The wind and light on Rocktop Hill, and his voice. And the rest, all the rest, all the days and lights and winds and years that would have been, and that would not be, that should be and were not, because he was dead. Shot dead on the road, in the wind, at twenty-one. His mountains unclimbed, never to be climbed.

If the spirit stayed in the world, Luz thought, that was where it had gone, by now: north to the valley he had found, to the mountains he had told her of, the last night before the march on the City, with such joy and yearning: "Higher than you can imagine, Luz, higher and whiter. You look up, and then up, and still there are peaks above the peaks."

He would be there, now, not here. It was only her own solitude she looked at, though it wore his face.

"Go on, Lev," she whispered aloud. "Go on to the mountains, go higher. . . ."

But where shall I go? Where shall I go, alone?

Without Lev, without the mother I never knew and the father I can never know, without my house and my City, without a friend—oh, yes, friends, Vera, Southwind, Andre, all the others, all the gentle people, but they're not my people. Only Lev, only Lev was, and he couldn't stay, he wouldn't wait, he had to go climb his mountain, and put life off till later. He was my chance, my luck. And I was his. But he wouldn't see it, he wouldn't stop and look. He threw it all away.

So now I stop here, between the valleys, under the trees, and I have to look. And what I see is Lev dead, and his hope lost; my father a murderer and mad; and I a traitor to the City and a stranger in the Town.

And what else is there?

All the rest of the world. The river there, and the hills, and the light on the Bay. All the rest of this silent living world, with no people in it. And I alone.

As she came down from the hill she saw Andre coming out of Southwind's house, turning to speak to Vera at the door. They called to each other across the fallow fields, and he waited for her at the turn of the lane that led to Shantih.

"Where were you, Luz?" he asked in his concerned, shy way. He never, like the others, tried to draw her in; he was simply there, reliable. Since Lev's death there had been no joy for him, and much anxiety. He stood there now, sturdy and a little stooped, over-burdened, patient.

"Nowhere," she answered, truthfully. "Just walking. Thinking. Andre, tell me. I never want to ask you while Vera's there, I don't like to upset her. What will happen now, between the City and Shantih? I don't know enough to understand what Elia says. Will it just go on the way it was—before?"

After a fairly long pause, Andre nodded. His dark face, with jutting cheekbones like carved wood, was shut tight. "Or worse," he said. Then, scrupulous to be fair to Elia, "Some things are better. The trade agreement—if they keep to it. And the South Valley expansion. There won't be forced labor, or 'estates' and all that. I'm hopeful about that. We may work together there, for once."

"Will you go there?"

"I don't know. I suppose so. I should."

"What about the northern colony? The valley you found, the mountains?"

Andre looked up at her. He shook his head.

"No way—?"

"Only if we went as their servants."

"Marquez won't agree to your going alone, without City people?"

He shook his head.

"What if you went anyway?"

"What do you think I dream of every night?" he said, and for the first time there was bitterness in his voice. "After I've been with Elia and Jewel and Sam and Marquez and the Council, talking compromise, talking cooperation, talking reason?—But if we went, they'd follow."

"Then go where they can't follow."

"Where would that be?" Andre said, his voice patient again, ironic and miserable.

"Anywhere! Farther east, into the forests. Or southeast. Or south, down the coast, down past where the trawlers go—there must be other bays, other town sites! This is a whole continent, a whole world. Why do we have to stay here, here, huddled up here, destroying each other? You've been in the wilderness, you and Lev and the others, you know what it's like—"

"Yes. I do."

"You came back. Why must you come back? Why couldn't people just go, not too many of them all at once, but just go, at night, and go on; maybe a few should go ahead and make stopping-places with supplies; but you don't leave a trail, any trail. You just go. Far! And when you've gone a hundred kilometers, or five hundred, or a thousand, and you find a good place, you stop, and make a settlement. A new place. Alone."

"It's not—it breaks the community, Luz," Andre said. "It would be . . . running away."

"Oh," Luz said, and her eyes shone with anger. "Running away! You crawl into Marquez's trap in the South Valley and call that standing firm! You talk about choice and freedom— The world, the whole world is there for you to live in and be free, and that would be running away! From what? To what? Maybe we can't be free, maybe people always take themselves with themselves, but at least you can try. What was

your Long March for? What makes you think it ever
ended?"

11

Vera had meant to stay awake to see them off, but
she had fallen asleep by the fire, and the soft knock
at the door did not waken her. Southwind and Luz
looked at each other; Southwind shook her head.
Luz knelt and hastily, as silently as she could, laid
a fresh square of peat behind the coals, so the house
would stay warm through the night. Southwind, made
awkward by her heavy coat and backpack, stooped
and touched Vera's gray hair with her lips; then she
looked around the house, a bewildered, hurried look,
and went out. Luz followed her.

The night was cloudy but dry, very dark. The cold
of it woke Luz from her long trance of waiting, and
she caught her breath. There were people around
her in the dark, a few soft voices. "Both there? All
right, come on." They set off, past the house, through
the potato field, toward the low ridge that lay behind it to the east. As Luz's eyes became accustomed
to the dark she made out that the person who walked
beside her was Lev's father, Sasha; sensing her gaze
in the darkness he said, "How's the pack?"

"It's all right," she said in a bare whisper. They
must not talk, they must not make any noise, she
thought, not yet, not till they were clear of the settlement, past the last village and the last farm, across

Mill River, a long way. They must go fast and silently, and not be stopped, O Lord God please not be stopped!

"Mine's made of iron ingots, or unforgiven sins," Sasha murmured; and they went on in silence, a dozen shadows in the shadow of the world.

It was still dark when they came to Mill River, a few kilometers south of where it joined the Songe. The boat was waiting, Andre and Holdfast waiting with it. Hari rowed six across, then the second six. Luz was in the second lot. As they neared the eastern shore the solid blackness of the nightworld was growing insubstantial, a veil of light dimming all things, a mist thickening on the water. Shivering, she set foot on the far shore. Left alone in the boat, which Andre and the others had already pushed off again, Hari called out softly, "Good luck, good luck! Peace go with you!" And the boat vanished into the mist like a ghost; and the twelve stood there on the ghostly, fading sand.

"Up this way," said Andre's voice out of the mist and pallor. "They'll have breakfast for us."

They were the last and smallest of the three groups to leave, one group a night; the others were waiting farther on among the rugged hills east of the Mill, country where only coney trappers went. In single file, following Andre and Holdfast, they left the river-bank and set off into the wild land.

She had been thinking for hours and hours, step after step, that as soon as they stopped she would sink right down on the dirt or the mud or the sand, sink

down and not move again till morning. But when
they stopped she saw Martin and Andre, up at the
front, discussing something, and she went on, step
after step, till she came up with them, and even
then did not sink down, but kept standing, to hear
what they were talking about.

"Martin thinks the compass isn't reading true,"
Andre said. With a dubious look, he held the in-
strument out to Luz, as if she could judge its inac-
curacy at a glance. What she saw was its delicacy, the
box of polished wood, the gold ring, the glass, the
frail burnished needle hovering, trembling between
the finely incised points: what a beautiful thing,
miraculous, improbable, she thought. But Martin was
looking at it with disapproval. "I'm sure it's pulling
east," he said. "Must be iron-ore masses in those
hills, deflecting it." He nodded toward the east. For
a day and a half they had been in a queer scrubby
country that bore no ringtrees or cottonwools but only
a sparse, tangled scrub which grew no more than a
couple of meters high; it was not forest, but not open
country; there was seldom any long view. But they
knew that to the east, to their left, the line of high
hills they had first seen six days ago went on. Whenever they came up on a rise in the scrublands, they saw
the dark red, rocky skyline of the heights.

"Well," Luz said, hearing her own voice for the
first time in hours, "does it matter much?"

Andre chewed his lower lip. His face looked bone
weary, the eyes narrowed and lifeless. "Not for going
on," he said. "So long as we have the sun or some
stars at night. But for making the map. . . ."

"What if we turn east again. Get over those hills. They aren't getting any lower," Martin said. A younger man than Andre, he looked far less tired. He was one of the mainstays of the group. Luz felt at ease with Martin; he looked like a City man, stocky, dark, well muscled, rather curt and somber; even his name was a common one in the City. But for all Martin's comfortable strength, it was to Andre that she turned with her question.

"Can't we mark the trail yet?"

Unwilling to make any trail that could be followed, they had tried to map their course. A map could be brought back to Shantih by a few messengers, after a couple of years, to guide a second group to the new colony. That was the only reason for making it that they ever spoke of. Andre, the map maker of the northern journey, was in charge of it, and he felt his responsibility as a heavy one, for the unspoken purpose of the map was always in their minds. It was their one link to Shantih, to humankind, to their own past lives; their one assurance that they were not simply wandering lost in the wilderness, aimless, without goal and, since they could mark no trail, without hope of return.

At times Luz clung to the idea of the map, at times she was impatient with it. Martin was keen on it, but his keenest care was that they keep their trail covered; he winced, Italia remarked, when anybody stepped on a stick and broke it. Certainly they had left, in the ten days of their journey, as little mark of their going as sixty-seven people could leave.

Martin was shaking his head at Luz's question.

"Look," he said, "our choice of route has been so obvious, the easiest way, right from the start."

Andre smiled. It was a dry crack of a smile, like a crack in tree bark, and narrowed his eyes to two lesser cracks. That was why Luz liked to be with Andre, drew strength from him, that humorous patient smile, like a tree smiling.

"Consider the options, Martin!" he said, and she saw what he was imagining: a party of City men, Macmilan's bullies, guns and whips and boots and all, standing on the bluffs of the Songe, looking north, east, south, over the gray rusty-ringed rising falling rain-darkened unending trackless voiceless enormous wilderness, and trying to decide which, of a hundred possible directions, the fugitives had chosen.

"All right," she said, "let's cross the hills, then."

"Climbing won't be much harder than slogging through this scrub," Andre said.

Martin nodded. "Turn east again here, then?"

"Here as well as anywhere," said Andre, and got out his grubby, dog-eared sketch map to make a note.

"Now?" Luz asked. "Or camp?"

They usually did not camp till near sundown, but they had come a long way today. She looked around the shoulder-high, thorny, bronze-colored bushes, which grew spaced a meter or two apart so that millions of pointless winding trails led around and between and amongst them. Only a few of the group were visible; most of them had sat right down to rest when the halt was called. Overhead was a lead-gray sky, featureless, one even cloud. No rain had fallen for two nights, but the weather was getting colder every hour.

"Well, a few more kilos," Andre said, "and we'd be at the foot of the hills; might find some shelter there. And water." He looked at her judgingly, and waited for her judgment. He, Martin, Italia, the other path-finders, often used her and a couple of the older women as representatives of the weak, the ones who could not keep the pace the strongest would have kept. She did not mind. She walked each day right to the limit of her endurance, or beyond it. The first three days of the journey, when they had been hurry-ing, afraid of pursuit, had exhausted her, and though she was growing tougher she never could make up that initial loss. She accepted this, and saved all her resentment for her backpack, that monstrous and irascible, knee-bending, neck-destroying load. If only they didn't have to carry everything with them! But they could not push carts without making, or leaving, paths; and sixty-seven people could not live off the wilderness while traveling, or settle in it without tools, even if it were not late autumn getting on to winter. . . .

"A few more kilos," she said. She was always sur-prised when she said things like that. "A few more kilos," as if it were nothing at all, when for the last six hours she had longed, craved to sit down, just to sit down, just to sit down for a minute, a month, a year! But now they had spoken of turning east again she found she also craved to get out of this dreary maze of thorn-scrub, into the hills, where maybe you could see your way ahead.

"Few minutes' rest," she added, and sat down, slipping off her pack straps and rubbing her aching shoulders. Andre promptly sat down too. Martin went off to talk with some of the others and discuss the change of course. None of them was visible, they had all vanished in the sea of thorn-scrub, taking their few minutes' rest already, flat out on the sandy, grayish soil littered with thorns. She could not see even Andre, only a corner of his pack. A northwest wind, faint but cold, rustled the little dry branches of the bushes. There was no other sound.

Sixty-seven people: no sight of them, no sound of them. Vanished. Lost. A drop of water in the river, a word blown off on the wind. Some small creatures moved a little while in the wilderness, not going very far, and then ceased to move, and it made no difference to the wilderness, or to anything, no more difference than the dropping of one thorn among a million thorns or the shifting of a grain of sand.

The fear she had come to know these ten days of their journeying came up like a small gray fog in the fields of her mind, a chill creep of blindness. It was hers, hers by inheritance and training; it was to keep out her fear, their fear, that the roofs and walls of the City had been raised; it was fear that had drawn the streets so straight, and made the doors so narrow. She had scarcely known it, living behind those doors. She had felt quite safe. Even in Shantih she had forgotten it, stranger as she was, for the walls there were not visible but were very strong: companionship, cooperation, love; the close human circle. But she had walked away from that, by choice, and walked out into the wilderness, and come face to face at last with the fear that all her life had been built upon.

She could not simply face it, but had to fight it when it first began to come upon her, or it would blot out everything, and she would lose the power of choice entirely. She had to fight blindly, for no reason stood against that fear. It was a great deal older and stronger than ideas.

There was the idea of God. Back in the City they talked about God to children. He made all the worlds, and he punished the wicked, and sent good people up to Heaven when they died. Heaven was a beautiful house with a gold roof where Meria, God's mother, everybody's mother, tenderly waited for the souls of the dead. She had liked that story. When she was little she had prayed to God to make things happen and not happen, because he could do anything if you asked him; later she had liked to imagine God's mother and her mother keeping house together. But when she thought of Heaven here, it was small and far away, like the City. It had nothing to do with the wilderness. There was no God here; he belonged to people, and where there were no people there was no God. At the funeral for Lev and the others they had talked about God, too, but that was back there, back there. Here there was nothing like that. Nobody had made this wilderness, and there was no evil in it and no good; it simply was.

She drew a circle in the sandy dirt near her foot, making it as perfect as she could, using a thorny twig to draw it with. That was a world, or a self, or God, that circle, you could call it anything. Nothing else in the wilderness could think of a circle like that —she thought of the delicate gold ring around the compass glass. Because she was human, she had the mind and eyes and skillful hand to imagine the idea of a circle and to draw the idea. But any drop of water falling from a leaf into a pool or rain puddle could make a circle, a more perfect one, fleeting outward from the center, and if there were no boundary to the water the circle would fleet outward forever, fainter and fainter, forever larger. She could not do that, which any drop of water could do. Inside her circle what was there? Grains of sand, dust, a few tiny pebbles, a half-buried thorn, Andre's tired face, the sound of Southwind's voice, Sasha's eyes which were like Lev's eyes, the ache of her own shoulders where the pack straps pulled, and her fear. The circle could not keep out the fear. And the hand erased the circle, smoothing out the sand, leaving it as it had always been and would always be after they had gone on.

"At first I felt that I was leaving Timmo behind," Southwind said, as she studied the worst blister on her left foot. "When we left the house. He and I built it . . . you know. I felt as if I was walking away and finally leaving him forever, leaving him behind. But now it doesn't seem that way. It was out here he died, in the wilderness. Not here, I know; way back up north there. But I don't feel that he's so terribly far away as I did all autumn living in our house, it's almost as if I'd come out to join him. Not dying, I don't mean that. It's just that there I only thought about his death, and here, while we're walking, all the time, I think about him alive. As if he was with me now."

They had camped in a fold of the land just under the red hills, beside a lively, rocky stream. They had built their fires, cooked, and eaten; many were already stretched out in their blankets to sleep. It was not dark yet, but so cold that if you weren't moving about you must either huddle to the fire or wrap up and sleep. The first five nights of the journey they had not built fires, for fear of pursuers, and those had been miserable nights; Luz had never known such a pure delight as she had felt at their first campfire, back in a great tree-ring on the south slope of the badlands, and every night that pleasure came again, the utter luxury of hot food, of warmth. The three families she and Southwind camped and cooked with were settling down for the night; the youngest child—the youngest of the whole migration, a boy of eleven—was curled up like a pouchbat in his blanket already, fast asleep. Luz tended the fire, while Southwind tended her blisters. Up and down the riverbank were seven other fires, the farthest no more than a candle flame in the blue-gray dusk, a spot of hazy, trembling gold. The noise of the stream covered any sound of voices round the other fires.

"I'll get some more brushwood," Luz said. She was not avoiding an answer to what Southwind had said. No answer was needed. Southwind was gentle and complete; she gave and spoke, expecting no return; in all the world there could be no companion less demanding, or more encouraging.

They had done a good day's walk, twenty-seven kilometers by Martin's estimate; they had got out of that drab nightmare labyrinth of scrub; they had had a hot dinner, the fire was hot, and it was not raining. Even the ache in Luz's shoulders was pleasant (because the pack was not pulling on them) when she stood up. It was these times at the day's end, by the fire, that counterweighed the long dreary hungry afternoons of walking and walking and walking and trying to ease the cut of the pack straps on her shoulders, and the hours in the mud and rain when there seemed to be no reason at all to go on, and the worst hours, in the black dark of the night, when she woke always from the same terrible dream: that there was a circle of some things, not people, standing around their camp, just out of sight, not visible in the darkness, but watching.

"This one's better," Southwind said when Luz came back with an armload of wood from the thickets up the slope, "but the one on my heel isn't. You know, all today I've been feeling that we aren't being followed."

"I don't think we ever were," Luz said, building up the fire. "I never did think they'd really care, even if they knew. They don't want to think about the wilderness, in the City. They want to pretend it isn't there."

"I hope so. I hated feeling that we were running. Being explorers is a much braver feeling."

Luz got the fire settled to burning low but warm, and squatted by it simply soaking the heat up for some while.

"I miss Vera," she said. Her throat was dry with the dust of walking, and she did not use her voice often these days; it sounded dry and harsh to her, like her father's voice.

"She'll come with the second group," Southwind said with comfortable certainty, winding a cloth strip around her pretty, battered foot, and tying it off firmly at the ankle. "Ah, that feels better. I'm going to wrap my feet tomorrow like Holdfast does. It'll be warmer, too."

"If it just won't rain."

"It won't rain tonight." The Shantih people were much weather-wiser than Luz. They had not lived so much within doors as she, they knew what the wind meant, even here, where the winds were different.

"It might tomorrow," Southwind added, beginning to wriggle into her blanket-bag, her voice already sounding small and warm.

"Tomorrow we'll be up in the hills," Luz said. She looked up, to the east, but the near slope of the stream valley and the blue-gray dusk hid that rocky skyline. The clouds had thinned; a star shone out for a while high in the east, small and misty, then vanished as the unseen clouds rejoined. Luz watched for it to reappear, but it did not. She felt foolishly disappointed. The sky was dark now, the ground was dark. No light anywhere, except the eight gold flecks, their campfires, a tiny constellation in the night. And far off there, days behind them in the west, thousands and thousands of steps behind them, behind the scrubland and the badland and the hills and the valleys and the streams, beside the great river running to the sea, a

few more lights: the City and the Town, a tiny huddle
of yellow-lit windows. The river dark, running in
darkness. And no light on the sea.

She reset a log to smolder more slowly, and banked
the ashes against it. She found her sleeping bag and
wriggled down into it, next to Southwind. She wanted
to talk, now. Southwind had seldom spoken much of
Timmo. She wanted to hear her talk about him, and
about Lev; she wanted for the first time to speak about
Lev herself. There was too much silence here. Things
would get lost in the silence. One should speak. And
Southwind would understand. She too had lost her
luck, and known death, and gone on.

Luz said her name softly, but the warm blanket-
bundle next to her did not stir. Southwind was asleep.

Luz settled down cautiously, getting herself comfortable. The river beach, though stony, was a better
bed than last night's in the thorny scrubland. But
her body was so tired that it felt heavy, unwieldy,
hard; her chest was hard and tight. She closed her eyes.
At once she saw the hall of Casa Falco, long and
serene, the silver light reflected from the Bay filling
the windows; and her father standing there, erect,
alert, self-contained, as he always stood. But he was
standing there doing nothing, which was not like him.
Michael and Teresa were off in the doorway, whispering together. She felt a curious resentment toward
them. Her father stood with his back to them, as if
he did not know they were there, or as if he knew it,
but was afraid of them. He raised his arms in a
strange way. She saw his face for a moment. He was
crying. She could not breathe, she tried to draw a long

breath but could not; it caught; because she was
crying—deep shaking sobs from which she could
scarcely gasp a breath before the next came. Racked
with sobs, lying shaken and tormented on the ground
in the enormous night, she wept for the dead, for the
lost. Not fear now, but grief, the grief past enduring,
that endures.

Her weariness and the darkness drank her tears,
and she fell asleep before she was done weeping. She
slept all night without dreams or evil wakings, like
a stone among the stones.

The hills were high and hard. The uphill going was
not bad, for they could zigzag up across the great,
open, rusty slopes, but when they got to the top,
among the rimrock piled like houses and towers, they
saw that they had climbed only the first of a triple or
quadruple chain of hills, and that the farther ridges
were higher.

In the canyons between the ridges ringtrees
crowded, not growing in rings but jammed close and
shooting up unnaturally high toward the light. The
heavy shrub called aloes crowded between the red
trunks, making the going very difficult; but there was
still fruit on the aloes, thick rich dark flesh wrinkled
about a center seed, a welcome addition to the scanty
food in their packs. In this country they had no choice
but to leave a trail behind them: they had to cut their
way with brush hooks to get on at all. They were a
day getting through the canyon, another climbing
the second line of hills, beyond which lay the next
chain of canyons massed with bronze trees and

crimson underbrush, and beyond it a formidable ridge, steep-spurred, rising in bare screes to the rock-capped summit.

They had to camp down in the gorge the next night. Even Martin, after cutting and hacking their way forward step by step, by mid-afternoon was too tired to go on. When they camped, those who were not worn out from path-making spread out from the camp, cautiously and not going far, for in the undergrowth you could lose all sense of direction very easily. They found and picked aloes, and several of the boys, led by Welcome, found freshwater mussels in the stream at the bottom of the gorge when they went for water. They had a good meal that night. They needed it, for it was raining again. Mist, rain, evening grayed the heavy vivid reds of the forest. They built up brush-wood shelters and huddled by fires which would not stay alight.

"I saw a queer thing, Luz."

He was a strange fellow, Sasha; the oldest of them all, though tough and wiry, better able to keep up than some of the younger men; never out of temper, totally self-reliant, and almost totally silent. Luz had never seen him take part in a conversation beyond a yes or no, a smile or head shake. She knew he had never spoken at the Meeting House, never been one of Elia's group or Vera's people, never been a choice-maker among his people, though he was the son of one of their great heroes and leaders, Shults who had led the Long March from the streets of the City Moskva to the Port of Lisboa, and on. Shults had had other children, but they had died in the first hard years on Victoria; only Sasha, last-born, Victoria-born, had lived. And had fathered a son, and seen him die. He never talked. Only, sometimes, to her, to Luz. "I saw a queer thing, Luz."

"What?"

"An animal." He pointed to the right, up the steep slope of brush and trees, a dark wall now in the fading light. "There's a bit of a clearing up there where a couple of big trees went down and cleared some room. Found some aloes at one end of it and was picking them. Looked over my shoulder—felt something watching. It was at the far end of the clearing." He paused a minute, not for effect but to order his description. "It was gathering aloes too. I thought it was a man at first. Like a man. But it wasn't much bigger than a coney, when it went down on all fours. Dark-colored, with a reddish head—a big head, seemed too big for the rest of it. A center eye, like a wotsit, looking at me. Eyes on the sides too, I think, but I couldn't see it clear enough. It stared a minute and then it turned and went into the trees."

His voice was low and even.

"It sounds frightening," Luz said quietly, "I don't know why." But she did know why, thinking of her dream of the beings who came and watched; though she had not had the dream since they were in the scrublands.

Sasha shook his head. They were squatting side by side under a rough roof of branches. He rubbed the beaded rain off his hair, rubbed down his bristling gray mustache. "There's nothing here will hurt us," he said. "Except ourselves. Are there any stories in the City about animals we don't know of?"

"No—only the scures."

"Scures?"

"Old stories. Creatures like men, with glaring eyes, hairy. My cousin Lores talked about them. My father said they *were* men—exiles, or men who had wandered off, crazy men, gone wild."

Sasha nodded. "Nothing like that would come this far," he said. "We're the first."

"We've only lived there on the coast. I suppose there are animals we've never seen before."

"Plants too. See that, it's like what we call whiteberry, but it's not the same. I never saw it until yesterday."

Presently he said, "There's no name for the animal I saw."

Luz nodded.

Between her and Sasha was silence, the bond of silence. He did not speak of the animal to others, nor did she. They knew nothing of this world, their world, only that they must walk in it in silence, until they had learned a language fitting to be spoken here. He was one who was willing to wait.

The second ridge climbed, in a third day of rain. A longer, shallower valley, where the going was easier. About midday the wind turned, blowing down from the north, scouring the ridges free of cloud and mist. All afternoon they climbed the last slope, and that evening in a vast, cold clarity of light they came up among the massive, rusty rock-formations of the summit, and saw the eastern lands.

They gathered there slowly, the slowest still struggling up the stony slope while the leaders stood waiting for them—a few tiny dark figures, to the climbers' eyes, against an immense bright emptiness of sky. The short, sparse grass of the ridge top glowed ruddy in the sunset. They all gathered there, sixty-seven people, and stood looking out over the rest of the world. They said little. The rest of the world looked very large.

The shadows of the ridge they had been climbing stretched a long way across the plain. Beyond those shadows the land was gold, a hazy, reddish, wintry gold, dimly streaked and mottled with courses of distant streams and the bulk of low hills or ringtree groves. Far across that plateau, at the very edge of the eyes' reach, mountains rose against the tremendous, colorless, windy sky.

"How far?" someone asked.

"A hundred kilometers to the foothills, maybe."

"They're big. . . ."

"Like the ones we saw in the north, over Lake Serene."

"It may be the same range. It ran southeastward."

"That plain is like the sea, it goes on and on."

"It's cold up here!"

"Let's get down over the summit, out of the wind."

Long after the high plains had sunk into gray, the keen small edge of sunlit ice burned there at the edge of vision in the east. It whitened and faded; the stars came out, thick in the windy blackness, all the constellations, all the bright cities that were not their home.

Wild bog-rice grew thick by the streams of the plateau; they lived on that during the eight days of their crossing. The Iron Hills shrank behind them, a wrinkled rusty line drawn down the west. The plain was alive with coneys, a longer-legged breed than those of the coastal forests; the riverbanks were pocked and hollowed with their warrens, and when the sun was out the coneys came out, and sat in the sun, and watched the people pass with tranquil, uninterested eyes.

"You'd have to be a fool to starve here," Holdfast said, watching Italia lay her snares near a glittering, stony ford.

But they went on. The wind blew bitter on that high, open land, and there was no wood to build with, or to burn. They went on until the land began to swell, rising toward the foothills of the mountains, and they came to a big river, south-running, which Andre the map maker named the Grayrock. To cross it they must find a ford, which looked unlikely, or build rafts. Some were for crossing, putting that barrier too behind them. Others were for turning south again and going on along the west bank of the river. While they deliberated, they set up their first stopping-place camp. One of the men had hurt his foot in a fall, and there were several other minor injuries and troubles; their footgear needed mending; they were all weary, and needed a few days' rest. They put up shelters of brushwood and thatchleaf, the first day. It was cold, with gathering clouds, though the bitter wind did not blow here. That night the first snow fell.

It seldom snowed at Songe Bay; never this early in the winter. They were no longer in the soft climate of the western coast. The coastal hills, the badlands, and the Iron Hills caught the rain that came in on the west winds off the sea; here it would be dryer, but colder.

The great range toward which they had been walking, the sharp heights of ice, had seldom been visible while they crossed the plain, snowclouds hiding all but the blue foothills. They were in those foothills now, a haven between the windy plain and the stormy peaks. They had entered a narrow stream valley which wound and widened till it opened out on the broad, deep gorge of the Grayrock. The valley floor was forested, mostly with ringtrees and a few thick stands of cottonwools, but there were many glades and clearings among the trees. The hills on the north side of the valley were steep and craggy, sheltering the valley and the lower, open, southern slopes. It was a pleasant place. They had all felt at ease there, putting up their shelters, the first day. But in the morning the glades were white, and under the ringtrees, though the bronze foliage had kept the light snow off, every stone and leaf of withered grass sparkled with thick frost. The people huddled up to the fires to thaw out before they could go gather more firewood.

"Brushwood shelters aren't what we need in this kind of weather," Andre said gloomily, rubbing his stiff, chapped hands. "Ow, ow, ow, I'm cold."

"It's clearing off," Luz said, looking up through a broad gap in the trees, where their side-valley opened out into the river gorge; above the steep farther shore of the Grayrock, the Eastern Range glittered hugely, dark blue and white.

"For now. It'll snow again."

Andre looked frail, hunched there by the fire that burned almost invisible in the fresh morning sunlight: frail, cold, discouraged. Luz, much rested by the day without walking, felt a freshness of spirit like the morning light; she felt a great love for Andre, the patient, anxious man. She squatted down beside him by the fire, and patted his shoulder. "This is a good place, isn't it," she said.

He nodded, hunched up, still rubbing his sore, red hands.

"Andre."

He grunted.

"Maybe we should be building cabins, not shelters."

"Here?"

"It's a good place. . . ."

He looked around at the high red trees, the stream rushing loudly down toward the Grayrock, the sunlit, open slopes to the south, the great blue heights eastward. "It's all right," he said grudgingly. "Plenty of wood and water, anyhow. Fish, coneys, we could last out the winter here."

"Maybe we should? While there's time to put up cabins?"

Hunched up, his arms hanging between his knees, Andre mechanically rubbed his hands. She watched him, her hand still on his shoulder.

"It would suit me," he said at last.

"If we've come far enough . . ."

"We'll have to get everybody together, agree. . . ." He looked at her; he put his arm up around her shoulders. They squatted side by side, linked, rocking a little on their heels, close to the quivering half-seen fire. "I've had enough running," he said. "Have you?"

She nodded.

"I don't know. I wonder . . ."

"What?"

Andre stared at the sunlit fire, his face, drawn and weatherbeaten, flushed by the heat.

"They say when you're lost, really lost, you always go in a circle," he said. "You come back to where you started from. Only you don't always recognize it."

"This isn't the City," Luz said. "Nor the Town."

"No. Not yet."

"Not ever," she said, her brows drawn down straight and harsh. "This is a new place, Andre. A beginning place."

"God willing."

"I don't know what God wants." She put out her free hand and scratched up a little of the damp, half-frozen earth, and squeezed it in her palm. "That's God," she said, opening her hand on the half-molded sphere of black dirt. "That's me. And you. And the others. And the mountains. We're all . . . it's all one circle."

"You've lost me, Luz."

"I don't know what I'm talking about. I want to stay here, Andre."

"Then I expect we will," Andre said, and thumped

her between the shoulders. "Would we ever have started, I wonder, if it hadn't been for you?"

"Oh, don't say that, Andre—"

"Why not? It's the truth."

"I have enough on my conscience without that. I have— If I—"

"This is a new place, Luz," he said very gently. "The names are new here." She saw there were tears in his eyes. "This is where we build the world," he said, "out of mud."

Eleven-year-old Asher came toward Luz, who was down on the bank of the Grayrock gathering fresh-water mussels from the icy, weed-fringed rocks of a backwater. "Luz," he said when he was near enough not to have to speak loudly. "Look."

She was glad to straighten up and get her hands out of the bitter cold of the water. "What have you got there?"

"Look," the boy said in a whisper, holding out his open hand. On the palm sat a little creature like a shadow-colored toad with wings. Three gold pinhead eyes stared unwinking, one at Asher, two at Luz.

"A wotsit."

"I never saw one close up before."

"He came to me. I was coming down here with the baskets, and he flew into one, and I put out my hand and he got onto it."

"Would he come to me?"

"I don't know. Hold out your hand."

She put her hand beside Asher's. The wotsit trembled and for a moment blurred into a mere vibration of fronds or feathers; then, with a hop or flight too quick for the eye to follow, it transferred itself to Luz's palm, and she felt the grip of six warm, tiny, wiry feet.

"O you are beautiful," she said softly to the creature, "you are beautiful. And I could kill you, but I couldn't keep you, not even hold you. . . ."

"If you put them in a cage, they die," the child said.

"I know," Luz said.

The wotsit was now turning blue, the pure, azure blue of the sky between the peaks of the Eastern Range on days, like this day, of winter sunlight. The three gold pinhead eyes glittered. The wings, bright and translucent, shot out, startling Luz; her hand's slight movement launched the little creature on its upward glide, out over the breadth of the river, eastward, like a fleck of mica on the wind.

She and Asher filled the baskets with the heavy, bearded, black mussel shells, and trudged back up the pathway to the settlement.

"Southwind!" Asher cried, tugging his heavy basket along, "Southwind! There's wotsits here! One came to me!"

"Of course there are," Southwind said, trotting down the path to help them with their load. "What a lot you got! Oh, Luz, your poor hands, come on, the cabin's warm, Sasha brought a new load of wood in on the cart. Did you think there wouldn't be wotsits here? We're not that far from home!"

The cabins—nine so far, three more half-built—stood on the south bank of the stream where it widened out into a pool under the branches of a giant single ringtree. They took their water from the little falls at the head of the pool, bathed and washed at the foot of it where it narrowed before its long plunge down to the Grayrock. They called the settlement Heron, or Heron Pool, for the pair of gray creatures who lived on the farther shore of the stream, untroubled by the presence of the human beings, the smoke of their fires, the noise of their work, their coming and going, the sound of their voices. Elegant, long-legged, silent, the herons went about their own business of food gathering on the other side of the wide, dark pool; sometimes they paused in the shallows to gaze at the people with clear, quiet, colorless eyes. Sometimes, on still cold evenings before snow, they danced. As Luz and Southwind and the child turned aside toward their cabin, Luz saw the herons standing near the roots of the great tree, one poised to watch them, the other with its narrow head turned back as it gazed into the forest. "They'll dance tonight," she said, under her breath; and she stopped a moment, standing with her heavy load on the path, still as the herons; then went on.

BIOGRAPHICAL NOTES

CYNTHIA FELICE was born in Chicago, but now lives in Colorado Springs, Colorado, with her husband and two small sons. She has been writing seriously for four years and has sold stories to *Universe* and *Galileo*. *Godsfire*, her first novel, was published in 1978.

MARILYN HACKER has won the Lamont Poetry Award and the National Book Award (1975). She coedited the speculative fiction quarterly *Quark* with Samuel R. Delaney, and put together certain issues of the poetry magazine *City*. She spent the 1976/77 academic year commuting between Washington, D.C., where she conducted a writing workshop at George Washington University, and New York City, where she taught a course in twentieth-century women poets. She has one daughter.

URSULA K. LE GUIN is one of today's most honored science fiction writers. She has won four Hugo Awards, three Nebula Awards, the Jupiter Award, and the 1969 Boston Globe–Horn Book Award. She was twice nominated for the National Book Award, and in 1975 won it for *The Farthest Shore*, part of a trilogy that includes *A Wizard of Earthsea* and *The Tombs of Atuan* (a 1973 Newbery Honor Book). Ms. Le Guin lives in Oregon.

ELIZABETH A. LYNN was born in New York City in 1946, and currently lives in San Francisco. At twenty-nine she quit her job as a medical secretary to be a full-time writer and promptly sold a dozen stories. She has taught courses called "Women, Reality, and Science Fiction" and "The Feminist Imagination" in the Women's Studies Department of San Francisco University. Ms. Lynn's first novel, *A Different Light*, will be published in the fall of 1978. She has said that science fiction allows her to get outside cultural trappings and to explore sexual identities.

DIANA L. PAXSON was born in Michigan in 1943, but was brought up in California, where her father was one of the original staff of the Rand Corporation. She was graduated from Mills College in 1964 with a major in English. In 1966 she received an M.A. degree in Comparative Literature from the University of

California at Berkeley. She is married to science fiction writer Jon DeCles (Donald C. Studebaker), and they have two sons.

Ms. Paxson was the originator of the Society for Creative Anachronism, Inc., a national organization which recreates the culture of the Middle Ages. Her first published story, "Message to Myself," recently appeared in Isaac Asimov's *Science Fiction Magazine*.

JOAN D. VINGE has a degree in anthropology and has worked as a salvage archeologist. "Science fiction," she says, "is a lot like anthropology in some ways—it lets you glimpse other possible life-styles, other ways of looking at things, other ways of dealing with problems." Ms. Vinge has had stories published in *Analog*, *Orbit*, *Women of Wonder*, and other magazines and anthologies. Her first novel, *The Outcasts of Heaven Belt*, will soon appear in serial form in *Analog*.

CHERRY WILDER, Australian-born and -bred, pulled up roots and in 1976 moved to West Germany to live, "forever." Ms. Wilder spends her time at home raising her children and writing. Her first novel, *The Luck of Brin's Five*, was recently published for young adults.

Bestsellers

- [ ] **A Stranger is Watching** by Mary Higgins Clark $2.50 (18125-9)
- [ ] **After the Wind** by Eileen Lottman $2.50 (18138-0)
- [ ] **The Roundtree Women:** Book 1 by Margaret Lewerth
  $2.50 (17594-1)
- [ ] **The Memory of Eva Ryker** by Donald A. Stanwood
  $2.50 (15550-9)
- [ ] **Blizzard** by George Stone $2.25 (11080-7)
- [ ] **The Black Marble** by Joseph Wambaugh $2.50 (10647-8)
- [ ] **My Mother/My Self** by Nancy Friday $2.50 (15663-7)
- [ ] **Season of Passion** by Danielle Steel $2.25 (17703-0)
- [ ] **The Immigrants** by Howard Fast $2.75 (14175-3)
- [ ] **The Ends of Power** by H. R. Haldeman
  with Joseph DiMona $2.75 (12239-2)
- [ ] **Going After Cacciato** by Tim O'Brien $2.25 (12966-4)
- [ ] **Slapstick** by Kurt Vonnegut $2.25 (18009-0)
- [ ] **The Far Side of Destiny** by Dore Mullen $2.25 (12645-2)
- [ ] **Look Away, Beulah Land** by Lonnie Coleman ..$2.50 (14642-9)
- [ ] **Bed of Strangers** by Lee Raintree and
  Anthony Wilson $2.50 (10892-6)
- [ ] **Asya** by Allison Baker $2.25 (10696-6)
- [ ] **Beggarman, Thief** by Irwin Shaw $2.75 (10701-6)
- [ ] **Strangers** by Michael de Guzman $2.25 (17952-1)
- [ ] **The Benedict Arnold Connection** by Joseph DiMona
  $2.25 (10935-3)
- [ ] **Earth Has Been Found** by D. F. Jones $2.25 (12217-1)

At your local bookstore or use this handy coupon for ordering:

DELL BOOKS
P.O. BOX 1000, PINEBROOK, N.J. 07058

Please send me the books I have checked above. I am enclosing $_____
(please add 35¢ per copy to cover postage and handling). Send check or money
order—no cash or C.O.D.'s. Please allow up to 8 weeks for shipment.

Mr/Mrs/Miss_____

Address_____

City_____State/Zip_____